A DCI SARA HOYLAND MYSTERY

All the best,
David Menon

DAVID MENON

EMPIRE
PUBLICATIONS

First published in 2013

EMPIRE PUBLICATIONS
1 Newton Street, Manchester M1 1HW
© David Menon 2013

ISBN 1901746 895 – 9781901746891

Printed in Great Britain.

ACKNOWLEDGEMENTS

For our own Beautiful Child, Helena, and for all the children who bite their lip but are still sent away.

And with special thanks to Gran for answering my prayers and to Danielle for making sure it wasn't too late.

Once again I'm indebted to Ash and the team at Empire for everything they've done to get me into the world of published authors. Today Manchester, tomorrow the world!

I'd also like to thank Wing Commander Ian Barke for being a true friend.

www.facebook.com/sarahoyland
www.twitter.com@ifanyonefalls
www.goodreads.com/davidmenon
www.davidmenon.com

CHAPTER ONE

The walls of HMP Manchester hold many secrets, most of which never get the chance to be revealed. Angela Barker had been working as a psychotherapist there for five years and her clients included some of the most dangerous men in the country. It wasn't the only place she worked. Employed by the NHS she practised her craft across several Manchester locations but she only dealt with the most serious cases of mental health disturbance. Just like anybody else she'd want to slap the kind of neurotic self-obsessed idiot who claims to have a low self-esteem problem because their parents never bought them the model of bike they wanted when they were a kid. No, Angela liked to delve deep into the mind and soul of someone with a more substantial history. Her husband thought it was highly amusing that she could talk to a mass murderer as if they were her neighbour but she can't sleep at night without leaving a light on because she's afraid of the dark. Even after all the years they'd been together he still teased her about that.

'The thing about therapy,' said Angela as she put her pen and paper down, 'is that it can only help you come to terms with the things that have been done against you. It can't take you back and stop them from happening.'

She was talking to Paddy, a man in his late forties who was in for having killed his girlfriend in front of their toddler son over twenty years ago. He was coming up for parole and it was Angela's job to assess him psychologically.

'Things?' said Paddy, his deep Australian drawl still

distinctive despite the rest of his character having fallen close to the abyss. He'd only been back in the UK a few short weeks when he committed his crime. He'd been born in the UK and spent the first five years of his life here. 'Is that what you'd call them?'

'For want of a better word,' said Angela who, try as she did, couldn't help focusing more than she should on the long jagged scar that ran downwards from his right temple to his jaw. It was as if the surgeon had been drunk when he'd taken his knife to Paddy's face. She didn't know where that or the limp that sometimes hindered his walk came from but she hoped all would be explained in due course.

'Well whatever the word, Doc, I think it's all a bit too late for me.'

'You elevate my status, Paddy,' said Angela, smiling affectionately at what she saw as a term of endearment, 'I've told you I'm not a doctor, I'm a psychotherapist.'

'Same difference to an old bloke like me, Doc.'

'What am I going to do with you, Paddy?'

'When I was younger I could've given you heaps of ideas, Doc.' said Paddy with a wink.

Angela threw her head back and laughed. 'I don't doubt that.'

'Sheila's like you always like a bit of rough.'

What was even funnier to Angela at that moment was the disapproving look on the face of the prison officer standing guard in the corner. She couldn't care less about it. Paddy had almost served out his time and it wasn't as if there wasn't enough misery in here. The place could do with the sound of laughter.

'Are we going to talk clichés all afternoon?' she asked.

'I don't know,' said Paddy, 'you probably know more of them than me so it wouldn't be a fair fight.'

Angela smiled again. She found herself doing it often to counter the crushing numbness of this sparsely furnished room with its grey walls. She was sitting on a plastic chair. Paddy was sitting opposite her on a similar piece of unremarkable furniture. She'd never seen the prison officer before although he looked as if he'd been in the job for centuries. In fact, apart from the uniform, he looked like many of the inmates. His head was shaved and it glowed, unlike his face which had been shaved almost to the point of tearing his skin. She deduced from his skin tone that he must have to sit in the shade when he went on holiday. Skin that white would require an industrial strength protection lotion. There were the usual bars at the small window that was just below the ceiling on the wall facing her. The unmistakable smell of the institution hung in the air like it did everywhere else in the prison. She'd always hated that smell. She looked up at Paddy whose grey eyes were far away.

'It isn't too late to open up your heart to me, Paddy.'

'Do you really think I've got one, Doc?' replied the inmate who didn't want to admit that he was finding it hard to talk today. The pain was like a steel claw scraping away at his insides, the result of an altercation with a fellow inmate who'd come off worse and ended up in the prison hospital. The Doc seemed like a good sort though, a real mercy child if it wasn't for the physical confines of his situation. Maybe he should try with the Doc. It could get him out of his cell and out of kitchen duty for a while.

'Everybody's got one, Paddy,' coaxed Angela, 'much as they like to try and disguise it.'

'And that's what I'm doing, is it?'

'It seems that way. I mean, you've told me precious little about yourself.'

'I'm not as open as some of the characters who pass

through here.'

'So why is that?'

Angela had grown rather fond of Paddy in the weeks since she'd been assigned to him. The authorities wanted to make sure they'd done all they could to sort out and assess his mental state. The Governor had called it a "Duty of Care" as well as being part of the parole process. Angela thought that for those like Paddy it was an injustice that it hadn't come before. Her view wouldn't be shared by the mass of populist opinion but she didn't care about pandering to those who thought the answers were always so simple. Despite what it said in Paddy's file about what he'd done, there were still the traces of the desperate child written right across that worn, craggy face.

'I'm not what you call touchy feely?'

'I might've agreed on that before I met you,' said Angela, 'but I'm not so sure now. Besides, I quite like you.'

'I'm honoured, Doc, but we've only got an hour.'

'I'm not clock watching, Paddy.'

Paddy tossed his thumb in the guard's direction. 'No, but they are.'

Angela laughed. 'Then we'd better start talking seriously.'

'Ah, just when I thought we were going to have a little fun, Doc.'

'I'm not here for fun, Paddy, I'm here to try and help you.'

'Help me? You think you can do that?'

'Paddy, I can help you stop the bad memories from stabbing away at you when you close your eyes and try to sleep.'

'Do me a favour, Doc. Don't ever take up writing situation comedy. You'd be lousy.'

'All this cracking jokes in your state,' said Angela, 'I'm

impressed.'

'You know I like to be up front.'

'You weren't trying to be funny then?'

'Well, maybe an attempt.'

'Well if it brings a smile to your face, which I can see that it has, then I'm glad.'

'You should've seen me in my younger days,' said Paddy, 'you'd have been impressed then.'

Angela blushed. Paddy had a way of doing that to her. There was something of a glint in his eyes even now. He'd have been a right one with the women if he'd managed to lead a normal life.

'What would you have liked to have happened in your life, Paddy?'

'Oh I gave up thinking about that a long time ago. Look, at the risk of becoming a boring old fart asking the same old bloody questions, why are you even bothering with me, Doc?'

'What do you mean?'

'Doc, I'm old before my time and you've read the notes on me. What else can I tell you?'

'Isn't that for me to find out during our conversations? Yes, I've read the notes on you, Paddy, but they only tell me the legal facts.'

'I was a bad person, Doc, so just go and read the notes again. That's where you'll find your answers.'

'I want to hear them from you, Paddy.'

'You're a bloody persistent sheila, I'll give you that!'

'Just tell me what's in your heart and soul, Paddy.'

'I've never talked about that.'

'Well I think that's the trouble, Paddy' said Angela. 'But it's never too late.'

CHAPTER TWO

Adrian and Penny Bradshaw walked up the hill to the local pub hand-in-hand. They were a good-looking couple. They were both still the right side of forty, Adrian still had a full head of thick black hair and Penny had the kind of figure that not only belied her age but also the fact that she'd had three children. The short pink cardigan that she'd kept unbuttoned over her short sleeveless cream coloured dress meant that she wouldn't feel any chill that suddenly wound its way through the early June air. They'd moved out to the hills of Saddleworth near Oldham and its infamous moors, when it was time for their two eldest to get bedded into the school system. It had been a good move, all three of their kids were doing well and village life so close to the city was good for the whole family. They felt they had the best of both worlds.

Adrian was wearing his usual beige chinos. Penny had ironed his favourite white linen shirt that she'd bought for his last birthday and he was wearing it with the top two buttons undone, showing off the thickness of his chest fur. She'd be the first to say that she was lucky. Adrian was tall and strong and though he was every inch the bloke, he still knew how to take care of himself. He went to the gym a couple of times a week and liked to watch what he ate. Not too seriously, he still liked his chips and his beer but he was disciplined when the weight started to creep up. Some of Penny's friends obsessed about their figures whilst their husbands expanded their beer bellies seemingly without any thought for how their wife saw them. But when she made love to Adrian she didn't have to do it with a giant balloon of flab pushing against her stomach like all those other women had to. He didn't have a six-pack but his stomach was flat and firm and he was still good at making her feel good. He never disappointed her. She rested her head against his shoulder as they walked.

'What's all this about?' asked Adrian.

'Nothing,' said Penny, who then gently stroked his freshly shaved face with the backs of her fingers. 'I'm just lucky to have such a handsome husband.'

'And how's my gorgeous wife?'

Penny smiled. She always went shy when Adrian paid her a compliment, even after all these years, and even after all the ways he'd used to make her believe in her own beauty. He blamed her parents. They'd always put her down in favour of her younger sister Natasha and Adrian had never been able to understand why. Penny had never given her parents any worry but Natasha had ridden all the wild horses she could find in the stable. You wouldn't think so now though. Now she was going out with a celebrity doctor and putting on an accent that made Adrian and Penny smile at the ridiculous falseness of it.

They managed to find a small table in the corner of the bar. A lot of the other customers were ordering food from the newly re-opened gastro pub side of the bar but the couple had already eaten with the kids.

'Your Mum loves looking after the kids,' said Penny, who was still holding hands with her husband. He was drinking a pint of bitter whilst she was sipping her way through a glass of dry white wine. 'I never have to ask her twice.'

'I know,' said Adrian, 'she's good to us.'

'She is' said Penny who'd always been envious of the

closeness of Adrian's family. He and his two brothers and one sister acted as one unit with his Mum. It was a million miles away from where her family was.

'Have you heard from your folks?'

'I've said I'll go around to Mum's this week to help her pack for their holiday to Malta.'

'I suspect you won't be helping your Mum pack,' said Adrian who knew how Penny's Mum liked to rush around the place saying she'd got loads to do whilst others around her actually got on and did it. 'I suspect you'll be doing the actual packing for her.'

'I expect so, not that I mind. It'll give us some time together.'

'You'll end up rowing.'

'No doubt.' she said, sipping her wine, 'You know us.'

'I know you and you're always so optimistic about things.' said Adrian. 'Your Mum and Dad have never done right by you but you still put a smile on for them.'

'It's what you do when they're your parents,' said Penny, unsure if she believed her own words or not. 'You keep on believing that one day it'll turn out alright.'

Adrian squeezed her hand. 'Like you always believed I'd get promoted even when I didn't.'

'Don't you make out like I'm one of those pushy wives.'

'You'd never be that,' he replied 'but you stepped in when I got discouraged. That's when I needed you most and like always, you were there. If it wasn't for you I'd still be Police Constable Bradshaw instead of Detective Sergeant.'

'You did all that by yourself, Adrian, by being a good copper.'

Adrian felt fortunate to have recently joined the squad led by DCI Sara Hoyland. He worked mostly alongside DI Tim Norris and fellow DS Joe Alexander. Norris was a brooding and sometimes hard to read bloke but Alexander was different altogether and they'd hit it off straight away.

'Anyway, what's it like working for that gorgeous Sara Hoyland?'

'The boss? She's alright actually.'

'She is gorgeous, Adrian.'

'Yes, she is, and I can't say I haven't noticed.' Adrian admitted, 'What man wouldn't? But she's knocking off one of the PC's, a young very fit looking lad called Kieran. He's the envy of all the unattached men at the station.'

'And some of the attached ones too?'

'Only those who are unhappily attached.'

'Ooh, right answer!'

'Years of practice, my love.'

'He must be younger than her?'

'He is,' laughed Adrian, 'by some years.'

'Go for it, girlfriend!' said Penny, 'Although I'd never trade you in for a younger model, darling.'

'I'm glad to hear it. There is some sort of tension between Tim Norris and Sara, some personal history thing but it doesn't really affect the squad.'

'Joe Alexander seems lovely.'

'He's a top bloke is Joe, no side to him at all.'

'He could do with losing a bit of weight though.'

'Yeah he could but... he's not morbidly obese or anything.'

'Just a bit cuddly.'

'That's it,' smiled Adrian, 'cuddly.'

'What's his attachment story?'

'Seeing a married woman. She lives on the same street, her husband is in a wheelchair apparently.'

'I can't help thinking that'll all end in tears' said Penny.

'You may be right. Just like you were about encouraging me and how you encourage the kids too.'

'Now come on, I'm not alone there, Adrian.'

'I do my best.' he said, 'Do you think your Natasha will have any kids with Charlie?'

'Natasha? I don't know. I've always thought she was too selfish for that but the other day she told me she had actually been thinking about it.'

'It must be part of some scheme she's cooking up.'

'Yes, that was my thought too,' said Penny. 'I mean, Charlie has already got two of course so who knows. He might not want anymore.'

'And do you think that'll stop Natasha if she's determined?'

'Well no, you've got a point there..'

'We'll wait and see' said Adrian.

'Adrian?'

'Yes?'

'Do you think that we could have just one more?'

'It's only nine o'clock, babes, I was hoping we were going to have at least a couple more.'

'No, you twit, I don't mean a drink. I mean a child.'

Adrian nearly spat his beer out. 'A child? You're not?'

' No, I'm not!' blushed Penny, before laughing at the terrified look on her husband's face. 'I just meant one more to finish off our family.'

'Penny, I'm more than happy with the three we've got and we're not exactly rolling in it. I don't think we could really afford another child'

'We could if we wanted to.'

'Penny, that's not fair. You've been working up to this, haven't you. I can tell you have.'

'The kids are growing up so fast. Tom's twelve, Amy's ten, Katie is five and ... '

'…yes, Penny, I do know the ages of our kids.'

'But what am I going to do when they don't need me as much?'

'Penny, that's life,' said Adrian firmly. 'You have kids, you do your best for them, then they grow up and find their own way leaving Mum and Dad to rediscover why they got together in the first place.'

'You old romantic.'

'Well I am trying to be practical too. I mean, we keep afloat financially because of what we get from your job at the school. Having another child would put a big financial strain on things for us.'

Penny enjoyed her job as a teaching assistant at the school where Katie, their youngest, went and she would also have to agree that the family finances had been easier since she'd gone out to work. But she was broody.

'I suppose it's my ticking clock talking,' said Penny.

'I didn't mean to be insensitive.'

'You weren't,' said Penny.

'To be honest, Pen, I just don't think I could go through the nappy and sleepless night stage again,' Adrian admitted, 'I like the fact that our kids are kids now and not babies anymore. There's a great thing going between the five of us.'

'I know' said Penny, smiling at certain memories. She'd always thought she'd be closer to her daughters and indeed she adored her girls. But in fact it was her son Tom who was her 'mate' amongst the three. She sometimes thought it may be because she saw so much of Adrian in Tom and that led to her being a little bit in love with her son like many mothers were.

'I'd like us to get the overdraft down and pay off some of the balance on the credit cards. You know, get rid of some of our debt.'

'Isn't that what you up your mortgage for?'

'Yes, but there's a limit to that, Pen, and we're very close to it considering the way house prices are at the moment.'

'I didn't realise things were that bad.'

'They're not,' said Adrian, 'we're in a better position than many others. We could just do a bit better than we do, that's all.'

She kissed him on the cheek.

'Now what have I done?'

'Nothing,' said Penny. 'I just felt like it, like I just feel like getting another one in and this time, I do mean a drink.'

A little while later they joined some of their friends and neighbours at the bar. As they talked Adrian kept a light hand on his wife's bottom and an intimate closeness that she responded to with equal affection. Her touch in the small of his back, the smell of her perfume as she stood so close, were just two of the things that made him glad that she was his wife. When they got home, Adrian's Mum had a coffee with them before leaving. Then Adrian and Penny went upstairs to bed and made love.

Just before one o'clock in the morning they had another baby on the way.

Canon Brendan O'Farrell of the Holy Saints Catholic Church in Salford had always been a very proud and fastidious man. It had been fifty years since he'd graduated from the seminary in Dublin and cut the ties with his native County Clare for a life in the priesthood. Holy Saints had been his very first posting and he'd been over in England so long he almost felt like he'd gone native. But whenever he went back home to 'Clare' his seven brothers and sisters reminded him that he was a thoroughbred Irishman. Brendan was the oldest and therefore the one who'd come under the most pressure from their late parents. One of the five boys had to become a priest and Brendan had found it impossible to resist. He had wanted to become a train driver but judging by how his chest had developed, perhaps God had been steering him away from all that steam that had surrounded the trains back then.

He was too old, he was now in his late sixties, to get up to do the morning weekday Mass but he had to give young Phillip a bit of a break. Father Phillip Evans had been holding the fort here at Holy Saints for the last couple of years and the poor lad was exhausted. It was a big church with a big parish and there just weren't enough priests to go around. He liked young Phillip. He seemed like a normal sort of bloke. He'd lost count of the amount of young priests whose promise had been sacrificed when they were moved around on account of being too fond of little girls or little boys. He didn't think Phillip would fall into that particular trap. He'd been wrong before but he felt pretty certain about Phillip. He didn't seem like the sort to have a 'side' to him.

Brendan was only going to be at Holy Saints for another couple of months. He'd already booked his ticket back home to County Clare on Aer Lingus, or rather he'd got young Phillip to do it on account of it having to be done on the internet if you wanted to take advantage of the cheaper fares. Just another couple of months and then he'd finally be allowed to retire. He had a small cottage waiting for him that overlooked the Atlantic Ocean that was next door to his sister Bernadette and her husband

Gerald who had retired there last year. His nephew had already fitted his satellite television. He couldn't wait.

After the Mass was finished he went into the kitchen to find his breakfast. He might've known that Ann Schofield, who was not only the priests' housekeeper but also one of Brendan's oldest and closest friends, would already be at her post, preparing a pot of tea along with toast, bacon, and eggs.

'Aw, Ann!' greeted Brendan warmly, 'Where would we be without you?'

'Sit yourself down, Brendan and I'll see to you.'

'I will sure enough, Ann' said Brendan who pulled out a chair and sat down at the table. He was in full priest's gear but he'd taken off his white dog collar and rolled up the sleeves of his black shirt. He'd miss these mornings with Ann. She'd always been more than just a friend and he'd miss her physical presence in his daily life. It would be one of the things that reinforced the loneliness he feared might overwhelm him once he didn't have the structure of the church to sustain him through the dark days.

Ann poured some tea for him. He always looked in need of nourishment when he came in from performing early morning Mass, that and the fags that he now had to smoke outside. Years ago in Ireland he'd signed the pledge never to drink alcohol. But he more than made up for it with the amount of cigarettes he got through. Sometimes those attending early morning Mass witnessed the burning of incense having the same effect on his throat and chest as the cigarettes did. Sometimes he could barely get through the Mass without constant coughing fits. It was why they were so poorly attended when people knew he was doing them.

'You've been a God send to Phillip since you came

here,' she said, 'there were nights when he almost seemed too exhausted to get himself to bed.'

'I know,' said Brendan, rubbing his chin, 'and what's going to happen to this place when both you and I retire in a few weeks' time? I still haven't heard from the Bishop about getting another priest to come here permanently to work with Phillip. And who could replace you, Ann?'

Ann blushed. 'You know who, Brendan. It's going to be Joan Fitzgerald.'

'Oh but she won't make cakes like you do!' he groaned.

'And why would you care? You won't be here so stop being so uncharitable.'

'Alright, boss,' said Brendan. He smiled at the plate of eggs and bacon that Ann placed before him. ' Just how I like it,' he said, 'the eggs runny and the bacon soft.'

'I should know what you like by now, Brendan, after all these years,' said Ann.

'And back then we didn't have any problem getting priests.'

'Back then the church didn't have any trouble getting priests to come to anywhere,' said Ann, 'but you've kept on coming back.'

'Like the proverbial bad penny.' Added Brendan with a wink at her.

'I wanted so much for our Matt to go into the priesthood,' said Ann, sighing like she always did when she thought of it, 'but it wasn't to be.'

'No,' said Brendan. ' It wasn't but Matthew has a very worthy career in medicine. Priests and doctors both give to the community we serve. And as for your Susie, well she's doing fine running the family business, Ann, which must make you very proud. I'd say your lot were doing alright.'

'I've much to be grateful for, Brendan,' said Ann.

'And much to look forward to,' said Brendan, 'like Susie's wedding for instance. That's going to be a grand affair.'

'It is,' said Ann, 'but I've still no grandchildren though, Brendan.'

'They'll come, Ann' said Brendan, 'I'm sure of it.'

'Well I don't know when Susie will feel inclined to give in to the natural forces of nature,' said Ann, 'she's too busy being a career girl. And as for our Matt... well he would've been headed for happiness if the devil hadn't got in his way and turned his life into darkness.'

'Is that your view or his, Ann?'

'It's mine, Brendan, as you well know.'

'Would you take all that bitterness out of your voice, Ann? I'd have been looking to you to show some love and compassion.'

Ann sniffed. 'Yes, well, let's just say I have to pray to God for the strength to do that where Matt's so-called lifestyle is concerned.'

'And I can see you're not listening to the Almighty's responses.'

'God always listens, Brendan,' said Ann, 'but I'm only human after all although I'll try. I'll try, Brendan. For your sake, I'll try.'

'Good.'

'But if our Matthew doesn't repent for his sin then I shall surely not see him in Heaven with me.'

'Love the sinner and condemn the sin, Ann.'

'Oh I know that, Brendan,' said Ann, impatiently, 'but I can't stop him from leading a sinful life.'

'Hope is the last thing you should lose in this instance, Ann.'

'But His Holiness the Pope said again just last week

in Rome that those who lead the sinful life that Matthew does shall not be welcomed into Heaven.'

'Then we must pray harder than ever that the blinding light of Christ shall rip the sin from Matthew's otherwise noble life, Ann.'

'We shall, Brendan.'

'And being a doctor is a noble life, Ann, no matter where else he lets life take him.'

'I know, Brendan, I know.'

'And he sticks to that practice right in the middle of one of the most impoverished areas of the city,' said Brendan, 'that's got to say something good about the man and his values.'

'You're right there, he does care for the people he sees, I've seen him in action and it makes me proud. Perhaps I expect too much.'

'And with regard to the Holy Pontiff, Ann, I don't believe he is always infallible.'

Ann gasped. 'Brendan!'

'Well I don't, Ann.'

'But isn't that what's wrong with the Church today, Brendan? People are picking and choosing whenever it suits them. This Pope is trying to bring back the discipline and the obedience that others have let slip.'

'This Pope needs to remember what it's like to be a human being, Ann.'

'I'm lost for words, Brendan.'

'Well I know you wouldn't expect me to talk like this but as I get closer to the exit door I find my tongue getting a little looser.' said Brendan. 'A little reflection does none of us any harm and if you can believe in Matthew as a good person…'

'…which I do, Brendan. He's the first one I ever turn to whenever there's anything wrong in the family.'

'...well then you can learn to accept that he finds happiness in ways that you wouldn't have chosen for him but which are not necessarily going to send him downstairs. Am I making sense or talking out the back of my arse?'

Ann laughed out loud. 'Brendan, you could always work your way through my worries with your words. How is that?'

'Simple.' said Brendan. 'I'm Irish and words were made for us. Now pour us both some more tea and we'll create ourselves a little bit of Heaven around this table before all the flotsam and jetsam of daily life starts turning it into Hell.'

CHAPTER THREE

Kieran Quinn was in the shower when he heard Sara let herself in. It was so much easier now she had her own key to his flat in Deansgate Locks, just south of Manchester city centre and his flat mate didn't mind especially as his girlfriend had one too. He wiped himself dry with a towel and then wrapped it around his middle. He walked through to the hallway and was already hard as he watched her strip down to her bra and pants. She was wearing the black lace underwear that he loved. Then she took off her bra and slid her pants down her long legs. Kieran curled up the corner of his mouth and breathed in deep.

'I got you some perfume.'

'I'll take it later,' said Sara.

They jumped on each other and she lifted up her legs and wrapped them around his waist. He'd been away for a week and she was desperate to feel him inside her. He pushed her up against the wall and started giving it to her.

She was wet, gloriously wet and he'd perfected the art of getting to the point of orgasm and then holding back just to drive her crazy. He was a strong young man and he could keep this going even as his muscles were holding her in such an indecent position. He could feel her hands grasping his hair and then her nails digging into the top of his back. They were both noisy with their gasps and moans and eventually he gave up control and let himself come. Sara could feel so much of it as he pulled himself out of her. They were breathless and panting. Sara let her feet drop to the floor and the muscles in her legs relax. Kieran leaned up against her and they kissed.

'Now how about a drink, DCI Hoyland?'

'I need one after that, PC Quinn.'

Kieran poured them each a glass of champagne and they lay down naked together on the sofa in the living room like two spoons in a drawer with Sara leaning back against Kieran who had his arm wrapped around her breasts. Her free hand was resting on the outside of his thigh.

'Well even by your standards, lover, that was pretty amazing,' gasped Sara.

'I aim to please, madam,' said Kieran who was glad to be home. Much as they liked to consider themselves to be free agents with no strings attached to their liaison, Kieran was getting more out of their relationship than just the sex of a lifetime. There was something about being with an older woman like Sara that he wished every man of his age could experience. He'd lost his virginity at the age of fourteen and since then he'd never gone short. But he'd never had anyone like Sara. When he was old and grey he'd remember these times with a woman who'd made him feel more alive than he'd ever dared to before. The only trouble was he couldn't imagine anybody being as free as Sara was. She wasn't hung up about anything to do with sex and for a young man of twenty-five it was as if the devil had sent him an angel. Nobody else would ever come close.

'I thought you might be all spent after your lad's holiday in Spain,' she said, running her fingernails up and down his leg.

'I backed out of going on the pull the last two nights of the holiday.'

'Really?'

'Yeah,' said Kieran, 'I was saving myself.'

'Well how sweet is that? I'm flattered.'

'You know I haven't even unpacked yet,' said Kieran, 'I didn't get in from the airport until just after three.'

'When are you back at work?'

'Late shift tomorrow.' said Kieran.

Sara threw her arm back and placed her hand around the back of his neck. She let out a sigh of contentment.

'Don't tell me you're satisfied already?' said Kieran.

Sara smiled. 'No,' she said, 'I'm just letting you know I'm glad you're back.'

Sara glanced around at these now more than familiar surroundings. The flat was such a lads place. Kieran and his flat mate had two calendars stuck on the wall featuring barely clad women and the stack of DVD's next to the TV were all action films containing little dialogue or characterisation beyond knowing why someone would want to shoot themselves around a city on the other side of the world.

'I'm glad to be back.'

'So what was your scorecard out there?'

'Five.'

'Five?'

'Well I was only there for seven nights and, like I said,

I did abstain on the last two nights.'

'I'll bet it was as easy as buying them a drink.'

'It wasn't tough.'

'Especially with this tan you've got.'

'You like it?'

'I love it,' said Sara, 'although judging by the size of your white bits your swimming briefs wouldn't leave much to a girl's imagination.'

'I'm proud of what I've got.'

'You should be.'

Sara turned herself over and took his face in her hands. One day he'd father the most beautiful children. She loved his thick dark blond hair and his green eyes. She loved his chest hair that was shaped like an upside down triangle and that tapered into a thin line down his stomach to his groin. Maintaining a physical attraction for him was easy. Knowing that she'd one day have to see him go off with some pretty young thing was beginning to bother her in a way that she found annoying. She hadn't counted on this happening and she'd have to be careful not to let it show.

'You did say it was alright?' he said.

'What?'

'Me going with other girls?'

'Oh yeah,' said Sara who certainly didn't want to give away that she'd actually missed him for more than just the carnal. 'I was just interested to know, that's all.'

★

Matt Schofield was getting ready to see his afternoon patients. The surgery was a single storey grey building with iron bars at the windows and a metal fence surrounding it. It had to be done up like Fort Knox because of all the break-ins. Usually it was down to local addicts who tried to help themselves to a different kind of currency from money. The surgery was in the middle of four tower blocks and at the top end of a two mile stretch of council houses that had been built in the 1950's and which had only just been modernised to bring the toilet inside, have a shower and a modern kitchen fitted and central heating installed. Some of the houses had two or three steps up to the front door and these had also had handrails fitted to make it easier for those residents who were no longer so agile on their feet. The modernisation work had brought a stream of residents into Matt's surgery though, all complaining about it all being 'too much of an upheaval' for them. Poor sods, Matt had thought. None of them had ever known what it was like to improve their lot and now they needed tablets to calm their nerves because the council, using government grants, was making life better for them. When Matt had asked one lady if she wasn't just a little bit pleased that it was all being done she replied, 'What do I want with a flaming shower, for God's sake? I have a good soak every Sunday night before Songs of Praise and that does me.' It had all proved to Matt that no matter how much is done for some people they are just never going to be happy.

There was a knock on his door and Matt's practice partner and best mate, Charlie Baxter, popped his head around. They'd been best mates since the day they met when they'd started medical school together.

'Hi! Got a minute?'

'Sure,' said Matt, 'so when do you want me to have the kids?'

'How did you know I was going to ask you that?'

One of the things Matt liked about Charlie was that he was always easy to read. He was a poor little upper class rich boy from the very right side of the Scottish tracks. He'd never had much in the way of bother from his career diplomat father and housewife mother. They'd sent him to boarding school whilst his father's career took him all over the world leading to his final posting as British ambassador to Norway. He'd recently retired and now Charlie's parents were living in what amounted to a mini castle up in the Border area near Berwick-upon-Tweed. Girls had always fallen at Charlie's feet. He had all the charm along with the sandy brown hair and green eyes and he just had one of those faces that would make him look about thirty all the way through to his fifties. It wasn't fair. Matt hated him really. He couldn't stand the sight of the bastard.

'Call it an educated guess,' said Matt.

Charlie ran a nervous finger along the inside of his shirt collar. 'The thing is, mate, Natasha has got this champagne lunch organised with some of her flying friends and some of the Cheshire set she knows from Wilmslow. She says the boys wouldn't enjoy it and that, quite frankly, they'd get in the way.'

'Charlie, this weekend is your time to have your boys as per your divorce agreement with Wendy.'

'Yeah, I know that mate, but I've got to make a go of things with Natasha. She's the best thing that's ever happened to me.'

Matt looked up at his old friend. 'Ever happened to you?'

Charlie blushed. 'Alright, after Wendy she's the best thing that's ever happened to me but that's only for your ears.'

Charlie's ex-wife Wendy was still one of Matt's best friends and Matt felt a tremendous sense of loyalty towards her but that wasn't why he couldn't stand Natasha,

Charlie's new girlfriend. She was an air hostess who served tea and coffee but she thought she was Cheryl Cole and it was her pretentiousness that Matt couldn't stand. She was serious when she said she couldn't possibly fly economy class or on any of the 'no-frills' airlines because they were full of what she called 'poor people.' It had to be at least Club class or nothing. She lived in what she called a 'cottage' in Wilmslow that was really a very nice looking two-up, two-down terraced house. She'd finally cooked all her chips with Matt when she referred to her parents as 'Mummy and Daddy.' He absolutely detested that in a grown woman and it really beat him why Charlie was so attracted to someone who was so obvious a fraud.

'You know the boys love their Uncle Matt.'

'Oh please, don't try that one on me.'

'Well do you have plans for Saturday?'

'No, but…'

'…well then. You're so good with them. You're better with them than I am.'

'Well that's not difficult is it because they see more of me than they do of you.'

'Ouch. I suppose I deserved that one.'

'You can't keep doing this to me, Charlie.'

Charlie winked at his best mate. 'You'll get your reward in Heaven.'

'I've told you before, Charlie, just like I've told my mother too, I don't want pie in the sky when I die I want meat on my plate while I wait.'

'And how is your mother?'

'She's fine,' said Matt, 'getting onto me about every five minutes about not going to Mass but apart from that, she's the adorable nag she's always been.'

'You exaggerate.'

'Yeah, I know.'

'So you'll have the boys for me on Saturday?'

'You knew the answer to that before you asked me.'

'Good man!'

'But I want you to collect them by seven on Saturday evening,' Matt warned, 'I want to go out on Saturday night.'

'I'll do my best.'

'Charlie!'

'Well I can't promise, mate.' said Charlie, his face full of appeasing gestures, 'It depends on how long this lunch thing goes on for and on what Natasha has got planned afterwards.'

Matt closed his eyes and pinched the bridge of his nose. 'I don't believe this.'

'Come on, mate, it's what goes on between men and women.'

'Oh and I suppose I wouldn't know anything about that'

'I didn't mean that, Matt.'

'No, I know you didn't.' said Matt, 'Alright, bring their pyjamas and overnight kit. I'll think of what to do with them between now and then. You just have yourself a good time.'

'She has silk sheets on her bed. I mean, how horny is that? She gets them cheap when she goes on trips to India.'

'Yes, and some ten-year old kid has probably gone blind stitching them in some sweat shop factory where he gets beaten if he doesn't work hard enough. Think about that lover boy the next time you're trying to avoid sleeping on the damp patch.'

'We don't do damp patches,' Charlie sneered, 'she gets up and changes the sheets after we've … you know.'

'Oh I've heard it all now. What happened to

spontaneous passion?'

'Oh there's plenty of that,' said Charlie, 'it's just that it has to be cleaned up afterwards or else she can't sleep. Absolutely nothing is out of place in her house. She's the Queen of the tidy girls.'

'Is she still calling you Charles when everybody else, including your own parents, call you Charlie?'

'Oh yes.'

'I rest my case.'

'She's very pretty.'

'That's only skin deep.'

'She's great in the sack.'

'Well that'll only last until you're married.'

'Yeah,' said Charlie, nodding his head, 'Good point.'

'Anyway, you've got patients waiting and so have I.'

'The pub after surgery?'

'Where's the lady Natasha?'

Charlie smiled. 'On her way to Chicago.'

' Then I'll be there,' said Matt, 'and I do believe it's your around.'

Joe Alexander got out of bed and put his boxer shorts back on. He was still hard from sex and had to negotiate his cock back under cover. Then he put his jeans back on and zipped them up carefully before pulling his light blue cotton t-shirt back over his head. He picked up Carol's watch from the bedside table and handed it to her as she came in from the bathroom.

'Thanks' said Carol, putting it on and fastening it.

Joe reached out and pulled her to him. She wrapped her arms around his waist and kissed him. Then Joe began to finger her hair away from her face.

'Have you got time to stay for a drink?' Joe asked.

'I'd better not,' said Carol, 'Richard will be expecting me and I'm already late.'

'That's a shame. I hate it when you have to rush off just after... you know?'

'Well it's your fault, tiger,' said Carol, lightly, 'I wasn't expecting it twice.'

'You bring out the stud in me.'

'I think I must do.'

'Carol, about the bruise underneath your arm ... '

'...don't Joe,' said Carol as she pulled away from him.

'You didn't fall over, did you?'

She looked at him helplessly and then she sat down on the end of his bed. 'What am I doing, Joe? I stay married to one man when I've got another who's a hundred times better.'

'So he did hit you?'

Carol looked up at him and nodded her head. Then he sat down beside her. She'd confirmed what Joe had suspected about her husband for a while.

'It all started after his accident,' Carol began, 'he's always been a proud man and not being able to go out to work just really gets to him, you know?'

'And that's an excuse to use you as a punch bag?'

'No, but... it doesn't happen every day. Just when he gets really down about everything and Joe, he was a fit, active man who ended up in a wheelchair at the age of thirty-seven. I can understand how frustrated he gets at not being able to do the things he used to and provide for his family.'

'Carol, I understand all of that but there's absolutely no excuse,' said Joe, 'and I'll never put any pressure on you, you know that. But if you lived here I'd cherish you, look after you, treat you like the lady that you are. The kids would have a good home here.'

'But how can I leave him when he's like he is?' she pleaded, desperately. 'He'd have nothing if he didn't have me and the kids.'

'Well I know how that feels.'

'Joe, don't say that.'

'Why not? It's the truth.'

'You deserve much better than me.'

'I'll be the judge of that,' smiled Joe, 'and I'm going to hold on until you come to your senses.'

Carol kissed him passionately.

'I can't ask you to do that.'

'You're not asking me,' said Joe who'd realised lately just how much he was in love with Carol and how much he depended on her coming around. 'I'm saying that I will.'

Carol looked into Joe's blue-grey eyes. 'I don't want you to waste your time. You ought to be out there finding someone.'

'I have found someone.'

'Oh Joe,' she said. Then she kissed him again and picked up her handbag. 'I'll go out the back way as usual'

'Okay.' said Joe, 'Saturday afternoon?'

'I'll be here about one,' said Carol who could've just burst into tears but she had to stay composed. It only took half a minute to walk from Joe's house at the top of the hill down to her own house further down. A difference of about ten houses. She touched his face. 'I'll be thinking of you.'

'And I'll be thinking of you,' said Joe.

'Stay safe on those streets,' said Carol.

'I will for you' said Joe.

She gave him her biggest smile and then she was gone.

★

Ann had prepared dinner and left it for Brendan and Phillip. All they had to do was heat it up but because there was so much of it Phillip was having to use every available means of heat source to do it. She'd done them a chicken pie made with short crust pastry just how Brendan liked it and there were so many different kinds of vegetables that Phillip got bored counting at five.

'Irish women are such big feeders,' muttered Brendan as they were finally able to sit down at the table and serve themselves up. 'It's in their DNA.'

'It would seem that way, Brendan,' said Phillip as he looked out across the table at the feast before them. He hadn't opened any wine because he knew that Brendan didn't partake and anyway, he had work to do himself later that evening. So instead he just poured them each a glass of orange juice.

'The English put the kettle on at the first sign of trouble while the Irish peel some more spuds.' chuckled Brendan, 'They think that if they pile a plate high with overcooked meat and vegetables then the boy they serve up this mothers meal to will forget he's being shagged to hell by some paedophile priest.'

Phillip almost choked on his piece of cauliflower. 'Jesus, Brendan, will you warn me before saying such things.'

'They'd think that would be enough for him not to say anymore about it. Then by the time his plate is clean the priest will have been moved to a parish on the other side of the country and no more would be said about that.'

'We can't be proud of the way we deal with such things, Brendan.'

'No, we can't,' said Brendan, 'now don't get me wrong.

This is a marvellous meal and Ann Schofield is a fantastic cook who simply wanted to show us her kindness. All I'm saying is that it is firmly in the Irish female tradition to use food as an avoidance tactic.'

'Comfort food.'

'In it's most basic sense, yes.' said Brendan.

'And is this really how you see the average Irish woman, Brendan?'

'It's how I see the average Irish anything, Phillip.' said Brendan, 'Still wrapped up in the values of a church that can do no wrong. It was my blinding faith in God that led me to the priesthood but it was also the recognition that I could use my status as a Priest to right some wrongs. What a bloody fool I was! What an idiot! And so bloody naïve. I couldn't change anything. You see, when I first became a priest back in Ireland we used to send young girls who got themselves into trouble to laundries where they were slave labour for sadistic nuns who used to beat the hell out of them if they didn't do as they were told. The church would decide when these girls would be set free but in the meantime none of the boys involved were ever sanctioned in any way. It was as if the girls had done it all to themselves and the injustice of it all made me so angry.'

'So what did you do?'

'We were a young democratic nation, we were the Irish Republic, we'd broken away from the yoke of British colonialism and yet we were imprisoning young girls just for being unable to stand up to boys who were determined to get inside their knickers.'

'That's not too far away from stoning women in Iran for adultery whilst letting their lovers get away with it.'

'It's no distance at all, Phillip!' Brendan replied, 'And at least in Iran there's some kind of a trial. Our girls didn't go before any court, we just sent them away. We didn't stone them but we committed them to a living death inside those blasted laundries. It was wrong, Phillip. It was very, very wrong. But it was part of the church being so entangled with the new Irish state. I was warned not to rock the boat and that if I wanted to get anywhere as a young priest I'd keep my mouth shut. I'll forever be ashamed for taking the advice and putting my career before justice for those girls. The laundries closed down eventually but not until after many more souls had suffered in them.'

'You're a rebel, Brendan,' said Phillip, 'but in the right way.'

'Oh I don't know. Maybe I'm just getting old.'

'They warned me you were a character, Brendan.'

Brendan smiled between mouthfuls of roast potato. 'Did they now?'

'Oh yes,' said Phillip, 'and they were right.'

'Well I'm not always proud of the ways of the church, Phillip.'

'So between the laundries and the issue of paedophile priests, nothing much went on?' said Phillip, his tongue very firmly in his cheek. 'It was all a breeze, wasn't it?'

'Well not exactly.' said Brendan as they both laughed. 'There was the little detail of the whole world blaming us for not helping the issue of poverty in developing countries by being opposed to contraception. Then there was the issue of the forced migration of children to Australia. That was a shameful business too, Phillip. It was an evil, shameful business.'

'Wasn't this very parish involved in all that, Brendan? '

'It was indeed, Philip.'

Phillip pointed out the kitchen window with his knife. 'Wasn't the children's home out the back there?'

'Yes,' said Brendan, 'before we sold the land and they built those lovely flats you see now. Scores of them went from here, Phillip, and again it's a shameful part of our history for which we should be on our knees every night praying for the Lord's forgiveness. We lied to them, Phillip. We lied to little children whose hearts were already shattered into pieces. We sent them into some horrible situations and some of them weren't even orphans. There was a trade going on with hard cash involved. It was nothing less than people trafficking, Phillip. Thank the Lord it was stopped eventually but long after it was too late for many.'

'Too late?'

'They'd already gone,' said Brendan, 'and there was no getting them back.'

CHAPTER FOUR

'Well now,' said Angela as she sat down once again across the plastic table from Paddy, 'two weeks ago you ended up telling me you didn't want to talk about it. Then I got your message yesterday saying otherwise. What's changed your mind?'

'Well you look like the kind of sheila who doesn't give up and I'm not in the mood for being pestered,' quipped the inmate, 'and I've nowhere to bloody run!'

Angela laughed. 'Oh Paddy, I'm so flattered. So what's the real reason?'

Paddy rubbed his stubble covered chin and looked thoughtfully at this good-looking woman with a kind heart and a ferocious brain who'd been sent to help him understand himself. He silently wished her the very best of luck. 'I think it's time, Doc,' he said, 'what you said before made a lot of sense but I'm not used to it.'

'Not used to what, Paddy?'

'People making sense to me.'

'Alright.' said Angela, keen to hold the momentum, 'So where do you want to start?'

Paddy lifted up a carrier bag that had been lying at his feet and handed it to Angela.

'There must be half a dozen folders in here,' said Angela as she pulled one of them out. They were full of pages and pages of hand written notes. 'What's in them?'

'The story, Doc,' said Paddy, 'the whole story, everything that's happened to me since that day in 1962.'

'I can read it all?'

'That's why I've given it to you,' said Paddy.

'I never knew you'd have something like this, Paddy' said Angela who was overwhelmed by Paddy's meticulousness. She had a quick look through the files and they were all in incredible order, detailing year on year every bit of Paddy's painful story. Except that they weren't written like a diary.

'I'm full of surprises, Doc.'

'Paddy, you've styled all this like a novel. It's all in the third person. Why have you done that?'

'I thought it might be less painful to…' Paddy folded his arms across his chest and stretched out his legs, '…well to think of all the shit happening to someone else. Does that make sense to you?'

'It does,' said Angela, 'but what do you intend to do with this? I mean, it's a manuscript. Do you want to get it published?'

'I guess it wouldn't be worth it otherwise.'

'Some would say you shouldn't profit out of anything in your situation.'

'They're the ones who haven't had the bloody life

I've had,' said Paddy.

Angela raised her head slightly at Paddy's deepening, firmer voice and the look of sheer anger shooting through his eyes. She'd obviously touched a nerve. 'You'll have to be prepared for it though, Paddy,' she said, 'you do realise that?'

'Yeah, I do, Doc' said Paddy.

'Okay,' said Angela who put down the file she'd been looking through and raised her eyes to take in once more the shadows all across his prematurely aged face.

'So you want to start in 1962?'

'Yes, Doc.' said Paddy. 'Like I said, the day before my fifth birthday. And what I should point out first of all is that I was called Sean back then. The name of Paddy came later.'

'Alright.' said Angela. ' Just a point before we start, though. Is there anything here that talks about the time before that day in 1962?'

'No.'

'And why is that?'

'Because I thought I was happy before then,' said Paddy.

'Thought you were?'

'Yes,' said Paddy, 'like I thought I had a mother who loved me.'

1962

'...he'd hit his little hand against the glass of the window so many times that the whole of his arm was aching. His Mummy had told him they were going to have tea with the Nuns. She'd told him there'd be cakes and jelly and ice cream. One of the Nuns had taken him out into the garden to play with some of the other kids and when he'd gone back to the room his Mummy had gone. The

Nun told him that his Mummy was very sorry but she couldn't cope with him anymore and was trusting him to the care of the Children's Home. He told them they were lying and one of them had slapped his face. He'd made for the door and they'd grabbed him. They held on to him as tight as they could whilst he screamed and cried and tried to kick his way to freedom. His Mummy couldn't have left him. Why had she left him? He'd been a good boy. He'd done everything she wanted. He hadn't been naughty. He'd eaten everything on his plate. Why would she want to do this to him? He'd just started school. The other kids had a Daddy but he'd never asked her where his Daddy was. The big man who'd started to come around hadn't talked to him. He'd tried to talk to the big man but the big man wasn't interested. 'Mummy!' he wailed. 'Mummy!' Why had she just left him there? He wanted to run all the way home but he didn't know the way. Maybe he could've got around to his Grandma's house but he couldn't remember how. His Mummy only took him there once in a while but his Grandma cuddled him and made him feel nice.

'I want to go home to my Mummy' he said.

'You can't, sweetheart,' said Rita, her heart breaking for him. When she'd got to work that morning she was asked by one of the Nuns if she could do something with the new boy. She knew what that meant. If he didn't shake himself out of it soon the Nuns would beat the shit out of him until he couldn't cry anymore.

'Your Mummy left you with us. We're going to take care of you now.'

'But I want to go home to my Mummy!'

'This is your home now, Sean,' said Rita. She was running out of time. Once the Nuns got hold of him he'd know about it. They could be cruel. They could be sadistic. Rita had witnessed them break the spirit of many a child. They always said that children born out of wedlock were an offence to God but Rita didn't buy any of that. The offence was made by the stupid parents who dumped their kids here and didn't seem to give a flaming damn. She remembered Sean's mother. She'd seemed respectable enough. Nice coat, nice shoes, leather handbag. Hair had obviously only recently been done. What the hell was she doing walking into a children's home with her son and walking out without him?

'This is not my home,' said Sean, 'and where's my Daddy?'

Rita held his hand. 'Sweetheart, you've got to get used to it. You've got to accept that your Mummy isn't coming back and you've got to start fitting in and behaving yourself. I know you can't make sense of any of it, love, but you've got to try. And I'll be here to help you. I promise. I'll be here to help you get through it.'

Sean was sobbing his heart out. 'Will I be able to see my Mummy?'

' No, sweetheart,' said Rita who then cuddled him close, 'but I'll be here. I'll be here always but you've got to promise me to be a good boy otherwise the Nuns will get cross with you and you don't want that. So promise me to do as you're told and try not to wet the bed.'

Whenever the nuns were getting a child ready for shipment they never gave a hint to the child as to what was about to happen to them. Packing their clothes, what little of them that some of them had, took place whilst the child wasn't near enough to notice. Rita hated doing this. She hated looking into the eyes of a child who'd already been rejected by their family and who was about to be sent to the other side of the world without them knowing anything about it or being part of the decision. They were already bewildered by what had happened to them so far but the nuns didn't have any thought for that. They could make some money for their association from trading children with other Catholic societies, even in a far off land. These children were mostly born from immoral acts as far as the nuns were concerned. That made them unworthy of the same consideration that was given to children born into normal families. Normal families? Rita herself had been lucky that George had wanted to marry her after she became pregnant with Michelle. If he hadn't then her child might've ended up in a loveless hole like this one. It sent a shiver down her spine to think that she'd come that close.

Rita had developed a special bond with little Sean. She'd love to get hold of his mother and demand of her how she could've been so cruel to just leave him there but her actual identity was a secret locked away in a filing cabinet in the Mother Superior's office. Rita had even put it to her husband that they might think about adopting Sean but her husband was dead against it. He didn't want to 'bring somebody else's bastard into our home' and he wouldn't hear anymore of it. But Rita worried about little Sean. There was just something about him that made her worry about his future. Call it a premonition or an instinct. But it was there.

It broke her heart to have to get his things together and pack them in the little suitcase. She was going to miss him and she knew that he was going to miss her. She could take the cowards way out and swap her shift so that she wasn't on duty when all the children left. But she couldn't do that to Sean. His own mother had kicked him in the teeth and she was about to do the same. Except she couldn't offer him her home and her family in which to nurture him and make sure he grew up feeling loved and wanted. She had to play her part in sending him off as if he'd done something so wrong and so terrible when the only thing he'd done was to be born.

She was about to take his little suitcase downstairs when she turned and saw him standing watching her at the door. It was written all over his face. He knew.

'What are you doing?' he asked.

Rita sat down on his bed and tapped the space beside her. 'Come and sit with me, love. I need to talk to you about something.'

Sean didn't move. 'What about?'

Rita held out her hand. ' Come on, Sean, love. Come and sit with me?'

Sean started to cry. Rita went over to him but he cowered away from her. She'd never felt more awful in her life.

She knelt down and held his shoulders. 'Sean, you've got to be a very brave boy for me. Do you understand? You're going away to a far away place and … '

'…why can't you come with me?' he pleaded, trying to untangle himself.

'I can't, sweetheart, I just can't. I'm sorry.'

As she tried to calm him down one of the nuns, Sister Philomena, a particularly nasty bitch who liked using a ruler on kids' knuckles, came storming down the corridor.

'Mrs. Makin!' she raged. ' I warned you about getting too attached to these urchins!'

'They're not urchins!' Rita retorted. 'They're in pain and they need love.'

'Oh I've never heard of anything so ridiculous,' snapped Sister Philomena. ' We, the sisters, give them a good home and you criticise us for it? Collect your cards from the Mother Superiors' office!'

Sister Philomena grabbed Sean so violently that the fear inside him made him wet his pants. She didn't like that one bit. She pulled his trousers and underpants down and rubbed his face in them before thrashing the living daylights out of him. Rita tried to intervene but Sister Philomena was stronger and she pushed her away. Sean disappeared, screaming in agony and hurt, his eyes full of fear, looking back and appealing to Rita as Sister Philomena dragged him along the floor by his hair. But Rita knew she was helpless.

'I'm sorry,' said Rita as she sobbed, her hands reaching out to him but not being able to go as far as he needed them to. 'I'm sorry, Sean. God bless you, sweetheart.'

'Rita! …Rita! …Ree – ta!'

★

'But how did you interpret what Rita Makin was thinking?' asked Angela. 'How did you work that out?'

'I didn't have to,' said Paddy, who was feeling tired after his great disclosures. He wasn't used to going down so deep into talking about himself. 'Rita used to talk to me a lot. I knew what she was thinking.'

'But you were so young.'

'But I remembered it, I soaked it all up because she was the only one who cared about me then. I didn't know what it all meant at the time. It was only later that it all started to make sense. Then when I was older I was able to work a lot of the other stuff out like when they were preparing a child for shipment for instance.'

'Even at the age you were then you still remember her words in such great detail?'

'Oh yes,' said Paddy.

'Do you still think of Rita Makin, Paddy?'

'Oh yes, Doc,' said Paddy, 'quite often.'

'But it was such a long time ago and you were so young.'

'Doc, you never forget those who show you love even if it was a lifetime ago,' said Paddy, 'you just never forget them.'

'I can understand that' said Angela.

'Especially when you've been shown as little as I have.'

'Is it sympathy you're after, Paddy?'

'No, Doc.' said Paddy. 'It's a recognition that I was done wrong against by the very person who should've protected me from any harm and that her actions sent me down a path to disaster.'

'Your mother?'

'Exactly, my mother. A crime is never simply a crime, Doc, despite what all the hang 'em and flog 'em brigade try and bullshit. A crime is just the end of the story.'

CHAPTER FIVE

Matt woke up and peered out from under his duvet at the small electronic clock on his bedside table. It was 6.09. He groaned and turned over and must've fallen back to sleep again because the next thing he knew was the sound of a hammering on his front door downstairs. Who the hell could that be? How embarrassing in this quiet tree lined avenue of Didsbury, the suburb of Manchester's thinking professional classes. This was where people liked to think of themselves as the middle class with a conscience. They used to vote Liberal Democrat because they'd fallen out with Labour over the Iraq war but now they'd fallen out with the Liberal Democrats over their support for the Tories so were going back to Labour. They read the Independent but sneak a look at their cleaner's Daily

Mirror when she's doing the upstairs. In short, they didn't do hammerings at the door.

He got out of bed and crept over to his bedroom's large bay window. He pulled the curtain back slightly and looked down. It was his sister Susie. He threw a robe over the t-shirt and shorts he'd been wearing in bed and went downstairs to let her in.

'What are you doing here at this time?' he asked as he stood to the side to let her through.

'Nice to see you too!' his sister replied. She was in full running gear and carrying a plastic bottle of water.

'Have you run all the way from Bowdon?' he asked as he closed the door behind her.

'No, you tit. I've just been to the gym and I thought I'd drop in on my big brother so that he can make me my breakfast.' She gripped his face. 'You look a bit second hand this morning. Late night?'

'No, I stayed in.'

'How many bottles of wine?'

'I just about remember getting through the second one.' Matt admitted.

'You doctors are all the same. You tell the rest of us to drink responsibly and yet you lot put away enough for all of us.'

'Yeah, well, those are the breaks,' said Matt who'd felt particularly lonely last evening and had used wine to help kill the pain. 'Come through and I'll put a pot of coffee on. Fried eggs on toast do you?'

'Lovely.' said Susie, following Matt into the kitchen. 'Got some tomato ketchup?'

'You know I don't buy it,' said Matt, 'I hate the stuff.'

'But what about your guests?'

'Well when you're a guest in my house you have to

abide by my rules' said Matt, smiling at her sulky face. 'So didn't Angus go to the gym with you? Or did you keep him up way past his bedtime last night?'

'Oh do you know you're so funny that you've missed your vocation and should be doing a turn at the Comedy Store in town,' she said, turning up the corner of her lip to match the sarcasm of her words. 'You know very well he's only six years younger than me. It's so bloody sexist. If it was the other way around nobody would bloody well notice.'

'Ladies and Gentleman, appearing at my kitchen diner for one morning only, it's Miss Germaine Greer!'

'Oh and they keep on coming.' Susie was smiling the self-satisfied smile of someone who was in love and thinking of how gorgeous her fiancé had looked after they'd made love in the small hours. Sex always brought out the best look on Angus, like a naughty boy who'd been allowed to play an adult party game.

'Well if you will be a cougar.'

'And what would I be if I were the man and he was the girl?'

'Lucky.' teased Matt, 'You know how it works.'

'Well that's where I rest my case.'

Matt laughed. 'Your face! Relax kid sister, I'm on your side.'

'That's only because you're a practicing homosexual with no moral code.'

'I'm not practising!' Matt protested. 'I'm very well accomplished in my role. So anyway, what did you do with my future brother-in-law?'

'He's on an early flight to Malaga,' said Susie, referring to Angus' job as a co-pilot for a holiday charter airline based at Manchester. 'Poor baby. He had to be at work at half-six. He'll be back the middle of the afternoon though and then he's got tomorrow off so we'll have a nice cosy weekend together.'

'How idyllic'

'It will be,' said Susie, noting the clear sound of envy in her brother's voice. She didn't like to come across like she was rubbing his nose in it but what could she say except the truth? She respected him too much for that.

Matt took a frying pan out of the cupboard and placed it on the cooker hob. He poured a little olive oil in and waited for it to get hot. He liked his kitchen. Everything was stored in an 'island' in the centre with only the sink, cooker, fridge, and dishwasher along the back wall. Susie was sitting at the diner on a high stool. She watched her brother pour them some orange juice into a couple of glasses and thanked him when he handed one to her. Matt thought about Susie's kitchen which had Angus' work roster pinned to the notice board and he wondered if his work roster would ever be pinned to anybody's notice board.

'So anyway,' said Matt, 'how's the world of trailer trash?'

Susie had taken over at the helm of the family business some five years ago when their father retired. He'd built it up over thirty years and now Schofield Caravan Parks had eleven sites at locations stretching across the northwest from Buxton in the Peak District right the way up to the Scottish border. They were all a mixture of long lease caravans that people tended to make their permanent home and holiday caravans that people came to for one or two weeks at a time. There were also large spaces available for those who brought their own caravans with them. Susie had just done a deal with a national pub chain that was going to open on each of the sites in time for next season. All four members of the family had equal shares in the business but Matt had never shown any interest in running it. Susie on the other hand had been at her father's side since she could talk so it had been entirely logical that he'd handed the reins to her.

'Don't be so disparaging. Anyway, it's booming and you should be grateful because the value of your shares are going up. A lot of people are downsizing because they can't afford their mortgage payments and many others are staying in this country for their holidays this year and I agree with them.'

'Well you would, it's your business.'

'Our business,' Susie corrected. 'We're all equal partners. I'm just the boss.'

'And despite your self-interest, do you think everybody should stay at home for their holidays this year?'

'Yeah,' said Susie, 'support the home economy and all that.'

'Remind me where you and Angus flew off to for two weeks last October?'

Susie narrowed her eyes at him. ' Malaysia.'

'And where is that in the Great British isles?'

'I would only let you get away with cornering me like that.'

'I know.' said Matt, laughing. 'Because I'm your big brother and therefore allowed.'

'Anyway, what are you doing with yourself today?' Susie asked.

'Charlie's coming over later with the boys' said Matt, 'I'm looking after them for the day and probably the rest of the weekend.'

Susie gave him a stern look.

'Don't start, Susie.'

'Matt, you're heading into the back end of your thirties and it bothers me to think that you spend your

Friday night getting pissed alone and then your Saturday looking after the kids of your totally irresponsible friend.'

'Susie, they're my God children and Charlie isn't totally irresponsible,' said Matt who leapt to Charlie's defence like he always did.' I could've gone out last night but I chose to stay in and that's an important difference.'

'But you're a social bunny,' said Susie, 'you always have been.'

'But I'm getting older, Susie,' said Matt.

'And you've not got many single friends left to run about with.'

'Yeah, that's right to tell you the truth.'

'Everybody is coupled up and you didn't feel like being the odd number at someone's house for dinner.'

'Sometimes I don't mind, last night I didn't feel like it.'

'But like you said, Matt, you're getting older and the picture of that house with the right man and a couple of dogs is fading.'

'Susie, you're talking as if I'm some kind of sad bastard who can't get a date.'

'That's not how I see you,' said Susie, 'I know you can get a date.'

'So?'

'So I'm convinced you won't get a date because you're in love with your straight best friend.'

'Susie!'

'Look me in the eye and tell me you're not in love with Charlie.'

'I'm not in love with Charlie, Susie.'

'Tell me like you mean it.'

'Oh Susie, give up.'

'You let him walk all over you. He's earning a fortune being the resident GP on Sky News. He's got a whole celebrity thing going on now as the dishy TV doctor.'

'He was on Loose Women last week,' added Matt. 'But Susie, I'd clam up on television.'

'Well what about his column in the Manchester Evening News? That all came out of the Sky News gig.'

'Granada are doing a new medical TV soap,' said Matt, 'they've asked him to be medical consultant on it.'

'And why didn't they ask you?'

'I don't…'

'…because everything that comes into the practice that pays hard cash goes to him.'

'Susie…'

'…whilst you get all the social work crap that has to be done out of the goodness of your bloody heart because he's too busy raking it in at your expense.'

'Susie, I'm not like you. I don't see a pound sign in everything I do.'

'Oh spare me the bloody socialist sermon.'

'Susie, I'm a doctor, I treat sick people, and I'm good at it. I'm happy enough doing that without all those extras that Charlie is much more suited for.'

'I don't believe you.'

'Well you're going to have to.'

'Just like I don't believe you about your feelings for him.'

'Well you're never going to get any other answer out of me than I've already given because it wouldn't be the truth.'

'Matt, I love you dearly, you're the best big brother a girl could have but I'm worried that you're going to end up a lonely old man because of your unrequited feelings for a straight man who's never going to give you what you want.'

Matt buttered the toast and made sure Susie's eggs

were still runny, just how she liked them, before placing them on top. He handed them to her and said 'Get tucked into them.'

Susie smiled.

'Or else?'

'Or else you'll be wearing them.'

★

DI Tim Norris and his wife Helen didn't have to worry too much about the pennies. They were both earning good salaries and despite Helen's tendency to be frugal, Tim could always persuade her to agree to them splashing out on occasions like tonight which was their anniversary. So it was a great dinner in one of Manchester's best restaurants where the clientele included soap stars, premiership footballers and BBC television presenters who'd moved up from London with the move to MediaCity in Salford Quays. And they were both in their best clothes. For Tim that meant a Hugo Boss suit in camel with a dark chocolate coloured shirt with which he wore his cufflinks. Helen was in a simple black strapless dress with a neckline that was low enough to show off her long flowing curly black hair to full effect but with a hem that was high enough to make Tim, and probably every other man in the place, feel the strongest desire. She did have the most fantastic legs and he never stopped believing how lucky he was to have this woman on his arm. He was also relieved that any feelings that Sara Hoyland might've stirred up in him had passed.

'If I have a dessert then I'll never fit into this dress again,' announced Helen after the waiter had presented them with dessert menus.

'It's our big night, baby,' said Tim, 'we're celebrating.

Six whole years.'

'And to think I thought I was going to lose you last year when Sara Hoyland came back into your life with her little bombshell.'

Helen had never been the kind of woman who was jealous of her husband's ex-girlfriends. She wasn't the kind of woman who had to believe that he couldn't possibly have ever been happy before she came along. That kind of attitude was for silly little girls and not grown women. But even Helen had been rocked by Sara's revelation that she'd had Tim's baby and given it up for adoption without saying a word to him. Helen hadn't been angry with Tim for having kept it from her once he knew. She'd understood his reasons for that. He hadn't wanted to upset her when they were in the middle of trying so hard to conceive themselves. Her distress had been caused by Sara's deception that had broken Tim's heart and because it spelt out loud and clear that Helen was the one with the fertility problem and that Sara had been able to give Tim what she couldn't.

'You would never have lost me, baby.'

'It crossed your mind though.'

'Helen, Sara was right' said Tim. 'If we'd got together all those years ago it would've only been because of the baby. Once I'd met you there was nobody else and never could be.'

'But I heard you in the pub that night … '

'…Helen, we've been through all this' said Tim with a note of exasperation, 'I didn't mean what I said that night. I was muddled. It was just because of…'

'…the baby?' said Helen. 'The baby that she can give you and I can't?'

Tim took hold of his wife's hands across the table. 'That means nothing to me, Helen. I'm not interested in what she can give me. I'm only interested in what you and I can give each other.'

'So you're sure about us adopting then?'

'Of course I am. And are you sure?'

'Yes. But she got one over on me where you're concerned and occasionally I don't think that grown up about it.'

'But it's you I love, Helen.' said Tim, 'Not Sara.'

Helen had never really doubted that deep down but if a woman turns up and tells a man that she had his baby five years ago but gave him up for adoption it's bound to have an effect on him. And Helen knew her husband. She knew how sensitive he was. She also knew that his character was strong. Otherwise, how could he carry on working with Sara?

'I know,' said Helen, 'I do know that and I do believe it.'

'Good,' said Tim 'because it's the truth.'

'Do you ever think of your son out there?'

'Now and then,' said Tim, 'you don't mind?'

'No, of course I don't.' said Helen. 'You're bound to think of him and of course I don't mind.'

'So you are ready to find out who we may be adopting ourselves?'

Helen and Tim had been through the adoption procedures and had passed all the tests. It was now time for them to be given a child and the social worker who was handling their case had called them in tomorrow to discuss it.

'Oh yes'

'It's exciting isn't it'

'It is,' said Helen 'and you know, if your son decided to find you when he grows up, that'll all be cool with me. You do know that?'

'I do,' said Tim who then lifted her hand and kissed it, 'and thank you. But let's see to our immediate future first and that means us becoming a family.'

Helen smiled. 'Happy anniversary, Detective.'

'Happy anniversary, Mrs. Norris' said Tim. 'Now what do you fancy for dessert?'

'Well it's not something you'll find on this menu.' said Helen, smiling that way that Tim loved. 'Let's go home.'

★

Time swept by so fast as it always did when Matt was looking after Charlie's boys. First of all they played some of the games on the Nintendo that Matt had bought especially for when they came to visit. Then he gave them Chilli con Carne for lunch which was one of their favourites and which he'd made the previous evening knowing that they were coming. After that he took them to see United thrash Sunderland by four goals to nil and then they headed back into Manchester city centre where he bought them a pair of shoes each after Wendy had told Charlie that they needed them. He asked them what they wanted for their tea and the answer was a unanimous 'pasta!' so he cooked some ravioli for them and served ice cream for dessert. He found it a joy to look after them and he didn't care about whatever his reasons for doing it were.

It was half past seven and he knew that Charlie wouldn't be coming to collect them now. Any moment he'd get a call from him to ask if he'd keep them overnight. And just as he was thinking that his phone started to ring. The caller ID told him it was Charlie's mobile.

'Hi mate' said Charlie.

'So what time tomorrow?'

'Are you sure you don't mind?'

'Charlie, I knew you wouldn't be coming back this evening so they're already in their pyjamas and watching 'Thunderbirds' on DVD.'

'Put them on and let me wish them goodnight.'

After Charlie had done his fatherly duties over the phone, his youngest son Harry handed the receiver back to Matt.

'That was short and sweet' said Charlie.

'They're watching Thunderbird 4 come out of the pod that comes out of Thunderbird 2.' Matt explained. 'It's a very complicated procedure and requires the absolute attention of our little International Rescuers here.'

Charlie laughed. 'I suppose so. Look, thanks Matt, I hope I haven't spoilt your plans for the weekend.'

Matt stood up and walked through to the kitchen with the cordless receiver in his hand. 'No, you're fine,' he said, 'but when can I expect you tomorrow?'

' Lunch with some more of Natasha's friends at some posh sort of restaurant in Prestbury' said Charlie. 'The boys wouldn't like it.'

'So when will you be picking them up?'

'About five?' Charlie ventured.

'So that means that for your entire access weekend the only time you'll have seen them will be when you drove them here yesterday and when you drive them back again to Wendy's house tomorrow'

'Will you take them to your parents with you for lunch?'

'You fucking know I will but that's not the point, Charlie.'

'I know, I know, and I'll make it up to them, I promise.'

'I hope you mean that,' said Matt. 'because they'll drift away from you otherwise and you'll only have yourself to blame.'

'I don't know what else to say, mate.'

'No? Well look, you get on with your Cheshire set weekend. I've got somebody else's children to look after.'

★

Penny was desperately upset when she came home from her parents' house. Her younger sister Natasha had done it again. Natasha had been saying how wonderful things were going with Charles and that she expected him to pop the question any time. Penny was genuinely pleased for her and hoped that Charles did make Natasha happy. But Natasha used her good fortune as an opportunity to have a stab at Penny and told her how she couldn't understand how Penny could've settled for so little in her life.

'She said what?' Adrian asked as they shared a coffee in the kitchen. They'd just had dinner and the kids were in the living room watching TV.

'She said that marrying a policeman and living in a semi with three kids is hardly having arrived. Then Mum joined in.'

'What did she say for God's sake?'

'That she didn't talk about me to her friends anymore because she thought my life was so boring,' said Penny. 'She said she only talked about Natasha now because her life was so exciting compared to mine.'

'I don't believe I'm hearing this,' said Adrian, exasperated at his in-laws insensitivity towards his wife.

'The thing is, they throw out their nasty remarks but if I retaliate then I'm the one who's accused of causing trouble. I can't win with them, Adrian, and it hurts, you know, it really, really hurts.'

'Oh, baby,' said Adrian taking her into his arms whilst she sobbed. 'They'll never have what we've got.'

'They wouldn't recognise what we've got,' said Penny. 'Remember what happened when Natasha split up with Robbie? She woke up and realised she didn't love him enough to marry him the morning after he told her that his business had failed and he had to file for bankruptcy. Did my parents give her a good talking to like they should've done for kicking a man when he was down? No. Did they tell her that they could see through her little gold digging act? No. But me, the one who marries for love and has three wonderful kids, I'm not worthy of being talked about by my own mother.'

'Your parents have never been able to see through all Natasha's crap,' added Adrian, 'I really don't know why.'

'Because they're like her, Adrian, especially Mum. I'm the black sheep for leading a normal, happy life without drama.'

'It must've been hard when you were a kid, baby?'

'Christmas, 1989,' said Penny, 'That was a hard time.'

'You've never spoken about it before?'

'I'd tried to block it all out,' said Penny.

'What happened?'

'After the school Christmas party I stayed out half an hour longer than I'd been given permission to. So Mum said that because I'd been so naughty and disobedient, she was cancelling Christmas for everybody.'

'What?'

'She said that I had to explain to Natasha why she wouldn't be getting any presents and to Dad as to why he wouldn't be sitting down to his usual Christmas dinner that he liked so much. I felt like the whole world hated me that Christmas. It was horrible. And do you know what? I found out from my grandparents on my Dad's side that they hadn't cancelled Christmas because of me. They'd overstretched themselves financially and couldn't afford it but instead of owning up to that they decided instead to put it all onto my shoulders and use the fact that I'd stayed out half an hour too long one night. Not Natasha who'd been suspended from school for bad behaviour and who'd admitted to having slept with half the boys in our street. Oh no, none of that was naughty enough to suspend Christmas for. But I'm late one time and I'm used to cover up their failings. And Mum could shout. She never hit me but she may as well have done with the way she shouted and bellowed at me in front of everyone all the time.'

Adrian held her tight. 'But why did she single you out?'

'I don't know,' said Penny. 'All I do know is that our Natasha could get away with murder but I was wrong every time I took a breath. Natasha said some horrible things today, Adrian. She said that if I wasn't her sister she wouldn't want anything to do with me.'

'Oh, babe.'

'Mum never offered me one word of comfort or support and when I left the house in tears neither of them came after me to see if I was alright.'

'I don't know what the hell is wrong with your Mum and Dad at times.'

'Natasha also said something else.'

'What more could she have said?'

'She said that I was so boring that she couldn't work out how you've stayed with me and had three kids and that you'd be off shagging if you got the chance.'

'I'll bloody swing for her!'

'It's not true though, is it, Adrian?'

'You know it's not true,' said Adrian, still holding her

tight in his arms. 'Penny, no other woman could ever hold a candle to you as far as I'm concerned. As for your Mum and Dad, well, I don't know what goes on inside their heads. What I do know is that they should be proud of their eldest daughter.'

'They never come and see the kids, do they. That's because they don't like me.'

'Oh Penny, sweetheart,' said Adrian as his wife broke her heart. 'They couldn't be more wrong. Natasha is jealous because we've got real love. That's something she wouldn't recognise if it leapt up and slapped her across the face.'

'I nearly slapped her one this afternoon.'

'You should've done.'

'My parents really would've really hated me then.'

'But you'd have got a lot of satisfaction out of it.'

'Too right. It's never even crossed my mind to slap any of our kids but my sister could turn me into a female boxing champion.'

'Well before you do, let's wait until the kids are all in bed and then curl up on the sofa with a bottle of wine and talk about how boring we are.'

'It's a date,' said Penny, looking up into her husband's face and smiling, 'I am happy, you know. More than I ever could say.'

'Me too, sweetheart' said Adrian.

Penny snuggled up to her husband and wondered how she was going to tell him that the familiar feelings of back ache and nausea had been sweeping over her again lately.

CHAPTER SIX

The atmosphere among everybody who worked at the
surgery was relaxed but it didn't stop Charlie and Matt
falling into the roles of good cop and bad cop with the
staff when necessary.

Charlie always got away with murder because he was
Charlie and everybody loved him. Any issues that came
up were left to Matt to sort out. There used to be two
phones on the receptionist's desk, one for surgery calls
and one for appointments, each with different numbers.
When Matt witnessed one of the receptionists tell a caller
off for ringing on the surgery line and then pick up the
appointments phone to the same caller only seconds later,
he decided that the surgery's patients needed to be treated
with a bit more respect than that, especially since many of
them couldn't afford to make multiple calls. So he cut the
two numbers and now patients ring just one number for
whatever they wanted. The receptionists hadn't liked this
because it had taken away some of their perceived power.
Then the nurses had been in a sulk with him because he'd
asked them to be more civil with the patients after some
of them had complained about the nurses being rude. So
it had fallen on Matt to tell everyone at the weekly staff
meeting that they were going to extend evening surgery
by one hour to make visiting the doctor easier for people
who worked full-time.

'It's about their convenience, not ours.' Matt had said.
'We're not here to serve ourselves, we're here to provide
healthcare in this community. I'm sorry if that doesn't

fall in with your childcare plans but things move on and develop. They don't stay the same and this practice will not be stuck in the arrogance of thinking that we're doing everyone we serve a favour.'

'But you're all doing a fantastic job,' Charlie added, 'we do want you to know that, don't we Matt?'

'Of course but this is how we're going to make a good job even better on behalf of the patients.'

Matt couldn't stand the mentality of people who think that everything should stand still and nothing should move with the times. Consumers of healthcare had changed, even though many of the practice's patients didn't have the stake in society that a job provided. But, in Matt's mind, that didn't mean that they were any less deserving than those who did. Even if someone doesn't have a job they need to prepare for when they do. They need to be part of the same stream in society. That's what Matt tried to get across to faces that looked back at him as if he was asking them to prostrate themselves before the local Bishop.

'Thanks for your support in there,' said Matt sarcastically as he walked into his consulting room followed by Charlie who closed the door behind him.

'You were doing alright,' said Charlie, encouragingly, 'you didn't need me.'

'That's not the fucking point! Why should I always have to be the one who plays the bad guy, Charlie? Why is it never you?'

'Because you don't need to be liked like I do?' Charlie offered, feebly.

'Oh for fuck's sake!'

'I'm just no good at that sort of thing.'

'Charlie, you are my partner in this place.'

'Er, that's something we need to talk about,' said

Charlie.

'What do you mean?'

Charlie took a deep breath. He knew Matt wasn't going to like this.

'I'm thinking of selling my share in the practice,' Charlie announced.

Matt felt like he'd been stabbed in the chest. 'Say that again.'

'Well the thing is, Natasha has got it into her head that this is a practice with too many poor people and she doesn't like me working here.'

Matt was livid. 'Now I've heard it all!'

'She wants me to move to a practice in a more acceptable area.'

'Acceptable?' Matt demanded angrily. 'Fucking acceptable? What the fuck does that mean?'

'She doesn't want to have to tell people that I work in inner-city Salford,' protested Charlie, 'she wants to be able to tell them that I only deal with the very top people of Cheshire.'

'And you've agreed to this bullshit?'

Charlie just shrugged his shoulders and smiled as best he could.

'I always knew you were weak where women were concerned but she's scraped the bottom of your fucking reserve tank.'

'Hey, that's not fair! It's funny though, I'll give you that.'

'You've only been with one real woman in your life, Charlie' said Matt. 'She gave you two beautiful children and, by your own admission, a very happy marriage and yet it still wasn't enough for you. You broke her heart because you couldn't keep your trousers on when all the gold-digging tarts came fluttering.'

'Have you finished?'

'Alright, well are you seriously telling me that you're going to piss down the drain everything we've worked for in this community for the sake of that airhead who wouldn't know a principle if it leapt up and slapped her across the face?'

'Don't put it like that, mate,' said Charlie, seeing all over Matt's face how badly the news was going down. 'I'll give you first refusal on buying me out.'

'Charlie, I'm the only other partner! We set it up that way, remember? So that we could do things our way without any interference from anyone else'

'I mean before I sell to anybody else.'

Matt took in a deep breath and tried to calm himself down. 'Sounds like you've got it all worked out.'

'Well it's what she wants, and women like Natasha are like little girls when they've set their heart set on something. And guys like me end up taking over from Daddy as the one who puts the smile back on her face by giving her exactly what she wants.'

Matt scoffed. 'And they say that women grow up faster than men?' He shook his head. 'Christ, I'm so glad I'm not straight and having to pander to this nonsense.'

'That's a point of view, mate.'

'And all so that you can continue to gain access to your girlfriend's front bottom.'

Charlie laughed. 'You always blind me with your wisdom, my friend. But look, Matt, can you can afford to buy me out?'

'Yes' said Matt. 'I may have to borrow some but I should be able to manage it. But that's not the point, Charlie.'

'I know, mate, I know, but it's not like we're ever going to stop being friends.'

'Well how could we? We're like a divorced couple with two kids to give us a reason to maintain contact.'

'Quite,' said Charlie, who was still feeling guilty about leaving the boys with Matt all through his weekend contact visit. He was feeling guilty about a lot of things to do with his 'old' life. 'It's just that we won't be working together, that's all.'

'But I'll miss that, Charlie,' said Matt with more tenderness than he'd wanted to give away.

'And I'll miss it too,' said Charlie, softly, 'but life moves on, mate. Sorry, but that's what it does.'

★

Brendan popped his head around the door of Phillip's study and saw that he was concentrating on the blank sheet of paper in front of him on his desk.

'Sorry, Phillip' said Brendan. I might've known that if a priest is sitting alone on a Saturday night it must be because he's working on his sermon for Sunday.'

Phillip held up the blank sheet of paper. 'Well as you can see, Brendan, I'm finding the inspiration a little hard to nail down tonight. So any distractions are welcome. Come in.'

Brendan went in and closed the door before sitting in the armchair that was at one end of Phillip's desk.' What is it you're wrestling with? I can tell there's something by your eyes.'

'I've got a married couple who are set on divorce,' said Philip, 'The more I try and talk to them the more intent they seem to be.'

'Do you think that all marriages should be saved regardless of what is or isn't going on inside them, Phillip?'

'Should that be a question a Catholic priest should be asking?'

'Brendan, we can level with each other, I believe, you'd be exactly like me if you were starting out today.'

'Would I now?' asked Brendan who was rather flattered by the young man's affirmation.

'You know you would be.'

'Yes,' said Brendan, thoughtfully, 'I believe we're cut from the same cloth, Phillip. And I don't believe that marriages should be kept together if the glue isn't there. We just make people miserable.'

'So what does that say about my future career?'

'Maybe you should try social work?'

'I thought I already was.'

They laughed and then Phillip began to probe Brendan's free spirit.

'It must've been hard to come into the church at a time of such conservatism, Brendan. Especially when you've always been such a radical thinker.'

'And you think it isn't wracked with conservatism now? No, it's been hard at times, I do confess. And I've nearly left on a couple of occasions. But my overriding faith in God has kept me here.'

'What type of occasions were they?'

'Have you ever heard of a group called the liberation theologists?'

'Oh yes,' said Phil, 'the group of Latin American priests from the eighties.'

'That's them. Latin America was one big torture chamber back then. Every government of every country was a fascist dictatorship and the United States under Reagan thought that was okay as long as they weren't communists. They didn't care how much the people suffered as long as the allegiance of the nation was to Washington and not Moscow. It used to annoy the hell out of me when I heard Reagan and Thatcher go on about the free world being anywhere that wasn't communist. They were so ideologically blind. Thousands of people simply disappeared off the streets of those countries during that awful, dark time and yet they call that freedom? Torture and repression, the rape of women, it was all part of the way those countries operated and the Vatican sucked up to every one of the administrations because they were all devoutly Catholic. It turned a blind eye because Pope John Paul II had been brought up in communist Poland and had a view of the world coloured by those experiences. But he should've seen beyond that and that's when I stopped believing in papal infallibility.'

'I'm glad there are no hidden microphones in this room,' joked Phillip, 'but where did the priests come in?'

'They were a group of priests who'd administered to the poor of Latin America for decades and were tired of the injustice of never seeing people's lives improve. They wanted the poor to be liberated from the land owners who kept them in poverty but who were in league with the dictatorships. So it brought the priests into conflict with the dictatorships who then turned to the Vatican for help. The Pope insisted that the priests stopped preaching their word of liberation for the poor and stuck instead to the official teachings of the church. Then along comes the Sandinista administration in Nicaragua and things really kicked off. They were a left wing party that took a lot from the liberation theology priests and they were democratically elected by the people. But of course, they wanted liberation from poverty for the people so Washington and the Vatican set themselves against them and made life as difficult as it could for them.'

'And all because they wanted justice for their people.'

'Precisely,' said Brendan, 'but the church isn't interested in justice, Phillip. It just craves obedience. It was during this time that the Reagan administration recognised the Holy See as a nation state, thus giving the Vatican the same recognition status as any other nation state even though you and I both know that it's no more the size of a park and nobody actually lives there, not even the Pope himself. But as a nation state it carries a great deal of influence and that's what the Reagan administration wanted in it's support of anything that wasn't communist, whether democratically elected or not. It's been a grave sin against the whole of mankind, Phillip.'

'So what are we doing here?'

'Because in our own small way we can bring a little Heaven into the lives of our flock. We can advise them as a compassionate Jesus would and not as some white-robed idiot in a dark version of Disneyland would.'

'You've given me a great idea for the sermon tomorrow.'

'Don't get yourself into any bother now,' Brendan advised, 'We need to keep free thinkers like you, Phillip.'

'Don't worry, Brendan,' said Phillip, 'I'll put a cloak around my words.'

★

Susie Schofield was sitting with her fiancé Angus having a sandwich lunch in her office at Schofield Caravan Parks headquarters. The company didn't have a grand suite of offices and didn't need one. They occupied half of the second floor of a two storey office block just a stone's throw from Manchester University on the Oxford Road going south out of the city. Susie had forty staff to help her deliver the company's objectives and got really pissed off with journalists who turned up to interview her and who only wanted to approach things from the perspective of her being a woman. Did she do anything differently from a man? How would she know? She'd never been one. She was her father's daughter and had inherited much of his character but she ran the business her way. Some of the staff liked her and some of them didn't, although she would say that she had more trouble from other women than from her male workforce. Some women really didn't like working for a female boss and it disturbed her that in this day and age women could still act that way. What about the sisterhood?

'Thanks for bringing these in, baby,' said Susie as she placed the last piece of her Tuna salad sandwich in her mouth. 'I wouldn't have had time to go out for anything'

Angus had brought his chair around to her side of the desk and leaned forward and kissed her. 'All part of the service'

She gently stroked the side of his face. He still gave her the butterflies. He worked on weights at the gym and his shoulders looked like they could raise his Airbus jet off the ground by themselves. He was in a black polo shirt and blue jeans and his thick, strong arms tapered into slim wrists and big hands. His wide chest did the same into his waist before giving way to his tree trunk legs. His hair was jet black and his dark eyes and square jaw gave him the look of someone off the cover of a man's fitness magazine. She was so consumed with lust whenever he was around. She knew she was a lucky girl.

'I missed you last night,' Susie said at last.

'You can show me how much later.'

'I shall look forward to that.' said Susie. 'So how was your night flight?'

'There and back to Ibiza' said Angus who'd only had a few hours sleep but didn't feel too bad. 'Nice and short, no dramas.'

Angus had been born and brought up in Surrey and had come up to the north for his first job after qualifying as an airline pilot. On his first night out in Manchester he'd met Susie who'd told him there and then that he was coming home with her. This wasn't difficult for Angus. Their mutual attraction was strong. That weekend he stayed at Susie's place and a couple of months later he gave notice at the shared house he'd been renting with two other pilots in Macclesfield. He hadn't anticipated meeting anybody as quickly as he'd met Susie. He'd been looking forward to playing the field where girls were concerned and having boys' nights with his housemates. But that wasn't to be and he wasn't complaining. Susie was the girl for him and he'd never given it a second thought that he wanted to spend the rest of his life with her.

'I'm looking forward to becoming Mrs. Angus Carleton too,' said Susie.

'Not long now. Just two short weeks.'

'I spoke to your Mum this morning,' said Susie. 'It's such good news about your Dad.'

Angus had spoken to his mother that morning too and she'd managed to settle a growing anxiety he'd had about the wedding. His parents were divorced and his father now lived in Hong Kong with his new wife. His father had been threatening not to come over for the wedding until Angus's mother apologised for remarks she'd made to his new wife on their most recent visit home to the UK. Angus's mother had finally found it in her heart to do that for the sake of her son's happiness.

'I couldn't have had the wedding without my Dad being there.'

'Well you don't have to now,' said Susie, 'but I think

we owe your Mum one. It must've taken a lot for her to back down. And if truth be told I don't know if I could've.'

'In front of the whole family she called Nancy a Chinese whore who should stick to frying rice.'

'I know,' said Susie, 'and that was unpleasant.'

'And it was racist.'

'Yes I know but taking that away and every wronged first wife would be able to identify with the feelings behind what your mother said. I've really got to know your Mum over the last few weeks and I like her, Angus. And she's not a racist.'

'I know that, Susie,' said Angus, 'I just wish she hadn't said it.'

Susie took hold of Angus's hand. 'I think she wishes that too, baby.'

'And why doesn't she move on? Malcolm has been part of her life for a long time now and he adores her. I know he's asked. So why doesn't she?'

'Because she hasn't quite stopped loving your father yet and until she does she won't be asking you to walk her down the aisle to marry another man, however lovely Malcolm is.'

'Well I love my Mum and I love my Dad and I'm relieved they'll both be there on the happiest day of my life.'

Susie kissed him. 'Me too. Now darling, can I ask you something?'

'Sure,' he said as he ran his fingers up and down her arm.

'You work with a lot of gay men in the airline business, don't you.'

'Yeah?' said Angus, munching on his chicken and bacon tortilla wrap. 'Where's this going?'

' Well have you ever been tempted? I mean, they say

that the difference between a straight man and a curious one is six pints of lager.'

'I kissed a guy once, yeah.'

'Kissed him?' asked a startled Susie. She hadn't expected him to say yes.

'Well I suppose you could say I snogged him to be honest.'

'Tongues?'

'Oh yeah.'

'Fuck's sake! Tell me more'

'He was a friend of mine at university' said Angus. 'One of my best friends actually. He was gay and I knew he was into me but I just ignored it because we were mates. Anyway, one night it just happened. We were drunk, we'd had a great evening out at the pub and it just happened.'

'But what did happen?'

'We were sitting together on the sofa, we were close and the next thing he kissed me. And I responded.'

'You responded?'

'I wanted to see what it felt like, yeah,' said Angus. 'but within seconds I knew that I wasn't even a little bit gay or even bisexual. I didn't like it. I didn't like the feel of stubble against stubble.'

' Did you get a stiffy?'

' Semi, yeah' said Angus. 'But it went down again once I'd realised it wasn't what I was into.'

'How did your friend react?'

'He called me a prick tease' said Angus, 'we were never the same after that.'

'The poor baby was in love.'

Angus blushed. 'Yeah, it seems that way.'

'Where is he now?'

'We graduated the same time and he joined the R.A.F.

He's flying the Eurofighter now. The last I heard he was part of a squadron that's seeing action in the Middle East somewhere. I've nothing but respect for him and I always wanted to forget about what had happened and stay friends. You know it makes no difference to me if someone is gay. But he felt differently.'

'You broke his heart.'

Angus blushed even more. 'Well if you want to put it like that.'

'Well how else could I put it?'

'Yeah, point taken.'

'So all those gay boys at work? There must be tons who fancy you?'

'Yeah, and I flirt and have a laugh but that's as far as it goes,' said Angus, 'but why all these questions about me and man love?'

'I was just thinking about my brother Matt,' said Susie, 'he's good looking, he's funny, he's intelligent …'

'…and he can't find anyone.'

'And he won't find anyone,' said Susie, 'because of Charlie fucking Baxter. God, I loathe that man. My brother is wasting the best years of his life over that user.'

'Are you sure Matt has got a thing for him?'

'Absolutely sure,' said Susie. 'You don't think he has?'

'I agree that all the evidence is there,' said Angus, 'but what can we do?'

'I don't know but I just worry about him ever finding happiness, Angus. I mean in gay years he's getting old.'

'You make him sound like a dog.'

'You know what I mean.' said Susie. 'Gays are so fucking youth orientated. I don't want him to be lonely, Angus.'

'You can't help who you fall in love with, Susie.'

'No. But if it remains unrequited then you have to

dump it and Matt is doing the opposite of that when it comes to Charlie Baxter.'

★

Rita Makin had been a widow for ten years. Her late husband George had worked at the local factory manufacturing shampoo and other personal hygiene items for all their married life but the pension still had to be supplemented by the state. Rita had worked all that time too. She'd worked in Catholic children's homes until vicious nuns had sacked her for wanting to show the kids some love. Then she'd spent the rest of her working days in a local flower shop, working alongside an owner whose husband had bought the shop for her as a means of tax avoidance. Rita had never been able to give herself to such luxurious thinking. She'd simply needed the cash and her boss, though friendly, had often subtly reminded Rita of their respective places in life. Rita had never really thought of herself as downtrodden. But she'd grown older believing that life could've offered her just a little more.

Which was why she wasn't feeling guilty about what she was doing now.

It had been difficult to get used to at first. She'd only ever been with one man before and neither she nor George had ever been particularly adventurous in the bedroom department. So the first time she'd been nervous. It had been painful as he'd initially penetrated her and a selection of creams and lubricants had been needed to ease his way inside her. But it hadn't been long before a whole wealth of feelings had gradually overwhelmed them both and she'd been as frustrated as him when he came too quickly. That had been an expression of his nervousness. So they'd practised their intimacy and until now she felt like a woman should feel about having sex with a man who clearly loved her despite the circumstances. But she closed her eyes to all that and celebrated the fact that this could happen to her at this time in her life. They'd both needed comfort. That's how it had happened. They'd each seen through the tears to something beyond. Now there wasn't a cloud in the sky when he smiled at her. That's what gave her the thrill she'd never known had been possible.

She still went to church, the same one that had once been attached to the children's home where she'd worked all those decades ago. When she thought back to all that she had seen and heard back then she knew she should've spoken up for those poor kids who suffered unmercifully at the hands of those sadistic bitches who called themselves Nuns. Discipline and obedience were all that they dished out to the poor little mites and they could be savage with it, causing many a child to cry themselves to sleep in pain at the physical treatment they'd been subjected to. If it had been this day and age she'd have reported them all. Just because they were Nuns didn't mean that they were above the law. She would've found it easy to report them now because the authorities these days made it easier for people like her to come forward and expose wrongdoing, particularly abuse against children who were supposed to be in someone's care. But back then it was a lot more difficult and almost impossible to go against authority, whether it was some public body or something like the church. Over the years she'd lost all faith in the structures of the church. She continued to go because her faith in God had remained constant and she used her prayers as a private conversation with Him and to ask him to take care of all the children who'd been so badly treated. She also prayed for the Almighty's forgiveness for not having spoken up to protect them.

She'd luxuriated in a long soak in the bath. Her cousin down in Derby had sent her some bath oil last Christmas and she kept it for special occasions such as when 'he' was coming around. The trouble was, she was having so many special occasions with 'him' that the bath oil was rapidly running down. She'd have to treat herself to another bottle.

She knew her body wasn't what it used to be but he didn't seem to mind. Her breasts were a joke compared to what they'd been when she'd married George but she couldn't help that. And it was another thing that he didn't seem to mind about. He seemed to celebrate the fact that she was a woman of advancing years who could still show a man how much she cared about him when they twisted their bodies together. She'd never known passion with George. It was always done in exactly the same way and in complete silence. George used to say that even any whispers and moans put him off. Now it was as if she'd been born into another world where the sheer pleasure found it's way into both their voices. She wanted to shout about it from the rooftops but she couldn't. This was their private world and would have to remain so until one day when perhaps the circumstances might change. God was really going to hate her for this. Every Catholic knows that adults shouldn't indulge in pleasure unless it resulted in children or misery. That way the church could claim responsibility for the child's welfare or the adults' salvation. Well Rita had decided that she didn't need saving. And more importantly, she didn't want to be saved.

She drew the curtains in the small conservatory at the back of the house and took her now empty coffee mug into the kitchen. She'd put on her best dress, the one he liked with the velvet collar, she'd taken great care over her make-up, and there wasn't a single hair out of place.

She'd even been to one of those lingerie boutiques and got herself something that she knew he'd like once her dress was off. She was excited. She felt that catapult in her stomach as the time drew near for him to arrive. She looked at her watch and saw that there was still half an hour to go. What on earth was she going to do to fill the time? She could try munching on something, nothing heavy, just a bit of salad but with no onions to linger on her breath.

She was just about to open the fridge door when she realised there was someone else in the room. She turned around and immediately recognised her visitor.

'How did you get in?'

'You shouldn't leave your back door unlocked, Rita,' he said. 'I've been telling you that for weeks.'

'Well forgive me but what do you want at this time of night? And why didn't you knock?'

'I didn't want you to send me away,' he said.

'But I'm expecting someone.'

'Yes, I know,' he said, 'you've been a very naughty girl.'

Rita didn't know what to say. She turned away from him but that was her big mistake. He grabbed her from behind. She tried to scream but his hand, covered in a black leather glove, was being held tightly over her mouth and she had no defence against his strength. Her body was consumed with absolute terror. Why the hell was he doing this? She'd never have thought him capable.

'Just relax,' he said in a slightly whispered voice that intensified her feeling of terror. 'The situation will be all be over a lot quicker if you do.'

She tried to scream but it was no use. Then a cold, sharp blade of steel ripped through her throat and she began the short journey into death.

CHAPTER SEVEN

Matt liked his Fiat 500 car. No, he loved his Fiat 500 car. It was groovy and red and gorgeous and he loved driving around in it, so did Charlie's boys, Freddy and Harry. He'd taught them Italian and whenever they were in the car together the three of them spoke it. Matt had learnt the language from his best friend Gabriella. She and Matt had grown up together and her parents were Italian. Ten years ago she married a big hunky Italian called Umberto and moved out to be with him in Rome. Matt flew over to see them once a year and Gabriella came back to Manchester for regular family visits too, although not as much since she'd had the children. He and Gabriella had been inseparable as teenagers which had led Matt's mother Ann to believe for years that they would one day get together. But that wasn't to be and Gabriella had known that long before Matt's mother.

'It's me!' he called out when he let himself into his parents' house. He could hear that the evening news was on the television and the current item was a piece from America about how difficult it was proving for the President to push through health care reform and Matt pricked up his ears. Some woman in a town hall meeting was opposed to the idea of universal coverage because she said it was a betrayal of freedom. So, thought Matt, the definition of freedom is being able to afford healthcare insurance when many of your fellow citizens can't? But nothing must be done to help the poor who can't afford healthcare because that would be a betrayal of freedom.

Well Matt thanked God for the NHS. He'd hate to live in a country where the less well off have to rely on the benevolence of rich folks through their fundraising dinners and their charitable donations.

He walked into the lounge which ran the whole length of his parents' detached house in the South Manchester suburb of Cheadle Hulme, just a few miles from his own place in Didsbury. His parents lifted themselves from watching Fiona Bruce and embraced him. They were looking well, a good ten years could be taken off their real ages. His mother had just turned seventy a couple of months ago and his father was a couple of years older. He was glad that his mother was giving up working at the presbytery. It was time for them to kick back and enjoy themselves.

'This is a nice surprise, love,' said Ann. She'd long had to look up at her son but either he was getting taller or she was shrinking but the gap always seemed to be widening. 'And to what do we owe this honour?'

'Nothing really,' said Matt, as he embraced first his Mum and then his Dad. They'd always been a physically affectionate family. Maybe that's why he'd always found it easy to show affection to friends and loved ones. He'd been taught well enough. 'Just felt like seeing you both.'

In truth Matt was feeling at a bit of a loss. Charlie's bombshell about selling his half of the practice had really shaken him. Nothing was ever going to be the same again and he wanted to talk to his parents about it.

'And you might've known I was making your favourite for dinner,' said Ann.

'Slow-roasted lamb?'

'It's been in the oven since just before two,' said Ann. ' and I've done roast potatoes cooked in goose fat too.'

'Oh Mum, I knew there was something pulling me

home tonight.'

'Come on through to the kitchen and get a beer for yourself and your Dad.'

Matt followed his mother through to where the smell of the lamb filled his nostrils and made his mouth water. It took him way back to when he'd first started dreaming of what life was going to turn out like for him.

'I'm glad you came,' said Ann who'd always felt especially close to Matthew, the protective older brother to Susie. When they were children he'd always been the one she could rely on to behave, the one who always helped her get the tea, the one who'd achieved the most academic success, gaining four A-levels and the highest marks of his year when he graduated from medical school in Birmingham. She was proud of him. But she still couldn't help but have a dig despite Brendan's recent words. 'I saw Heather at the shops yesterday.'

Matt smiled and hoped she wasn't about to start. Matt had been engaged to Heather before the truth of himself had led to him calling off the wedding a month before it had been due to take place.

'That must've been nice,' said Matt through clenched teeth as he took a couple of beers out of the fridge. 'Is she well?'

'Oh she's very well,' said Ann. 'Her little girl is just gorgeous too. I'm glad she found someone who could make her happy.'

Oh dear, thought Matt. He really wasn't in the mood for this. 'And do you wish the same for me, Mum? Do you wish I could meet someone who could make me happy?'

'Well it depends on what you want to call happy I suppose.'

Matt rolled his eyes. 'Mum, if I'd have married

Heather it would've made you happy and me miserable and sooner or later I'd have broken her heart. Now as my mother I thought you'd have been on my side.'

'Oh I am on your side, Matthew,' Ann insisted, 'it's just that you choose to live your life in a way that I'm not always comfortable with.'

'I don't choose to live it this way, Mum, I was born this way and I will die this way and that's because your God has made me this way in His own image.'

'I hate it when we argue' said Ann.

'Then just don't keep having a go, Mum. Okay? You're the world's worst for pressing my buttons and then acting all innocent.'

'Brendan gave me a right talking to about you.'

'He did?'

'He said I should just accept your sexuality and be done with it.'

'I shall buy him a packet of fags next time I see him.'

Ann laughed. 'You do that' she said. 'And I will try, son. Honest, I will. It's just that when I saw Heather and how happy she was it made me think of you all alone every night. I want you to be happy, son. I don't want you to be lonely.'

He kissed her. 'Mum, if I end up being lonely it won't be because I'm gay. It'll be because I didn't meet the right man for whatever reason and don't tell me that it never works for men like me because I can give you the names of ten gay couples off the top of my head who've been together for years and intend to stay that way.'

'But I want something to work for you, son.'

'You and me both, Mum.'

'Like I said, I just don't want you to be lonely.'

'But I'd feel even more lonely in a sham marriage to a woman like Heather, Mum. Don't you see that? Besides, it wouldn't be fair to her either.'

'I suppose, love.'

'Now do you want me to help you with dinner?'

'No, you're okay, love' said Ann. 'You know I like to do it all myself.'

'Then I'll take this beer out to Dad.'

Matt took a beer through to his Dad and clinked cans with him. 'Cheers, Dad.'

'Cheers, son.'

'You've got a hard life, Dad,' he said, 'a roast dinner in the middle of the week?'

'Oh I'm not complaining, son.'

'I'm glad Mum is retiring at last though, Dad' said Matt. 'She's spent her whole life running around after us lot and a load of priests. She needs a break.'

'That's true enough, son.'

'You've got to start insisting she takes it easy sometimes, Dad,' said Matt.

'Am I getting a bollocking off my own son?'

Matt laughed. ' Not a bollocking, Dad. Just the planting of a concern in that head of yours, that's all. I know you do your bit as much as Mum allows you to but perhaps you need to be more insistent, that's all.'

Bill had been married to Ann for over forty years and in that time she'd never let him so much as breathe in the kitchen unless she wanted him to, same with the housework. Matt was right though. He had to start insisting that bit harder.

'So what's new in your world, son?' asked Bill.

Matt grimaced. ' Charlie wants to sell his half of the practice.'

'What?' his mother exclaimed as she came through and joined them.

'You're kidding us?' said his father.

'I wish I was,' said Matt, 'I really wish I was, Dad. But it seems the lady Natasha, who apparently must always be obeyed, wants him to move out to a practice in Cheshire where his patients will be more to her liking.'

'I hope Charlie realises how much hard work she's going to be,' said Bill who didn't like Natasha at all. Charlie had brought her around to the party when Susie got engaged to Angus and Bill hadn't taken to her. He'd met many girls of her type in his time. She'd end up thinking herself as important just for being Charlie's wife.

'All fur coat and no knickers that one,' said Ann.

'Yeah, well, she's got her claws into Charlie alright,' said Matt.

'Will you be able to afford to buy him out, Matt?' asked Ann.

'I might need to borrow some, Dad.'

'Well we'll sort you out there, son,' said Bill.

'Of course we will' said Ann. ' But I can't believe that someone like Charlie would turn his back on you and the practice for the sake of that pretentious madam.'

'Well I've tried talking to him but it doesn't make any difference.'

'Do you think you'll find another doctor alright to replace Charlie?' asked Bill.

'Oh I don't think that'll be a problem, Dad' said Matt. 'A lot will jump at the chance of working in a busy inner city practice. Unless of course they've got an air stewardess girlfriend called Natasha who only works in first class and who looks down her nose at what she considers to be poor people.'

The telephone at the presbytery rang and when Ann Schofield answered it she was deeply shocked to be told that Rita Makin was dead.

'Who was that?' asked Brendan, who'd just come

back from hearing confession in the church.

'It was the police' said Ann, tearfully.

'Whatever is the matter, Ann?' asked Brendan. 'What's happened?'

'They'd been asked to contact us by Rita Makin's family' said Ann who could barely get her words out. 'Brendan, Rita is dead.'

'What?' Brendan questioned in a state of complete disbelief. 'But I only saw her last week. She didn't look ill. In fact she looked the picture of health and happiness.'

'She wasn't ill, Brendan' said Ann, gently. She could see that Brendan was clearly very distressed by the news. 'Apparently, Brendan, Rita was murdered.'

' Murdered?' Brendan gasped. He made the sign of the cross on himself. 'Oh for the love of God, no! Not Rita? Who on God's earth would want to murder her?'

'They found the body just this afternoon' said Ann. ' They said… they said that her throat had been cut.'

★

Rita Makin's kitchen had never been anything other than ordinary. As DCI Sara Hoyland stood in the small room at the back of the terraced house she took in the pink wallpaper with vertical broad cream stripes, the fake wood faced units, the automatic washing machine, the gas cooker that didn't seem to have a grill, the tall fridge freezer that had probably helped Rita Makin to budget her food bill. There was only just enough room for the table and four chairs in the corner.

'That wallpaper would have to go if I lived here,' said Sara when DI Tim Norris came into the room. The house, which had been cordoned off with uniformed police positioned both in front and behind the house, was full of forensics officers taking samples from anything that might be useful.

'Yeah, I guess it isn't really you,' said Tim who was really doing his best to get on with Sara and put their past behind them. It wasn't always easy but they were both trying.

'How did someone manage to kill her in here? There's hardly enough room to swing the proverbial.'

'No wonder there was blood everywhere' said Tim. 'It couldn't have been avoided.'

'So what do we know about Rita Makin?' asked Sara.

'She was a widow' Tim answered.

'Children?'

'One daughter.'

'Did she raise the alarm?'

'No' said Tim. 'Her daughter's married and lives up at Radcliffe with her husband and three sons. It was her son-in-law who discovered the body'

'Her son-in-law?'

'He'd popped around on the off chance that she might be in but instead of tea and biscuits he found something else.'

Sara stood in the small kitchen looking out the window at the view of several allotments beyond the back yard. Inside this small insignificant little space in the world a woman who'd led a no doubt pleasing but unremarkable life had met with a rather brutal and unpleasant death.

'Isn't it a bit unusual?' Sara posed before turning her eyes back to the room.

'What?' Tim questioned.

'A man to call in on his mother-in-law on his own?'

'I don't think it's that unusual outside the world of seventies comedians,' said Tim, 'I mean, I get on fine with my mother-in-law.'

'But would you call in and see her if you were passing?'

'Yes' said Tim. 'I mean, I haven't but I would.'

'And what does the son-in-law do for a living?'

'He's a butcher.' said Tim. 'Got his own shop in Newton Heath.'

'So he'd be good with knives then?'

'Sara, the man is in shock.' said Tim. 'Why are you going for his balls?'

'I'm not.' said Sara. 'I'm just throwing out ideas from what we know. At the moment he is all we know.'

'But why would he want to kill her?'

'I'm not saying he would, Tim.' said Sara. 'I'm just saying it's possible.'

Sara walked through into the lounge with it's two low brown leather sofas. There was an alcove either side of the old fireplace that had been bricked in and a gas fire was attached to the wall. There was a flat screen television sat on a free standing unit just under the window and there was a multi-coloured rug in the middle of the floor to break up the monotony of a plain beige carpet. It all reminded Sara of her Aunt's house in Leigh.

'So there was no sign of a forced entry?'

'No.' said Tim. 'The kitchen was the only room that had been disturbed.'

'So this wasn't part of any burglary that went wrong?'

'It doesn't seem like it, no.'

'He came to kill her,' said Sara, 'he came specifically to kill Rita Makin.'

'So far it certainly looks that way,' said Tim. 'Look, Sara, I know this is not a good time…'

'…but?'

' I need to speak to you about something' said Tim. 'It can't wait, I'm afraid.'

'Well here is not the best place,' said Sara. 'Come and see me after the team meeting tomorrow. Am I going to like it?'

'Well it's not about you and me if that's what you're thinking.'

'There is no you and me.'

'You know what I mean.'

'Yes, I do,' said Sara, 'and whatever the problem is I'll do my best. Okay?'

'Okay.' said Tim, 'Thanks.'

The house was at the end of a row of terraces which had made it easier to be cordoned off. Sara looked up and saw that one of the uniformed officers outside was having a conversation with a priest who was looking anxiously towards the house. Sara went out to speak to him.

'Father?' she said, holding out her hand. 'I'm DCI Sara Hoyland.'

'Brendan O'Farrell'

'I take it you knew Rita Makin?' The poor man looked utterly crestfallen. They must've been close.

'Yes,' said Brendan. 'I'm here about this terrible business.'

'Were you Rita Makin's parish priest, Father?' Sara asked.

'Yes' said Brendan, barely able to hold back the tears. He held out his arm and Sara linked hers with it. 'I'm sorry' he said, 'you must think I'm a stupid old man.'

'On the contrary, Father,' said Sara, 'you're clearly very upset.'

'Rita and I were very good friends who went back a long, long way.'

'Do you have any idea who might've done this to her?' asked Sara.

Brendan looked at her as if he was utterly bewildered

at her question. 'No' he said, emphatically. 'Rita could never have harmed anyone. She was kind, she had a good heart. She lived for her family. I'm sure that if I pray to God for the rest of my days I'll never understand it. It's beyond all reason.'

★

Natasha was over the moon now that Charles had finally popped the question. Of course she hadn't given it a moment's thought. Things were beginning to work out just as she wanted them to but there was some way to go before she'd managed to completely shape his life her way. There were a number of items on her list but one thing at a time. When she joined the airline a few years ago and discovered pilots who earned the kind of money that could well service her idea of a meal ticket, she'd gone all out to get herself one. But it hadn't quite worked out. She'd never met one who'd been willing to fall victim to her charms. One had even accused her of being a gold-digging slag. Well she'd decided that maybe these men and their flying machines were too clever for their own good so she'd hit the pubs and wine bars of Cheshire and that's where she'd met Charles one summer Friday night.

Some pilots were in her Wilmslow social circle and even though she no longer needed to look for a suitable husband she kept them in her social circle because they were the right kind of professional types she wanted to be surrounded by. Her job in flying also meant that she had to be away for several days at a time and that meant having to find a pilot to treat her like his special girl for the trip. She needed the attention of well off men. But her games were no longer motivated by the serious need to search for the right one. She wouldn't ever be unfaithful to her Charles. Not when he could provide her with so much. There was a moral line to be drawn after all and he was a poor darling having to stay at home whilst she was away. At least it gave him time to be with his kids. That was the only fly in the ointment as far as her relationship with Charles was concerned. She had no desire to be a step-mother to his boys and quite frankly if she could wipe them out of the picture she would.

As they sat across from each other at the breakfast table she held her hand out in front of her that had been adorned by Charles's engagement ring.

'It's beautiful, darling. Thank you so much.'

'It looks fantastic on you, I must admit,' Charles gushed.

Natasha leaned over the breakfast table and gave him a kiss. 'I'm such a lucky girl.'

'Well don't flash your ring too much in front of Matt,' said Charles, 'he's got a real thing about what are called blood diamonds.'

'Blood diamonds?'

'Diamonds that are mined in poor African countries with the proceeds used to buy weapons that kill innocent people in civil wars.'

'And what's that got to do with me exactly?'

'Matt thinks it's immoral for anybody to buy a ring with a diamond in it that could've been mined under those circumstances' said Charles. 'But I liked the ring so much and knew how fantastic it would look on you that I just went ahead and bought it without asking the guy in the jewellers anything about where the diamond had come from.'

Natasha stroked Charles's hand. 'Darling, I really couldn't care less about where anything comes from or who makes it or any of that kind of stuff. I just like what

I like and that includes this gorgeous ring and you. So don't go concerning your handsome head about anything other than me.'

Charles kissed her and she wiped a crumb from the corner of his mouth before buttering him another slice of toast and handing it to him.

'And as for your friend Matt he can keep his bleeding heart to himself,' Natasha went on.

'Now don't be like that, darling,' said Charles.

'Like what?'

'Matt is my best mate,' said Charles.

'Yes, I know but I'm your baby girl.'

'And it's important to me that the two of you get along' said Charles. 'Matt has always cared about stuff. It's one of the things I've always admired about him.'

'Yes, well, there are those that care and those who employ accountants to get out of paying tax. I'm glad to say that we'll be falling into the latter category.'

'It wouldn't do for us all to be the same, darling,' said Charles.

'Yes, quite,' said Natasha who now wanted to move things on to a matter she'd been wanting to target since she and Charles had got serious. 'Anyway darling, we need to sort out our finances before we're married.'

'Our finances?'

'Well yes,' she said as she scooped the last drop of yogurt out of the container with her spoon. 'I know a lawyer. He lives down the road here. He specialises in re-negotiating divorce settlements.'

'Sorry?'

'Well don't look so surprised, darling' said Natasha. 'Wendy has got away with it for far too long.'

'Got away with what?'

'Sponging off you,' said Natasha, 'she doesn't go to

work.'

'She used to before she had the children.'

'And so she can go back again,' said Natasha, 'and that house is far too big for her and the children. You've said so yourself.'

'Yes but without any intention of doing anything about it, Natasha.'

'Even so,' said Natasha, 'now that I'm around to fight your corner, the former Mrs. Baxter has got something of a shock coming. You're paying two mortgages after all.'

'And I can well afford it.'

'That's not the point, darling,' said Natasha. 'I really think you've let her get away with emotional blackmail for too long, Charles.'

'She's never emotionally blackmailed me' said Charles, nervous about where all this was going. 'She's always been very reasonable. More reasonable than I deserved and I pay two mortgages to keep a roof over my children's heads and so their mother can take care of them.'

'Oh' said Natasha, 'so what I want doesn't matter?'

'I didn't say that, darling...'

'...I should hope not, darling. I should certainly hope not.'

★

Brendan had moved one of the armchairs in the sitting room into the space provided by the open French window and sat there in the semi-darkness smoking a cigarette. He'd had one on the go almost constantly since he'd heard about Rita's horrific death. It was almost nine o'clock and the summer evening air had grown heavy as if a storm might be approaching. It would never be like this once he'd retired and moved to County Clare.

The fresh power of the Atlantic Ocean always kept the air clean and that pleased him. He'd never been one for the heat. He'd once gone out to Zambia to see a friend who was a missionary out there and the heat had almost finished him off. He liked the temperature to be warm enough to be able to walk around in shirt sleeves but not so bad that just the placing of one foot in front of the other brought him out in a sweat. And he didn't have the skin for tanning. Too many Irish freckles, the skin too white, the hair now too grey. If it hadn't been suitable before it certainly was never going to be now.

Brendan and Rita had been almost the same age. He'd first met her when her daughter Michelle was only tiny and he'd been there for her throughout all the ups and downs of her marriage to George. He'd ministered to George too. Brendan knew that Rita was no saint and that their problems, just like any other married couple's, were often a case of six of one and half a dozen of another. But Rita was different. Rita had been a true and valued friend, someone he'd come to concur with on many issues.

He looked up when Phillip came into the room. 'Sorry' he said, holding up his cigarette. 'I know I shouldn't, Phillip, but I'm relying on your Christian charity.'

'Don't worry, Brendan' said Phillip as he held up the bottle of scotch in his hands. 'I don't mind if you don't.'

Brendan smiled before getting up and, assisted by Phillip, he moved the armchair back into the room and sat down. Phillip sat on the sofa beside him.

'Then let's indulge each other in our respective vices,' said Brendan.

'You'll be in trouble in the morning when Ann Schofield comes in and smells the smoke,' Phillip teased as he poured himself some scotch.

'Yes, well I've got more on my mind than a telling off from Ann.'

'Who could've done such a wicked thing to Rita Makin?'

'I shudder at the thought of what happened to her,' said Brendan. 'I can barely imagine her going through such evil.'

'We must pray too for the perpetrator,' said Phillip. 'We mustn't forget that.'

'Yes, well I'll let you do that,' said Brendan. 'I'm about to hang up my collar. I've been as good a priest as I could've been these decades. I think I'll be forgiven if I don't pray for the soul of someone who took the life of one of my best friends, Phillip. It's a challenge to my faith that I'm unable to meet just now.'

'What would you like to see happen, Brendan?'

'I'd like to see them catch the bastard and throw away the key.'

CHAPTER EIGHT

'You'd been taken to the other side of the world, Paddy, and you were still a child whose mother had abandoned you,' said Angela as she sat with Paddy during another session at the prison. She was beginning to appreciate just how to handle him. If she pushed him too much he'd close up and ask to go back to his cell which would be a pity seeing as they were making great progress. He seemed more tense than usual this morning. Maybe recalling his past was taking more out of him than he'd thought it would. He certainly looked like he hadn't had much sleep. 'I need you to tell me how that felt because I can't imagine.'

'You had good parents?'

Angela felt a little guilty answering that one. 'Well yes I did.'

'They loved you? Cared for you? Made sure you had everything you needed?'

'Yes, Paddy.' said Angela, 'They did.'

'Remind me to ask you one day what that feels like' said Paddy as he looked down and shuffled his feet around on the floor. 'I'd like to know.'

Angela smiled, out of sadness instead of joy. 'I will, but back to you now.'

Paddy shifted in his seat. 'It was called the Brothers of St. Peter Home for Boys although the definition of home had become a bit twisted in all their shit. Anyway, it was in North Sydney, New South Wales in Australia and it had taken me the best part of two months to get there. I remember there was this big iron gate at the head of the short drive to the house itself that had a padlock and chains all around it. Life had turned on me and I'd done nothing to deserve it. It was supposed to be the lucky country. That's what they called Australia back then but I felt anything but lucky, Doc.'

'Hardly surprising.'

'But that was only the first home I was taken to,' said Paddy. Then he laughed lightly. 'You could call it the reception class. Anyway, I actually grew up at another home further north on the edge of the city. It was on top of a hill and overlooked the ocean...'

1963

Sean had never wanted to see another ship again after he'd gotten off the one that had brought him to the other side of the world after nearly two months at sea. At first during the voyage he held himself tightly and didn't speak to anyone. But gradually the noise and the chatter of the other children made him open up and by the time they reached Australia he'd made several friends. None of them had known what had happened to their Mums or Dads. Some had been told by the Nuns that their parents were dead and some had been told that their parents simply didn't want them anymore and that they should be grateful to the church for taking care of them. But the fact was that all of them needed each other to hang onto. They had nobody else in the world and they'd been brought to this strange land where people spoke with funny accents and they'd been told not to go into the woods because of all the snakes.

But what Sean was getting used to was people coming into his life one minute and being gone the next. None of the girls on the ship had been brought to the first children's home he'd gone to and only a handful of the other boys had gone there too. They were fed. They were given drinks of water. Then they were beaten every night. Then when he was moved to this home and the years rolled by, the monks would come along with their straps and lash the palms of their hands as a warning against masturbation when they went to bed. They were getting into being 'that age' they were told and the almighty God working through the Catholic church considered masturbation to be a sin. The fact that many of the boys didn't know what masturbation was didn't matter. They had to be brutally warned against doing it.

Then one night it had all changed. Not for the other boys but for Sean. Brother Michael had come to Sean's bed and asked if he was alright. Shaking and terrified he answered that he was. Then Brother Michael slid his hand under the blanket and placed it on Sean's private parts.

Sean froze. He felt something happening and he didn't know what to do. Then Brother Michael told him to quietly get out of his bed and come along to his study with him. When he got there Brother Michael made him lie down beside him under another blanket. He didn't dare say a word as Brother Michael told him exactly what to do.

'Do you want to carry on, Paddy?' asked Angela, breaking a silence that had fallen onto the room.

'What's that?' asked Paddy. It was almost as if he'd been in a trance. Angela's voice had carried him out of it.

'I was asking if you wanted to carry on? We can pick it up next time if you like?'

'Sorry, Doc,' said Paddy. 'I'm going back into a place inside my head that's so dark... but no, I do want to carry on. If I break now I'll never get started again.'

'Okay,' she said, softly. 'Whenever you're ready.'

1969

Sean developed a way of using his 'special' times with Brother Michael as a means of maintaining a quiet life. Nobody bothered him. He was never lashed for anything which was a blessing in itself considering that some of the boys were lashed to within an inch of their lives just for trying to hold their own. There was a dungeon in the home and nobody who ever went in there came out without having to be supported just to stand up.

But something else was puzzling him more than the daily brutality of life in the home. Why wasn't anyone coming for them? They'd been told on the ship time and time again that families all over Australia were just waiting to take them in and give them good homes. But if that was the case then where were they? True enough many of the boys had gone but many still remained to work as slaves for the brothers and other sections of the church. Some were hired out to local farms and Sean thought they had it best. At least they came into contact with men who didn't want to stick it up them. But then again, being around normal people for eight hours made it seem even worse when they came back to their abnormal life at the end of the day and some of the farmers didn't treat the boys much better than the brothers did.

Sean spent hours just watching local school kids of his own age walking along; laughing, talking, joking and fooling with each other. He wondered what they'd done that was so right and what he'd done that was so wrong. They had Mums and Dads to take care of them. All he had was a man in a gown who pounded his arse every night.

The boys never went to the beach like all the local kids. They didn't have television sets at the home. They didn't have bicycles to ride or board games to play. The hours were long, especially at the weekends and during the holidays but absolute obedience always had to be maintained. Their birthdays were never noticed. Christmas Day was never more than one long church service where the boys were expected to be thankful for what they'd got. They were never touched unless it was to abuse. Nobody ever told them that they loved them. When they reached their teenage years like Sean had all they were told was that nobody was ever going to come now and they'd better get used to it. It was too late because they were too old. They'd have to work through their time until the church kicked them out and told them to fend for themselves.

'And yet, Doc, inside I was shouting and screaming. I had a Mum! She'd left me at the home that day but maybe if they checked she might've changed her mind. They acted as if my life had only started the day she left me at the home back here in England. I had to erase everything about before then.'

'Which is another reason why you've left it all out of the book?

'Yes,' said Paddy. 'I'd gotten so used to doing that.'

'Blanking out the happiness.'

'Yeah,' said Paddy. 'That puts it perfectly. But then again, Doc, this was the sixties. Everybody was supposed to be feeling free. Men were landing on the moon but I'd had my life ripped away from me and nobody bloody cared about my feelings. I was surrounded by priests who saw me as nothing more than an arse to fuck. Every day was relentless. It was like being in a long dark tunnel with no sign of light at the end of it. It was hard, Doc. It was so fucking hard I can't tell you and that's why those bastards who say I shouldn't profit from getting my story out are wrong, Doc. I'm owed, Doc! I'm fucking well owed the fucking world!'

Paddy then put his head in his hands and wept.

Angela went back to the prison the next afternoon at the request of Paddy who said he wanted to keep on talking. Before she got there she spent some time researching. The children's home he'd been sent to as a boy had long since closed down. The church it had been attached to was still there though and she was planning to go and speak to someone who might be able to shed some light on the church's former policy of sending children to Australia. She'd looked it all up on the internet and been able to find out a lot of 'facts.' But now she wanted to add the 'personal.'

'So how are you today, Paddy?'

Paddy looked mischievously at her. 'Aw, you know,

Doc' he said 'I keep up my walks in the park, I go down to that little Italian near the docks because I really like the way they make their lasagne, oh and I think I might go up to Scotland for the weekend.'

Angela smiled shrewdly at him. 'It's only the bars inside that I can take away, Paddy. The rest will be subject to the findings of the parole board.'

'I know, I know, Doc,' said Paddy. 'I shouldn't tease you like that.'

Angela sighed and felt humble. She's the one who shouldn't ask questions that were so stupid to someone whose actions had led to his freedom being taken away. It was what had led him there that she was interested in.

'Paddy, we'd got through to your teenage years' said Angela. 'Tell me how the Paddy of that age was feeling about life and what was happening to him?'

'Aren't you going to be any fun today, Doc?' said Paddy. 'We always have some fun as well as dealing with all the serious shit.'

'Let's talk first.'

'I felt abandoned.' said Paddy after a pause, 'Still after all the years I'd been left at the children's home, I felt abandoned. I felt like nobody loved me.'

'Which they didn't?'

'Which they didn't.' said Paddy. 'Or else how could my Mum have left me like that? I was still a child. In some ways I think I always will be that little boy who had to grow up a lot faster than he should've done.'

1972

The boys' home was halfway up a hill that stretched from the ocean at the bottom to the main town at the top. It was where Sean came to sit and think about what he was going to do when the church threw him out. Some of them talked about trying to get home to England but Sean didn't know how he would ever start with that. They were all mouth. Where would they get the money? Nobody would help them. They'd end up getting jobs and dirty little units in the not so nice parts of towns that they were never meant to see. They'd forever be the kids that had been dumped by their own parents and taken in by a church that thought it was no good showing them any love. They had to prepare them for the cruel world out there by beating the hell out of them or using them for sex.

He could always tell when Brother Michael was near by and approaching. Even up here on the hillside where the smells of the elements and the view of the vast open sea gave Sean some temporary relief from the misery of his existence, Brother Michael's signature aroma managed to pollute Sean's moments with nature.

'Hello, Sean,' said Michael who sat down beside him on the ledge that overlooked the ocean. He felt rather precarious. 'You're not afraid that a snake might slither along here? This is just the sort of habitat they like.'

'I've never been bothered by one so far,' said Sean who'd rather have to face one of Australia's most venomous reptiles than have his arse pounded by this sick bastard every night..

'You know you're not supposed to be down here? There's no danger signs or cordoned off parts but you're told not to come.'

'You've just got to be careful,' said Sean.

'Well it can be part of our secret' said Brother Michael. 'If you behave yourself. You come here every day, don't you?'

'Yes.'

'I see you' said Brother Michael. 'My window overlooks this spot as you well know young man. But it's only my window that overlooks this spot. It's only me who knows you come down here.'

Sean closed his eyes and tried to dream the filthy pervert away. His little piece of the world had now been contaminated. He could see his skin, his fingernails, his face looking as if nothing he was doing could ever be wrong. He could see his big legs slapping against his own when he was fucking him and his hands holding him steady at the shoulders.

'Well,' said Brother Michael 'You've had your little taste of freedom. Come back with me now.'

Sean took a deep breath and then said 'No.'

'What did you say?'

'I said "No".'

'Repeat that again.'

'No.'

Brother Michael slapped Sean around the head. Sean leapt up to his feet.

'Leave me alone!'

Brother Michael was so shocked he still hadn't thought about standing up. Sean was almost as tall as he was and this sudden onslaught of courage was worrying.

'Sit down, Sean.'

'No!'

'Do as you're told, Boy, or you'll know what will happen to you.'

'I said and I meant "no".'

'You want to go in the dungeon with Brother Charles? You won't come out for days if I have the right word with him and I've never known a boy last for more than three in there.'

'You don't get it' said Sean. They'd never get him in

that dungeon. They'd have to fucking catch him first. 'I'm not letting you do all that shit to me anymore.'

Brother Michael was incensed at this show of disobedience. 'You'll do as I say when I say…'

Sean didn't know quite how it happened but as Brother Michael tried to stand up he must've caught his legs in his floor-length gown and he couldn't get his balance. He was teetering on the edge with the backdrop of the ocean behind him. Sean smiled. Brother Michael locked eyes with him and Sean smiled again.

'Sean, help me!'

Sean placed his hand in the middle of Brother Michael's chest and pushed him over. Brother Michael fell backwards, his face contorted in shock, and then twisted through the air to the sharp rocks below. Sean watched as Brother Michael's body dropped into the Pacific with a rapidly expanding slick of blood around it. Sharks had been seen in the area in recent days. That brought a smile of satisfaction to Sean's face. Time for dinner, boys and girls.

Sean's moment of pleasure was short-lived however. He turned and saw Andy Cook, who was the same age as Sean, but not nearly as clever. Andy was unusual at the home because he was an actual Australian.

'I'm telling' said Andy.

'Telling who about what?'

'Don't try it with me Sean!'

'Oh am I meant to be scared by that? Look, you'll keep your stupid little mouth shut.'

'And what if I don't?'

Sean almost laughed at the stupid little prick's bravado. He walked over to him.

'If you know what's good for you, you'll keep your mouth shut. Okay?'

'Why? Are you going to kill me too?'

'It might come to that,' said Sean. 'I'll do anything to survive this place until I can get out. And I mean anything.'

'Yeah? Well I'll do anything too and that's why I'm telling.'

Andy turned to run back to the main house when Sean grabbed hold of him and swung him around. Andy fell to the floor but kept on rolling and before either of them knew it he was over the edge and hurtling towards the same fate as Brother Michael. Sean hadn't intended that but there was nothing he could do about it.

Sean looked around. Nobody had seen. But soon the police would be all over the place and everybody knew about his special relationship with Brother Michael. The brothers would direct the police to him with no problem. They wouldn't tell of the abuse of course. They'd say that he was a liar who was always accusing poor Brother Michael of abusing him. He wouldn't stand a chance. As for Andy Cook, Sean felt desperate about that but at least it meant that Andy wouldn't be talking. Andy wouldn't be doing anything from now on. And Sean felt sick about it. Andy wasn't a bad kid and he'd suffered just like the rest of them had. But now wasn't the time to reflect on the life and times of Andy Cook.

Now was time to run as fast and as far as he could.

'What do you think now when you think of Andy Cook?' Angela asked.

'Like I really am a murderer' said Paddy as the tears began to flow down his cheeks. 'Doing what I did to poor little Andy was the worst of my crimes, Doc. I've felt that way for a long time now.'

'Why?'

'Because he was the only one who didn't deserve it.'

CHAPTER NINE

Sara had gathered her team together in the squad room for a briefing on the Rita Makin murder. Superintendent John Hargreaves was also there. DS Adrian Bradshaw was sat at his desk, shoulders forward, hands clasped together on the desk, eyes wide and keen. DS Joe Alexander was leaning back in his chair, looking more relaxed but his attention clearly focused. Superintendent Hargreaves was perched on Joe's desk, his legs dangling, his arms straight and his hands on the edge. The only one missing was DI Tim Norris, who'd rang Sara and excused himself so that he could attend to some 'personal business.' She'd not been entirely pleased and it had raised the Superintendent's eyebrows too.

'How long had she been dead, ma'am?' asked Adrian.

'About three days, DS Bradshaw' Sara answered. 'According to forensics there were two other traces of finger prints in the room. We've run them both through the national database and it's come up with nothing. There are no known matches for either. But there was no sign of a disturbance or of a burglary.'

'What about the rest of the house, ma'am?' asked Joe.

'One of the other sets of prints were found all over the rest of the house, Joe,' replied Sara, who'd been a bit concerned about Joe lately. He hadn't been his usual cheerful self. She wondered if it might be women troubles or a lack of them. She didn't want to get into the habit of playing Mother Hen to her squad but she liked Joe and would want to help if she could.

'So what are your theories, DCI Hoyland?' John Hargreaves asked at last.

'That Rita Makin knew her killer, sir. The door hadn't been forced open. She'd got herself dressed up and there was a bottle of wine with two glasses on the coffee table in the living room.'

'She'd been expecting someone?'

'Clearly, sir' said Sara.

'A lover perhaps?'

'Perhaps, sir' said Sara before turning back to the big white board with Rita Makin's photo on it and notes that had been scribbled on it with a thick black marker pen. 'That may account for why one of the traces of prints are all over the rest of the house but again, with no sign of a disturbance. So we may be looking for someone who was intimately involved with Rita Makin but we'll start our enquiries with her family, her friends, see if any of them knew if she was seeing someone. She had one daughter, Michelle, married to Warren and they have three boys. He says he was on his way home from his own parents and decided to call in. Rita was also well known at the local Catholic Church too and was close friends with the priest there, Canon Brendan O'Farrell.'

'There doesn't seem like much to go on, ma'am,' said Adrian.

'You're right, DS Bradshaw, there isn't but something is going to lead us to finding out who would have the motive to kill a seemingly harmless woman in her mid-sixties living out her ordinary life in the suburbs.'

'Ordinary except for the fact that she may have been having some kind of an affair, ma'am,' said Adrian.

'Oh so do you think that women stop having urges when they get to a certain age, DS Bradshaw?'

Adrian blushed crimson. ' I didn't mean that, ma'am,'

he said, 'I suppose I'm thinking of my own mother who's the same age as Rita Makin.'

'I know,' said Sara. 'And I do know what you're saying. But I don't want her judged as being too old to have some fun. She was a widow and therefore a free agent after all.'

'So is my mother,' said Adrian.

'The man she was entertaining may not have been a free agent,' said Joe Alexander who knew all about affairs given his situation with Carol.

'That's the most likely scenario from what we know, I think,' said John Hargreaves, another with the knowledge of how to play effectively away from home, although his most recent affair with WPC Sharon Howells hadn't shown much in the way of expertise. Sharon hadn't taken it well when he ended the affair and she sent every present he'd bought her to his wife along with a detailed summary of every time they'd met and where. It had been an act of pure spite that had caused him a lot of problems at home for a while but Mrs. Hargreaves was used to her husband's indiscretions and after a while things had settled down again.

'But look, let's not get carried away,' said Sara, a real note of caution in her voice. 'Rita Makin was murdered in a very brutal but very precise manner and whoever did it clearly believed they had a motive. Now she might not have been having an affair as such. She might've been having a relationship with, say, a widower of the same age.'

'Well if that was the case, ma'am,' said Adrian, 'then why hasn't he come forward so that we could at least eliminate him from our enquiries?'

★

Sara once had a boss who liked to set people up for failure. She'd give them a task that she knew they wouldn't be able to complete because of a lack of knowledge, time, or experience and then make a big show of riding in and rescuing the situation from the 'incompetent.' Then she'd use the example to belittle the person and make them feel useless. Sara had been the only one to stand up to her and as a consequence Sara had been moved out of the offending inspector's squad. The last she'd heard of the infamous bully was that she'd had to retire early after suffering a severe nervous breakdown. The general consensus was that it couldn't have happened to a nicer person. It appeared too that she'd fallen foul of the demon drink. Well, Sara had vowed to herself, nobody was ever going to be able to accuse her of taking her insecurities out on the people who worked for her.

Last year one of her detective sergeants, Steve Osborne, had gone out on a limb and got himself killed for it. Sara had taken it harder than she'd ever admitted to anyone. Although everybody had said that it wasn't her fault and that she couldn't possibly blame herself for what had happened, she still couldn't help but do just that. Deep down in a corner of her soul the death of Steve Osborne would weigh heavily for a very long time.

But what could she do? She couldn't keep an eye on everyone twenty-four/seven and neither could she micro manage their every move. She had to trust them to get on with whatever they were assigned. Steve's place in the squad had been taken by Adrian Bradshaw, who Sara had taken to be a bright, capable officer, happily married with the kind of rugby player looks and build that make some girls go weak at the knees and wet in the fanny. The general consensus amongst all the girls at the station was that Mrs. Bradshaw was a very lucky girl and Sara hadn't dissented from that view. But she still hadn't spent enough time with him and she was determined not to let Adrian Bradshaw pretend to be close when he was far enough away to risk his life like Steve Osborne had done.

'My parents used to live around here' said Adrian as he drove his boss through Prestwich, one of the leafier suburbs of North Manchester, on the way to Radcliffe, a suburb of Bury where he and Sara would interview Michelle and Warren Clarke, Rita Makin's daughter and son-in-law.

'Used to?' asked Sara.

'Well Dad died a few years ago and Mum lives a couple of miles away from us now. I'm the only one in the family with kids and she likes to be near.'

'Convenient baby sitter for you and... is it Penny?'

'That's it,' said Adrian.' Mum loves to come and look after the kids so yes is the answer to your question.'

'And would you find it hard for her to be with someone else? I mean, that's what you intimated earlier in the squad room.'

'No,' said Adrian, 'and I'm sorry if I gave that impression. If she was to meet a good bloke who made her happy then none of us in the family would stand in her way.'

'Well you wouldn't actually have any right to stand in her way,' said Sara who hated that way it is in some families where someone is given 'permission' to live their life by the rest. The thought of losing either of her parents absolutely terrified her but if the one that was left met someone else and could be happy again then she'd be delighted for them. She wouldn't want to see them lonely if they didn't have to be.

'How long have you and Penny been together, Adrian?'

'Getting on for about fifteen or so years now,' said

Adrian.

'And how did you meet?'

'In a restaurant in Didsbury, Sara,' said Adrian who was still getting used to calling his boss by her first name when it was just the two of them. But that's how she wanted it so he complied. 'She was there with two couples and I was there with a couple of mates. I said that she must be feeling like the odd one out and would she like to join us for a drink.'

'How gallant.'

'I don't know about that,' said Adrian, 'lust was my main motivator.'

Sara laughed. 'Then how gallant and how honest. Go on.'

'Well I walked her home, we arranged to meet the next day, and that was it. Fifteen years and three kids later we're still going strong and I can't see past her.'

'You're lucky.'

'I think so, Sara,' said Adrian who wondered what his boss would say if she knew about his little demon. 'Believe me, I think so.'

'So you'd say she was your best friend and all that?'

'Oh yeah.' said Adrian. 'We compliment each other, you know? We each bring something different to the party. We've got some things in common of course but we're opposites too. Take our respective tastes in music for instance. Or rather I should say that I've got some taste in music but Penny hasn't.'

Sara laughed again. 'That is such a bloke thing to say. What's wrong with Penny's taste in music?'

'She's into anything that for me is totally bland and meaningless.' said Adrian. 'Like Celine bloody Dion.'

'Well I'm on your side there,' laughed Sara, 'I can't stand Celine Dion or any of those other so-called singers whose stock-in trade seems to be bloody power ballads.'

'Sounds like you've got more of a masculine taste in music, Sara.'

'Oh I have,' said Sara who then decided to have a bit of fun with him. 'And I'm like it in bed too. I always prefer to be on top.'

Adrian blushed and coughed. 'Well I'll have to take your word for that, Sara.'

'Yes you will because I never play with married men even if they ask me very nicely and are as good looking as you.'

'Are you always this disarming, Sara?'

'Oh didn't you know? All the girls at the station think you're a bit of alright.'

Adrian blushed again and smiled. 'Is that right? Then I'm flattered but tell them they're all about fifteen years too late I'm afraid.'

'Oh I can hear the sound of breaking hearts from here to police college!'

Adrian laughed. 'You like to have your fun, don't you, Sara?'

'Well the job is serious enough! But don't mistake me for someone who doesn't care. I want the job done to the very best of everyone's abilities.'

When they got to Michelle and Warren Clarke's house it was in the middle of a long tree-lined avenue of semi-detached houses that were all painted in white on the outside. There wasn't a car in any drive that was less than three or four years old. It was quiet. Most people were out at work at this time on a Thursday morning.

'Warren Clarke is a butcher,' said Sara. 'There must be a lot of money in meat if they can afford to live in a place like this.'

'Might be worth checking out his finances,' said

Adrian.

'Good idea' said Sara. 'Money being one of the two biggest motives for murder.'

'And the other?'

'Well sex of course' said Sara. 'Lust, betrayal, adultery, crimes of passion. I know you're married, Adrian, but surely you remember all the emotions released by doing what comes naturally?'

Adrian smiled. 'Oh you don't need to worry about me, Sara. I get my fair share.'

'Well Mrs. Bradshaw would be mad if you didn't.'

They were led into the house by Warren Clarke who wasn't saying much. They sat down in the front lounge. Sara and Adrian were on the sofa whilst Michelle and Warren sat in separate armchairs at opposite ends of the room. Sara thought that strange. In most situations of this kind couples tended to sit closely together and hold hands. These two could barely look at each other.

'I'd first like to say how sorry we are for your loss,' said Sara.

'Thank you' said Michelle Clarke, with a smile that came and went almost like an afterthought. She tucked her hair behind her ears with her fingers and played with a paper tissue in her hand. It was clear she'd been crying but that was no surprise.

'We'll be doing everything we can to find whoever did this, Mrs. Clarke,' said Sara.

'I'm sure you will' said Michelle. 'It's just that I don't have much faith in anything at the moment.'

'Well that's understandable,' said Sara. 'Mrs. Clarke, where were you the night your mother died?'

'I was here at home,' Michelle replied, 'on my own. We have a busy family life, inspector, with three boys to take care of. I preferred to have some time to myself.'

You're a liar, thought Sara who out of the corner of her eye could see Michelle's husband Warren slowly smouldering like a fire that could burst into flames at any moment. She was wondering what was taking him so long. What were these two hiding and, more importantly, why?

'Is that so?'

'Yes, inspector, it is.'

'Mrs. Clarke, can you think of anyone who might've had the motive to do something so despicable to your mother?'

Michelle closed her eyes as the tears began to fall again. She turned her head away from everyone and raised her hand to her mouth. 'My mother and I had not been getting on lately.'

'Oh? Why was that?'

'Oh you know how it is in families sometimes,' said Michelle, still tearful. 'But now she's gone and in such an evil way... well I wish we'd made up, you know?'

'I understand' said Sara.

'Why? Has your mother been murdered too?'

'Michelle, for God's sake!' said Warren Clarke. 'These officers need answers.'

'Well why don't you give them some then?' snarled Michelle. She was looking daggers at her husband. 'Why are you still here anyway? '

'I'm staying with my children,' Warren insisted, through a voice of restrained emotion.

'Not if I say you can't!' Michelle roared.

'Hey, now, calm down, both of you,' said Adrian who'd never seen such an appalling display from relatives after the death of a supposed loved one. 'I'm sure this isn't getting anybody anywhere.'

'Just mind your own fucking business!' Michelle

ordered in a voice raised as far as her emotions would take it.

'Alright, that's enough!' said Sara. 'Whatever the situation, Mrs. Clarke, I don't allow my officers to be spoken to like that. Now I know that grief hits people in different ways but there's clearly something else going on here.'

'Well if there is I repeat it is none of your business.'

Warren stood up and marched out of the room. 'I've had enough of this shit.'

'That's it! Walk away! You've never been any good to me.'

★

Tim Norris followed Sara into her office the moment she got back from interviewing Michelle and Warren Clarke.

'How did it go?'

'There's definitely something for us to find out there,' said Sara.

'Oh?'

'The elephant in the room was so big we almost couldn't move because of it,' she added as she sat down at her desk. 'Adrian is going to see Warren Clarke at his work tomorrow to see if he can get anything out of him when he's on his own.'

'Adrian seems to be settling in well,' said Tim.

'He is.' Sara agreed. 'Now Tim, I have to say that I don't think the Superintendent was impressed with your absence at the briefing.'

'I'm sorry if it put you in an awkward position.'

'Well it didn't do that but I can't cover for you unless I know what's going on?'

'I did say I needed to talk to you.'

'I know' said Sara. 'So what's up?'

'I need some time off, Sara.'

'Time off? Your timing isn't brilliant'

'I know,' said Tim who was feeling guilty. 'But when is it ever in a squad like this?'

'Okay' said Sara. 'So what's the reason?'

'Helen and I are adopting a baby and I'm entitled to paternity leave.'

The news hit Sara like a block of concrete being thrown at her chest. It brought back all too sharply the memory of the baby son she'd given up for adoption five years ago. The baby son that his father, Tim Norris, hadn't know about until she'd joined the squad last year.

'Sorry,' she said.

'No, I'm sorry, Sara,' said Tim. 'I didn't mean to upset you and clearly I have.'

'It's just all a bit sudden.'

'Well we've been planning it for a while obviously,' he added, 'ever since we found out that Helen couldn't conceive. But you know that, Sara.'

Sara couldn't deny that. 'What are you having? A little boy or a little girl?'

'A little girl' said Tim 'She's called Jessica and she's six months old. We couldn't, well at least, I couldn't adopt a little boy after... well, you know.'

'Yes, you don't need to say anymore,' said Sara who knew exactly that Tim was talking about their baby son who was out there somewhere.

'So can I have the time off?'

'Of course you can,' said Sara who was putting on a brave face but felt very emotional inside, 'and I wish you all the best, Tim, you and Helen and Jessica. I really hope it goes well. I mean that.'

Tim managed a smile as he left. 'I know. Thanks.'

CHAPTER TEN

Adrian parked his car about fifty metres short of the row of half a dozen shops where Warren Clarke's butcher's shop was located. The area of Newton Heath around it was a mixture of social housing and streets of two up, two down terraces that could still be snapped up for a bargain price.

'Thank you for seeing me,' Adrian began as he joined Warren Clarke in a small office at the back of the shop. There was barely enough space for them both to be in there comfortably and the bars at the small window made it feel even tighter. But there were two chairs and a small wooden desk and they both sat down.

'It's the least I could do after the little show my wife and I put on yesterday,' Warren answered by way of an apology.

'So what was it all about, Mr. Clarke?' asked Adrian. Warren Clarke was looking everywhere except directly at Adrian. His elbow was on the desk and he was rubbing his face almost constantly. He was clearly uncomfortable and if Adrian's hunch was right then he had good reason to be.

'My marriage has been in trouble for months,' said Warren. 'Something like this happens and it's supposed to bring you together but it's way too late for that for me and Michelle.'

'It's driven you further apart?'

Warren nodded his head. 'It hasn't always been like it is now between us. We've got three boys. We have had some happy times.'

'So what went wrong?'

'I don't know to tell you the truth,' said Warren. 'My wife has always been very demanding. It's no surprise as she's an only child. She was always used to having everything her own way and that's stayed with her. Her father was the only one who could stand up to her. I certainly couldn't and Rita certainly couldn't.'

'Did you get on with Rita, your mother-in-law?'

Warren paused before answering. 'Yes, I do... I mean, I did,' he said.

'Warren, did you know that she might have been seeing someone?'

Warren didn't answer.

'Warren, was it you Rita was expecting that night?'

Warren put his head in his hands and then lifted his face back up again, wiping his mouth and under his eyes with the back of his hand. 'It had only been going on a few weeks' he declared. 'But it was becoming something very special for both of us.'

'So it was you? You were having the affair with Rita?'

'Yes, it was me.'

'But how did that come about? I mean, the age gap for starters and she was your mother-in-law?'

'Rita was lonely,' said Warren. 'So was I. I was lonely inside my marriage. Michelle was giving me a hard time over nothing one night and I stormed out of the house and got into my car. Without really thinking about it I drove around to Rita's place. I cried on her shoulder and one thing led to another. Perhaps I should be ashamed but I'm not. If I could go back I'd do it all again. Rita made me feel good about myself again. I hadn't known that for some time. So to be the one who discovered her body... well I'll never forget that as long as I live.'

'But she was expecting you the night she died?.'

'I waited three days after discovering the body before I reported it to the police.'

'Why did you do that?'

'I don't know!' cried Warren. 'I suppose I didn't want people to think it might've been me who'd killed her.'

'And did Michelle know about the affair?'

'Yes, she knew.'

'Must've caused something of a rift between Michelle and Rita?'

'You could say that,' said Warren, 'but it drew Rita and I closer together.'

'United against a common enemy.'

'Something like that,' said Warren. 'Yes I know there was an age gap but Rita and I never noticed that when we were together. And she was still an attractive woman. At least she was to me.'

'Warren, I think we should carry this on down at the station.'

Warren looked up aghast. 'You can't think that I... that I did it?'

'I just think it would be better.'

'I didn't kill her!'

'Then you won't have anything to fear from answering some further questions down at the station,' said Adrian. 'Now come on. Don't make me have to arrest you.'

'You can't arrest me!'

'Mr. Clarke, you've admitted to discovering the body of Rita Makin but not telling anybody about it for three days. You've also admitted to having been in an intimate relationship with Rita Makin. I'd say we've got an awful lot to talk about. Wouldn't you? We will also need to take your finger prints and a DNA sample. It would help you ultimately if you co-operated'

★

'Good work, Adrian,' said Sara as they walked down the corridor towards the interview room where they were holding Warren Clarke.

'Well I just put two and two together, ma'am,' said Adrian.

'Do you think Clarke is the killer?'

'I'm keeping an open mind, ma'am, until we question him more thoroughly,' said Adrian. 'I don't know if he's capable of actual murder but then he's covered up some important facts up till now.'

DS Joe Alexander walked up and handed Sara a file.

'Ma'am,' Joe began, 'this gives details of Warren Clarke's financial situation. He's on his uppers, ma'am. The way things are going he's about two months away from bankruptcy. He's desperate for cash and Rita Makin changed her will only a week ago.'

'Don't tell me' said Sara. 'She bequeathed everything to Clarke?'

'She did, ma'am,' said Joe. 'Rita Makin wasn't wealthy by any means but she had a private pension and there was a considerable amount of equity in her house. If it had all been put together it would've given Clarke enough to save his business.'

'Thanks, Joe.'

Sara turned to Adrian. 'I'd say this changes things a little?'

'I'd say that too, ma'am,' said Adrian. 'Maybe I shouldn't have given him the benefit of the doubt. But we'll see what he says.'

★

The tape was rolling in the interview room as Sara

and Adrian, sat on one side of the desk, began their interrogation of Warren Clarke, who was sat on the other side. Warren had his arms folded across himself and he was looking away from them.

'Mr. Clarke?' Sara began. 'Your prints and DNA sample match one of the traces we found in Rita Makin's house.'

'Well that's hardly surprising,' said Warren who was terrified at what was being played out. 'I was there a couple of times a week, sometimes more. And I discovered the body.'

'But you didn't tell us for three whole days, Mr. Clarke.'

'I told you before I was scared someone would think that I did it!'

'Well to be honest that's what I'm thinking at the moment.'

Warren slammed his hand on the table. 'You can't! You can't think that! I loved Rita. I could never harm her!'

'Oh come on, Mr. Clarke! You told us that you called in on the way home that night on the way back from your parents. But seeing as your parents live twenty miles away that's quite a detour just to claim you were passing. Then there's the question of where you were the night you deemed to report having found Rita's body.'

'I just drove over there,' Warren claimed. 'I knew I had to do something to put things right.'

'Classic avoidance tactic that,' said Sara. 'The murderer calls in the murder to the police and thinks that will insure them against any suspicion.'

'I didn't kill her.'

'What was it like in those intervening three days,

Warren?' asked Adrian.

'It was like a living hell.'

'How did you manage to look your wife in the eye?'

Warren shook his head. 'I don't know! Christ, this is a nightmare.'

'If you were brave enough to murder her mother then you were more than capable of keeping up the pretence,' said Adrian. 'Come on man, it stands to reason.'

'You're in trouble financially, aren't you, Warren?' said Sara.

'What's that got to do with anything?'

'Did you know that Rita had changed her will recently?'

Warren looked up and paused. 'Yes.'

'Leaving everything to you with the proviso that you passed everything on to her grandsons when the time came?'

'Yes!'

'Did your wife Michelle know that her mother had cut her entirely out of her will?'

'Oh yes' said Warren. 'She knew alright.'

'How did she find out?'

'I told her one night in the middle of a row' Warren admitted.

'And how did she react?'

'She came at me with a carving knife. Look, if anyone had a motive to kill Rita it was Michelle. It's her you should be talking to, not me. I loved Rita and I didn't kill her.'

★

Matt wasn't feeling particularly well disposed towards Charlie but he'd still agreed to look after the boys again. He couldn't help it. Charlie always knew exactly what to do to touch his heart and he'd done it again. He'd just put the boys to bed when their mother Wendy rang him. He felt a bit awkward. He didn't want to drop Charlie in it with his ex-wife but at the same time he did want to hurt Charlie for taking him for granted.

'Hi!' said Matt. 'This is a lovely surprise. I haven't heard from you in a while.'

'I know' said Wendy. 'I've been a bit… a bit busy with stuff, which is no excuse I know but you know how it is.'

'I do,' said Matt, noting the edge in her voice. Something was wrong. 'What's the matter, love?'

It took Wendy a few seconds to compose herself before answering. 'Oh Matt.'

'What is it?'

'I really need my old friend,' said Wendy, tearfully.

'Well I'm here but tell me what the matter is, sweetheart? Is it Neville?'

Neville was the bloke Wendy had been seeing these past few months. He was a hill farmer up in the Lake District and Matt liked him. He was so into Wendy and Matt thought he was making Wendy happy. 'If he's hurt you I'll burn his fucking barn down.'

'No, no, it's the other way around,' said Wendy. 'I've hurt him. I've dumped him and I didn't even have the decency to give him a good enough reason. And I was happy with him, Matt. I felt happier than I've been for a long time.'

'Sweetheart, you don't dump somebody because they make you happy.'

'I know'

'Look, why don't you come over? We can talk'

'I can't drive,' said Wendy. 'I've already had nearly a bottle of wine already and a second one is looking very tempting at this point.'

'Get a taxi' said Matt. 'I can't come and fetch you because I've got the boys here and they've just gone to bed.'

'You mean, they're with you?' Wendy questioned. 'Again?'

Charlie and Wendy had certainly had an amicable divorce, more amicable than Charlie deserved thanks to Wendy's strength of character and dedication to her children's welfare. Wendy had never expected any of their friends to take sides even though she was the injured party but despite all the grown up attitudes, there were still areas of contention. Charlie and Wendy had once been in love with each other and that meant that upsets can still occur that made it difficult for those who were in the middle.

'He had something on tonight, Wendy,' said Matt, lamely.

'That's more important than maintaining a relationship with his children?'

'I don't know what to say, Wendy,' said Matt.

'I know,' said Wendy. She had absolutely no problem with Matt looking after the boys but Charlie seemed to dump them on him all the time which wasn't right. Charlie was their father. He should be using the time to maintain his relationship with them. 'I wouldn't expect you to, Matt.'

'I know that,' said Matt, 'now are you going to get that taxi?'

'Have you got plenty of wine in?'

'Is the pope German?'

Wendy laughed. 'Silly me for asking. Alright, I'll ring for that taxi. But I warn you, it's not good news I've got to tell you.'

'I didn't think so,' Matt replied, 'so it's a good job I'm not a good news only friend.'

'You're much more than that' said Wendy. 'Always have been.'

'Then get that taxi booked and get over here.'

'I look a mess' said Wendy, 'I didn't put any make up on today.'

'Well I think I'll let you off' said Matt. 'And bring an overnight bag. I may as well do breakfast for all three of you'

Less than an hour later, Wendy turned up on Matt's doorstep. Her auburn hair rested gently on her shoulders and though she wasn't wearing any make-up, she still looked every inch the woman in her late thirties who shouldn't have to prove herself.

'I'm so glad to see you,' she said as she fell into Matt's arms and he held her tight.

'Sweetheart, whatever is it? I've never known you like this. You had some dark days when you and Charlie split up but nothing compared to this. Please, Wendy, tell me, what is it?'

'Are the boys asleep?'

'Dead to the world' said Matt, ' I checked on them a couple of minutes ago.'

'Can I just go in and see them?'

'You're their Mum,' said Matt, 'why ask?'

Wendy went in to see her boys, her two beautiful boys and managed to kiss them both without stirring them enough to wake them.

'They look like they're at home in there,' said Wendy as she walked into the kitchen where Matt was waiting. He'd opened a bottle of Rioja and poured them each a glass. He handed one to her.

'They seem relaxed with their Uncle Matt.'

'They are,' said Wendy, 'and thank God for you.'

'Wendy...'

'...I'm dying, Matt. I've got cancer. The latest prognosis is not good. There's nothing else they can do.'

Matt almost coughed his wine back up. 'What do you mean there's nothing else they can do? How long have you known this?'

'A long time,' said Wendy, 'please don't be angry with me, Matt. I couldn't bare it if you were angry with me.'

Matt took her in his arms again and hugged her. 'I'm not angry with you, Wendy. I could never be. But what are we going to do?'

'I don't know'

'I take it Charlie doesn't know?'

'No' said Wendy, 'I've arranged to meet him next week but I just had to tell someone before then. You were the only one I could tell.'

'So your parents don't know?'

'No,' said Wendy, 'apart from my doctors you're the only one who knows. And there's something else.'

'Christ, Wendy, what more?'

'I've had a letter from a firm of solicitors in Wilmslow.'

Matt had a sinking feeling about where this was going. 'Go on?'

'Matt, Charlie wants to re-open our divorce settlement,' said Wendy before breaking down. 'His submission says that I've taken too much of an advantage of his financial means and that I could contribute more.'

Matt could barely control his anger. 'Well we both know who's behind this,' he said 'It'll be Natasha.'

'Matt, tell me what to do?'

'You've got to tell Charlie you're ill, sweetheart,' said Matt, holding her tight as she cried on his shoulder. 'Maybe then he'll drop the case.'

'Do you think?'

'Well if he doesn't I'll bloody flatten him.'

'Why is all this happening, Matt?'

'I don't know, my love,' said Matt, who was ready to burst into tears himself. A mixture of pain and anger ran through his soul. Pain at the terrible illness Wendy was going to have to face up to and anger at what Charlie was threatening to do to her financially. If Natasha was standing in front of him right now he'd fucking well kill her. 'This isn't fair, this isn't fair at all but I'll be there for you throughout everything. I promise you.'

Wendy cried out 'Oh Matt, what's going to happen to my boys? My beautiful, beautiful boys'

★

The next morning Matt saw that Wendy was okay and took the boys to school before heading into work. He checked with the receptionist that Charlie didn't have a patient with him and then he marched up to his door and burst into his consulting room before slamming the door shut behind him.

'What the hell's wrong with you?' asked a startled Charlie.

'What's wrong with me? I'll tell you. I used to know someone called Charlie Baxter and he would never have put the mother of his children under the pressure of having to re-negotiate his divorce settlement!'

'Ah' said Charlie as he put his pen down on his desk. 'Wendy's told you.'

'How could you, Charlie?'

'Matt, I'm making a new start with Natasha and I need to sort out my old life before I can do that.'

'I'd never have heard that from your lips before Natasha came along.'

'But that's part of what love is about! Someone comes along and points out where you've gone wrong. I wouldn't expect you to understand that.'

'What do you mean?'

'Well you've never known the kind of love that I've got with Natasha or, for that matter, that I had with Wendy. You don't know what it's all about, Matt, because you've never experienced it or anything like it.'

'You utter bastard.'

'I'm sorry,' said Charlie, 'but I'm not going to let you keep me on the receiving end all the time.'

Matt was floored by what Charlie had said but he did manage to have the last word before he left to go to his own consulting room.

'One day Natasha will have dug out all of your pot of gold and then she'll dump you for someone with an even bigger pot. And when that happens, and I know it will, don't bother to come running to me to get you out of it like you normally do.'

CHAPTER ELEVEN

When Matt got home he was in a heavy, foul mood. He put his key in his front door, stepped through and kicked it shut with the heel of his foot, walked straight through to the kitchen, threw his bag down on a chair, went for a bottle of his favourite French Bordeaux, opened it and slugged down a whole glass before filling it up again. He loosened his tie, tossed his jacket over the back of a chair and then thought about getting himself something to eat. He couldn't believe what Charlie was doing to Wendy. He couldn't believe how Natasha had changed Charlie. The old Charlie would never have been so cold.

But he could handle all that. He could face both Charlie and Natasha down despite what they were going to do. But what he couldn't fight was Wendy's illness. He'd deliberately avoided ringing his Mum today. He didn't want her trying to claim that Wendy's illness and the fact that she was going to die and leave her sons behind was all part of God's fucking plan.

He had some spinach and ricotta cheese ravioli which he boiled in a pan of water to which he'd added some salt and olive oil. He emptied a jar of spicy arrabiatta pasta sauce into another pan and heated that up and turned his oven on high to bake some garlic bread. By the time it was all ready he'd drunk half the bottle of wine but he didn't care. When it was gone he'd open another one. He thought about taking it easy considering all he'd got on his mind but then he told the thought to get to fuck. He needed comfort tonight and if he found that in a bottle of wine then so be it.

He was halfway through his dinner when the doorbell rang. He cursed. He really wasn't in the mood for any visitors tonight but as he walked down the hallway and saw the outline of who it was through the patterned glass panels in his front door, his face broke out into a smile. It had been some time.

'Well' said Matt after he'd opened his front door. 'Detective Sergeant Adrian Bradshaw. To what do I owe this honour?'

'I know it's been a few weeks, Matt,' said Adrian who knew he didn't deserve to expect anything from Matt. 'What can I say? I'm a bad boy.'

'Then it's a good job I like bad boys' said Matt who thought Adrian looked great in his grey suit, white shirt, and dark purple tie. He had one hand in his pocket and was holding his car keys and his mobile in the other. His dark eyes were bearing down intensely into Matt's and he knew what that meant. 'Come in.'

Adrian went through into Matt's kitchen and started helping himself to wine and food like he lived there and was just late home for supper. He wiped some of the pasta sauce up with a piece of garlic bread and wolfed it down.

'I'm a cheeky bastard, aren't I.'

'It's always been part of your charm,' said Matt leaning against the door frame.

'I haven't eaten anything since breakfast,' said Adrian, 'and this wine is a bit bloody nice. You know how to live, Dr. Schofield.'

'Glad you're enjoying it' said Matt who'd like to give Adrian his dinner every night but that was a dream that he'd long since dismissed as impossible.

Adrian lifted up his arms up. 'Do you think I'm keeping in shape?'

'It looks like you are.'

'I've been going out running with one of my neighbours.'

'Up and down those Saddleworth Hills? That really will keep you fit.'

'I'm sorry I haven't been in touch for a while, Matt,' said Adrian.

Matt shrugged his shoulders. 'Well you could've sent me the odd text now and then but I know what the score is with a married man, Adrian.'

Adrian had agonised endlessly about why he kept coming back to see Matt. He'd never been with another man before he'd met him and he still didn't consider himself to be even bisexual. He certainly never looked at any other men and he'd never admit to being unfaithful to Penny. Matt was a man not a woman and being unfaithful meant going with another woman. It was just something about Matt. They'd become friends after Matt had done a stint as the police surgeon at the station Adrian had been working at. Then one evening Adrian had given Matt a lift home after a few of them had been at the pub and Matt asked him in for some coffee. Matt had been a bit drunk and he'd started asking Adrian if he'd ever thought what it would be like with another man. Adrian had laughed initially and then Matt had asked him why he'd come in for coffee. That had been followed by a moment during which Matt had decided to make his move. There was just something about Matt that Adrian couldn't explain. He'd been flattered that Matt had found him attractive. He'd never had a friend who was gay before but he'd have to admit that the more he got to know Matt the more curious he had become. He was still straight. It was still women who turned his head. He just felt lucky that life had thrown him a different kind of sexual experience with a guy as lovely as Matt was. Just something about the person Matt was that had found something inside Adrian's soul. But his marriage would never be threatened by it.

'A straight man who likes a bit of cock on the side is nothing but heartache for a man like you, eh?'

'Now don't go all poetic on me,' said Matt who didn't believe that any man who went to bed with another man was completely straight but he'd let Adrian off with that one.

'No chance of that, mate' said Adrian who then walked over to Matt and stood close. 'If you want to tell me to piss off then I'll go.'

'I'm actually really pleased to see you, Adrian.'

Adrian placed his hands on Matt's shoulders and leaned forward until their foreheads were touching. 'I'm glad I'm here. I've wanted to come a few times but you know how it is'

'Not really,' said Matt, 'I'm not married. But you're here now and I want to make the most of it. How long have you got?'

'A couple of hours.'

'Then let's not waste anymore time talking.'

They kissed passionately and their hands were all over each other. Then Matt took Adrian upstairs where they made up for lost time.

★

Angela had never been much of a church goer. She went there for weddings, funerals and christenings – in other words, all the times when others invited her to their rituals of religious symbolism. Faith, in a religious sense, was just something she'd never understood. She wasn't religious, neither was her husband, and when they got married they did so in a registry office. But despite that she liked the architecture of church buildings and when she did step inside them she couldn't help but get a strange sense of peace and calm from being inside such a cavernous structure. That's why she'd arrived for her meeting with Brendan O'Farrell early so that she could sit down in a pew in Holy Saints church and gather her thoughts.

'Can I help you at all?' said Phillip as he walked up the aisle towards the smartly dressed woman sitting near the front.

Angela turned around. 'Oh sorry father, I ... '

'...no, no, don't apologise,' said Phillip, holding up his hand, 'I just wondered if I could be of any help.'.

'No, I'm fine, thanks,' Angela answered before smiling and holding out her hand. 'I'm Angela Barker. I've got an appointment to see Canon O'Farrell at half past.'

Philip shook her hand. 'And I'm Father Philip Evans. Welcome to our church, Angela.'

'Thank you,' said Angela who rather liked the look of this fresh faced young man. She could imagine confessing all to him without any qualms at all. Why did they saddle these guys with celibacy? What a bloody waste.

'You're the psychotherapist?'

'That's right' said Angela.

'You want to talk to Brendan about this particular church's involvement in the migration of children to Australia back in the fifties and sixties? Is that right?'

'The forced migration, father.'

'Sorry, yes, I have to acknowledge it was a forced migration and I think you'll find Brendan does too.'

'That's good,' said Angela, 'because that means progress on the part of the church.'

'Well of this particular church anyway,' said Phillip. 'We're a little independent, a little revolutionary here but don't tell or else you'll get us into trouble.'

Angela smiled. 'Don't worry' she said, 'your secret is safe with me.'

'That's good to know'

Phillip led Angela from the church across the short yard to the presbytery. Inside it reminded Angela of everything she used to hate about school. The walls were in the standard nondescript magnolia with dark brown wooden polished tiles on the floor and the coldness punctuated only by pictures of the Pope, Christ and various saints. There didn't seem to be anyone else there as Phillip showed her into an office just off the main hallway. The sun was beaming through the window as Brendan, who'd been sitting at the desk, stood up and gave her the big beaming smile of an old man who'd used it to get through life. His hair was grey but his face was wearing well, she thought, and the skin on his neck showed little signs of sagging. He took her hand in both of his and gestured for her to sit down in one of the two armchairs. He sat in the other.

'Well now you're a psychotherapist,' said Brendan. 'That's a very modern profession now, isn't it.'

'I suppose it is, Canon, yes,' said Angela. Despite the warmth of his greeting she was still wary of him. She'd had some of her fiercest confrontations with members of the clergy, both Catholic and Protestant. She liked to think she offered practical help to the people in her care whereas priests can only offer prayer.

'Phillip will bring some tea in shortly,' said Brendan. 'Now how can I help you?'

'I want to talk to you about a patient of mine,' said Angela.

'Oh yes?'

'Yes. He's an inmate at Manchester prison which is one of the places where I work.'

'And you'll have your work cut out for you there, I expect?'

'It's a challenge, yes,' said Angela, 'but a worthwhile one.'

'Are you a Christian woman, Angela?'

'No, Canon, I'm not.'

'But you perform in a very Christian profession,' said Brendan, 'ministering to some of the most needy in society.'

'Well I happen to think that the people who demonstrate Christianity are those who don't go to church,' said Angela who immediately regretted saying it. She was making herself out to be as truthfully righteous as those she accused of being falsely righteous. And she didn't think of herself in that way at all. It was a kind of reverse snobbery and she couldn't fucking stand that.

Brendan let his head fall back as he laughed. 'I see,' he said, 'and why do you say that?'

'You really want me to tell you?'

'Yes' said Brendan. 'You're a professional woman and I value your opinion.'

Angela teased herself with the thought of making a cheap shot about how unusual it was for the Catholic Church to value the opinions of a professional woman but she decided, at the outset of her relationship with the Canon, that she would keep it buttoned and simply amuse herself with that idea.

'Well I'm an agnostic, Canon' said Angela. 'I don't know for sure that there's no truth to religion which is why I'm not an atheist. But to me churches are full of people who think their hypocrisy filled lives will be redeemed by an hour on a Sunday morning when they're seen to be going to church.'

'Go on?'

'Well a large part of my job is to not judge anyone,' said Angela.

'And you've just judged my entire congregation.'

Angela could feel herself blushing. Why did priests always have the apparent ease to do that to her? Talking to a priest like Canon O'Farrell was like talking to her father. He could always corner her arguments too.

'But I'm not claiming to be a Christian and I thought that Jesus came to teach us not to judge?'

'Well,' said Brendan. 'I think you've enunciated a basic truth about some who profess to be Christian.'

'Which is?'

'That many of my flock don't seem to know the difference between the old testament and the new testament. Now you're making me feel like an activist in some political party who thinks he should beg you to join.'

Angela laughed. 'Well I wasn't making a pitch, Canon.'

'No, I know, just indulge me,' said Brendan, 'I'm an old man about to retire and I like to have some fun.'

'Good for you, Canon.' said Angela. 'But could we now get back to why I'm here?'

'Of course' said Canon. 'I promise not to sidetrack us again.'

'Okay. I want to talk to you about my patient who, as a young child of five, was left here by his mother and then as an orphan sent to Australia back in 1962.'

'1962? I wasn't here then, Angela, but I agree that the whole forced migration scheme was a most shameful act on the part of the church.'

'It was, Canon,' said Angela, 'many of these children ended up leading pretty awful lives and my patient is an example of that, a fairly extreme example, but an example nonetheless. His name is Sean Patrick O'Brien and although he's still behind bars at the moment he is up for parole soon and I know he wants to come back to where it all started for him.'

'So what is it you want from me?'

'I want to know if you have records for these children and if so then I'd like you to show me the record for Sean Patrick O'Brien.'

'Angela,' said Brendan, sitting forward in his seat and wishing that Phillip would come in with the tea. 'What good do you think that would serve now?'

'That's not for either of us to judge, Canon. It's for Sean Patrick O'Brien.'

'Well then I'm going to have to disappoint you, Angela,' said Brendan. ' I'm afraid all records of the orphanage were destroyed in a fire at diocesan headquarters in the seventies. I'm sorry.'

★

Charlie Baxter got around to Natasha's house just before
seven. He was burdened with worry about Wendy. She'd
finally told him her diagnosis and the news had devastated
him. This was the woman he'd fallen in love with all
those years ago and who'd given him his two wonderful
children. The woman he'd let down so badly. .

'You said you'd be here at six,' said Natasha, flatly.

'I had to go and see Wendy,' said Charlie, his face
barely lifting from staring at the floor. 'I did tell you.'

'And I told you that we needed to have an early
dinner tonight because Toby and JJ are coming around
for drinks later.'

'JJ?' he questioned, wondering what the fuck she was
talking about.

'It stands for Jennifer Jane,' said Natasha, irritably as
if she were reminding a child for the sixth time that his
Grandma was about to visit. 'I did tell you.'

'My ex-wife has been diagnosed with cancer, for
God's sake. I think I can be forgiven for having had one
or two little items on my mind that prevented me from
holding information about someone called fucking JJ.'

'Well are you sure she's not spinning you a yarn?'

'I beg your pardon?'

'Well it just seems very convenient that she comes
up with this cancer thing just after you've told her you're
going to renegotiate the divorce settlement.'

Charlie didn't want to lose his temper with her but
remarks like that would make it a real struggle. 'Natasha,
Wendy is one of the most honest people I've ever known
and ever will know. You're way off the mark with that.'

'I'm only saying, darling boy,' said Natasha, sensing

that she may have gone too far and moving on him. She wrapped her body around his. 'I'm only looking out for you, Charles, you know that.'

Charlie pulled her arms off him. 'Not now, darling.'

'Charles, I'm not having our evening dictated to by her,' said Natasha as the scales fell from her eyes. 'I brought the prawns all the way back from the fish market in Seattle and now they're overcooked and ruined.'

'Well if that's all you've got on your mind then you're a very lucky girl,' said Charlie as he picked up his car keys and went for the door.

'Charles! Don't you walk out on me you bastard!'

'I think that's what I am doing.'

'But what about Toby and JJ?'

'Fuck Toby and tell whoever JJ is that she's a pretentious bitch!'

Natasha started crying. Charlie heard her and it made him stop. She wasn't as strong as Wendy. She wasn't as mature as Wendy. He couldn't leave her like this. He turned and went back and embraced her. She was his future. He had to bring her with him or else he'd be lost.

'Go and have a shower, my darling,' said Natasha, wiping her face with her fingers. 'I'll rustle up something for us to eat for when you come back down. You must be hungry.'

'Not really, to tell you the truth.'

'But you must eat something, darling boy,' said Natasha. 'Toby and JJ like their booze and you'll need to keep up with Toby in particular or else he might think you're being unsociable.'

'Natasha, I'm putting a hold on everything,' he said. 'The re-negotiation of my divorce settlement from Wendy and the selling of my half of the practice. It's all going on hold. It wouldn't feel right to go ahead with any of it just now.'

Natasha had to work hard to contain her anger. She wasn't going to let something like her lover's ex-wife's cancer get in the way of what she wanted.

'Darling, I know how awful everything is at the moment but don't you see? This is exactly the right time to make the changes we need.'

'You mean this is when everybody is feeling vulnerable so let's kick them when they're down.'

'No of course I didn't mean that, Charles! I'm really hurt that you could even think that.'

Charlie put his arms around her again as she began to get upset. 'Okay, okay, I'm sorry.'

'Whatever I do is all for us, you know? Our future happiness is all that matters to me.'

'I know' said Charlie who then kissed her head. 'I'll go and take that shower'

'We will need to talk about it though, Charles,' said Natasha. 'I'm not comfortable with leaving things as they are.'

'And there's the boys to think of, Natasha' said Charlie.

'What do you mean?'

'Well they'll have to come and live with us' said Charlie. 'They're my children and I'll be the only parent they have left.'

'But you'll be starting your new life with me, Charles' said Natasha who hadn't counted on Charles' brats having to come and live with them. Well she wasn't going to have it. Why should she have to take them on just because their mother's dead? She'd see them in care before that happened. They've got bloody grandparents to go to for fuck's sake. Let somebody who cares wipe their bloody noses.

'Yes' said Charlie, 'and that will have to include my kids

now that the circumstances have changed so dramatically. They'll need stability and security and that means being with me, their father. Surely you understand that, darling?'

'But what about when we have children of our own, darling boy?'

'What about it?'

'Well I want people to think that our children are your first.'

Charlie was in disbelief over what he was hearing. He'd always known that Natasha wasn't the brightest but he'd got carried away with lust for such a pretty girl. And because she made him feel intellectually superior. That was important and that's why it hadn't worked with Wendy.

'Natasha, the children I've already got are my priority for the time being. This is an awful situation and nobody would've chosen it, especially not Wendy. But it's here now and we're going to have to deal with it in the best way we can. I need your support, Natasha. I really need you to support me on this.'

Natasha decided to play for time whilst she decided what to do. 'Of course' she said. 'And I do support you, darling boy, and of course the boys too. I'm by your side, now and always, no matter what.'

CHAPTER TWELVE

Angela had been less than pleased with her meeting with Canon O'Farrell at Holy Saints church. He'd been good enough to go through the history of the church and how over two hundred children had been dispatched from it's orphanage into the forced migration programme to Australia that the church had been in cahoots with the government over. He'd been refreshingly frank about how dirty a trade it had been and how he didn't believe the church should ever have been involved in it. But he hadn't been able to confirm anything about Sean Patrick O'Brien. Angela didn't believe a word of his claim that all records relating to the orphanage had been destroyed in a fire. However much of a facade Canon O'Farrell had put up with his charm and his wit and his manner that had bordered on the flirtatious, she couldn't help but feel that he could help her further if he wanted to.

But two days later when she sat down with Paddy she didn't know how to break the news to him about Rita Makin. Rita had made such an impression on him when he'd been at his most vulnerable. How was he going to take the news of what had happened to her? He obviously hadn't found out for himself yet or else he would've mentioned it. But still, she decided to wait until it felt like the right moment.

'Paddy, tell me what happened after you ran away? Did they catch up with you?'

'No, Doc,' said Paddy, 'It's surprising how much you can live off your wits when you're forced into it. I had almost a year of living rough, running from town to town, not making relationships with anyone.'

'How did you survive though, Paddy? I mean, how did you eat?'

'When I could,' said Paddy. 'You'd be surprised at how much food people throw away that's perfectly edible. Well, as long as you're not fussed about having a table to eat off and plates and knives and forks.'

'You can't have been more than what, twelve, thirteen, fourteen?'

'I was about fourteen,' said Paddy. 'Once I was out of

the routine of the children's home I had time to think and all the bewilderment about how my mother could've just left me came over me again. The pain from that was truly relentless at times.'

'How did you deal with that?'

'I didn't,' said Paddy, 'I just did what I could to get through each day. I didn't know where the fuck I was going. I only knew where it was I'd come from.'

'And what followed on from this period?'

'I was on the outskirts of Melbourne,' Paddy recalled, 'I was sitting in a park in some suburb or other. I hadn't seen the news or anything for days so I didn't know how dangerous it was for a boy of my age to be in that area on my own at that time.

1972

'You look a bit lost, mate' she said.

Sean didn't answer. He was sitting on a bench in the park next to the street where all the Greek restaurants were. He'd never been to a restaurant. He'd heard of a place called Greece. And now he knew something about Greek food from all the stuff the restaurants throw away that he'd been able to salvage and eat. He didn't know what any of it was called. But it tasted alright.

'I've seen you around here a few times,' she carried on, trying to find a way in.

Sean still didn't say anything. He just kept staring into space and ignoring his companion. As soon as he was able he'd run. He was good at running. He'd been doing it for the last year. If she'd noticed him a few times then others were bound to have done too. It might be time to move on to be on the safe side. Last night he'd found a place in the woods to sleep but he hadn't had a good night. All he could dream about was the face of his mother on the day she left him with the Nuns. He'd woken up in tears. He wondered what she was doing now and if she ever thought about him. He wondered why she'd sent him to Hell whilst he was still alive.

'Do you want a smoke, mate?'

Sean looked down at the packet of cigarettes the woman was holding. It was tempting. So was she. She was pretty with blond hair and wearing a short blue dress. She had red painted nails and a curve to her breasts.

'Go on,' she said encouragingly, 'you know you want to.'

Sean took a cigarette and leaned forward to let her light it for him.

'Thanks' he said. Smoking had become one of his acquired skills whilst he'd been on the run.

'Well now you've taken one of my ciggies, do I get to know your name?'

'It's… Patrick,' said Sean. Patrick was his middle name and it was the one he'd been using on the run whenever he'd had to engage in conversation with anybody.

'Why don't I call you Paddy? It's a bit more relaxed, right?'

'Paddy' shrugged his shoulders. He didn't want to admit it but he rather liked the idea of becoming 'Paddy'. It was like he was becoming someone else. It didn't make any difference to him being on the run. He'd managed to find newspapers that told him he was wanted for questioning in relation to the deaths of Brother Michael and Andy Cook. No surprise there. Not long after running away from the boys' home he'd crossed over from New South Wales into Victoria and eventually made his way all the way down to Melbourne. He felt safer in the city. People in the country were too suspicious of unfamiliar faces.

'Well I'm Eileen,' she said, offering one of her small hands to shake with Paddy's.

'Hello,' said Paddy who'd been starved of basic human contact for so long that he didn't know what to do, especially given his circumstances. He decided to shake her hand.

'That's very formal,' she cooed, 'and quite sweet really. So where are you from Paddy?'

'Here and there.'

'Secretive, eh? Good for you, my little vegemite. You don't want all and bloody sundry knowing your bloody business. You're fairly boyish looking but I'm guessing you're a bit older? Just on the edge of being a man?'

Paddy didn't know why but he laughed. 'Yeah, I reckon.'

'Look, Paddy, I reckon we're likely souls, you and I. Why don't you come back to my place, have yourself a bath, get yourself something to eat? You look like you've been making do for ages.'

'Who are you?'

'Nobody you should fear,' said Eileen. 'I'm not the police but I'm guessing you're running from someone or something.'

'How do I know if I can trust you?'

'You don't,' said Eileen. 'You just need to take the risk.'

★

'So why did you take the risk with her, Paddy?'

'I needed some company, Doc' said Paddy. ' I mean, have a fucking heart.'

'No, I do understand, Paddy,' said Angela.

'Yeah, I know you do, Doc' said Paddy as he stretched out his legs under the table and folded his arms across his

141

chest. 'I guess you have to be a bit obvious, a bit probing to make sure I'm telling the truth.'

'Well it's not really like that, Paddy,' she said, although Angela would have to admit she couldn't have put it more succinctly than Paddy had done.

'Are you okay today, Doc?'

'Me? Why do you ask?'

'You seem a bit... well, tense,' said Paddy. 'I'm used to you being all relaxed and sort of laid back. That's your style. Oh don't get me wrong, I'm not saying you don't care or anything because I know that you do. I'm just giving you my impressions of how you work.'

'Thanks, Paddy, but you're supposed to be the patient.'

'I know but I see it as a fair exchange.'

'I'm grateful, Paddy,' said Angela. 'And once more you've surprised me. But I'm okay, truly. Now, tell me what happened after you went back to Eileen's house?'

'She turned me into a man, Doc.'

'You had a sexual relationship with her?'

'Yes, I did.'

'Did she force you into it?'

'Well if she did then you could say that I was willing to be forced.'

'Did you enjoy it?'

'Of course I did' said Paddy. 'What fifteen year old boy wouldn't enjoy sleeping with an older woman who could show him what to do? The only trouble was she had a boyfriend and I didn't realise that she was only sleeping with me so that I'd work for him.'

'You couldn't get out of the situation?'

'No,' said Paddy. 'They found out I was the young lad they'd seen on the news who was on the run. And they used that. That's when Hell really started.' He threw his head back and laughed sardonically. 'I'd thought for just one marvellous second that maybe the Gods were giving me a break when I met Eileen but I really should've known.'

CHAPTER THIRTEEN

'Well just look at you' said Matt as he walked back into the bedroom from the bathroom. He was naked and his cock and balls swung slightly as he walked. 'Sitting up in my bed with your post-coital cigarette and showing off your hairy chest to the world. You look like Sean Connery in all those early Bond films.'

'Well does that make you Miss Moneypenny?' asked Adrian in an attempted Connery voice that made Matt fall about laughing. 'Why are you laughing?'

'Because that was the worse Sean Connery imitation I've ever heard!'

Adrian grabbed Matt and brought him close. 'I'll bet Connery doesn't kiss like I do, he said before sweeping Matt onto the bed and kissing him with the same extraordinary passion that had driven their love making. He then lifted the duvet and tapped the space inside with the palm of his hand. 'Now get back into bed.'

'Yes, Sir,' said Matt as he crawled in and snuggled up to Adrian. If only it could stay like this. He didn't want Adrian to go home. He wanted to hold onto this feeling and yet he knew that it would be wrenched away from him like a child who won't give up his toy at bedtime. 'You seem a lot more relaxed than when you first got here.'

'Well I've had a thorough examination from the good doctor so I'm tons better now.'

'Is it work that's stressing you?'

'Yes' said Adrian. 'We've got a big case on. I was lucky to get away to be honest.'

'Murder?'

'Oh yes,' said Adrian. 'You might've read about it in the papers? A woman called Rita Makin?'

'Yes, I did' said Matt as he recalled reading the report in the Manchester Evening News. 'Somebody got into her house and cut her throat for apparently no reason?'

'That's the one' said Adrian.

'Horrific,' said Matt, 'poor woman. Her poor family.'

'You might not say that if you'd met them' said Adrian. 'Anyway, lets not talk about it anymore. I know what I meant to ask you. Are you going on holiday this year?'

'Well, yes,' said Matt who was somewhat surprised by the question.

'Where are you going?'

'I'm going to Italy in August. My friend Gabriella lives in Rome so I'll stay with her and her family for a week or so and then we'll all go down to the coast near Naples for another week. It's beautiful down there. Have you ever been?'

'No, can't say I have,' Adrian replied. He'd not been abroad that much. Since the kids had come along he'd not been able to afford it. It was alright for men like Matt who don't have any dependents. Adrian wouldn't swap his kids for the world but they did mean that his own life was on hold whilst he saw to theirs. That's one of the reasons why he needed this time with Matt. It was something he didn't have to share with anyone else in the family but himself.

'Anyway, can you just picture you and me on some faraway beach then?' asked Matt his voice rich with fantasy.

'Well I can picture it, mate, but it's not going to

happen.'

Matt wished Adrian wasn't quite as blunt as he sometimes could be. He took a deep breath and then asked 'So why did you ask me?'

'Well, the thing is, I told you my Dad died years ago?'

'Yeah?' Matt asked, noting that Adrian hadn't apparently noticed the pause in their conversation. But then why would he? Adrian had everything he wanted at home and away.

'Well my Mum has decided to give me and my brothers and sister part of what we were going to inherit when she died. She wants to give us something now so she can get the pleasure out of seeing what we do with it. My Dad has missed out on so much with his kids and his grandkids and I think my Mum just doesn't want to miss out on as much. Anyway, it's not a lot of money, Matt, not really. We'll get about six grand each but it'll be enough to spend some of it on a holiday for me and the family. I just wondered if you had ideas as to where we might go.'

Matt didn't really want to answer that. He wanted to go on holiday with Adrian. He didn't want to advise him of where he could go with someone else even if that was his wife and his children.

'I've always loved Italy' said Matt. 'I don't think you can go wrong there. The food, the wine, the buildings, the culture, just the general way of the place.'

'Too full of Italians.'

'Watch it, you. My friends Gabriella and her husband Umberto and their family mean a lot to me.'

'Okay, but not Italy.'

'Well how about France? For all the same reasons as Italy.'

'Too full of the bloody French,' said Adrian. 'Look, I don't want to go to any country that doesn't speak

English.'

'I beg your pardon?'

'Okay, so I'm a lazy Brit who won't try.'

'You're not prepared to make any effort to speak someone else's language?'

'No, sorry. I'm very English when it comes to things like that. It's up to them to speak English not the other way around.'

'Christ!' Matt exclaimed, 'I didn't realise what a little Englander you were.'

'Yeah, well that's me.'

'That's a pity because it would be great for your kids and learning another language opens up a whole new culture to you.'

'I'm quite happy with my English culture thank you very much.'

'You were quite happy with straight sex until I came along.'

Adrian laughed. 'Oh touché!'

'You see' said Matt. 'You can speak another language.'

'Well what's touché?'

'It's French you idiot.'

'I never knew that.'

'Oh puh—lease!'

'No seriously, I didn't.'

'Mange tout, Rodney, mange tout.'

'So do you speak French?'

'Yes'

'And do you speak Italian too?'

'Yes' said Matt. 'But it's the language of love so that's why I never speak it to you.'

'Oh ha, ha, my sides!' laughed Adrian. 'Anyway, I think it's going to be Florida.'

Matt pulled a face. 'Florida? You'd have to pay me to

go there.'

'At least they speak English.'

'Of a sort. I'm sometimes able to understand people who don't speak English more than I can understand Americans. I certainly feel more in tune with other Europeans than I do with America.'

'Well I'm of the opposite view,' said Adrian. 'Sorry. Europe means nothing to me. America is the real deal.'

'Oh I hate their absurd puritan values,' said Matt. 'They wanted to impeach Clinton because he'd had an affair. It had nothing to do with anybody else but those directly involved.'

'So you're saying that if our Prime Minister was found out to have been having an affair with one of his staff, it wouldn't bother you?'

'Not a bit.'

'Why not?'

'Because it would be his business to sort out with his wife and his lover,' said Matt. 'Just like it was Mitterand's business in France when it was discovered he had a daughter with a woman who wasn't his wife. Nobody else bothered. The French public just shrugged their Gallic shoulders. They took the more mature view.'

'But what about the morality that goes with being in that office?'

'I think it's a bit rich of you, Mr. Married Man, to be climbing onto the moral high ground when you're lying here in bed with me.'

'But this is different.'

'Why is it?'

'Because I'm not the Prime Minister.'

'But there's the duplicity, don't you see? In Britain and America we've got to grow up about these things. We're forever banging on about how we want our politicians to be more human and then when they do show they're human we condemn them for it.'

'Well, yeah, I can see what you're saying,' said Adrian who then lowered himself down and kissed Matt. 'You think a lot deeper than I do.'

'That isn't difficult.'

'Don't push it, mastermind.'

Matt cradled Adrian's face in his hands. The stubble on his face made it feel like sandpaper to Matt's smooth hands and it got him hard.

'Remember when you wouldn't kiss me on the lips?' said Matt.

'Yeah' said Adrian. 'What a twat I was.'

'You'd fuck me from here to next week but you wouldn't kiss me on the lips because you said that would really make you gay.'

Adrian laughed at his own stupidity. 'I know' he said and then kissed Matt again. He did have the softest lips. 'I can't get enough of it now.'

'Is that why you've never asked me to fuck you?'

'I don't understand?'

'Well that really would be making you perhaps more gay than you want to be' said Matt. 'The penetration and all that. You know what I mean, Adrian.'

'Yeah I do and I suppose that's true, yeah. But I've never really thought about it, Matt, until you mentioned it. I get what I need from being inside you.'

They kissed again and Matt felt his erection twitch against Adrian's. 'Do you have time?'

'Yes,' said Adrian as he reached for another condom and picked it open with his teeth. 'But this one will have to be a quickie though. It's KFC bargain bucket night at our house and Penny normally goes for it about seven.'

'Oh you sure know how to make a boy feel valued.'

They'd just finished making love when Adrian's mobile rang. He reached out and picked it up. He said it was Penny calling and asked Matt to keep quiet whilst he answered it. Matt did as he was told just like he always did but it annoyed him. Listening to Adrian say 'darling' this and 'darling' that just really pissed him off.

'She's a wonderful woman, my wife,' said Adrian after he'd finished the call from Penny, 'I'm so bloody lucky I can't tell you.'

'I'm very pleased to hear it.'

Adrian looked up at hearing the tone in Matt's voice. 'What's all that about?'

'Do you have to say that every time you're here?'

'I don't' Adrian protested.

'You fucking do,' said Matt. 'You may use a slightly different form of words but it amounts to the same thing. I know I'm only your bit on the side, Adrian, but you don't have to rub my nose in it.'

'I didn't think you had a problem.'

'I don't,' Matt insisted, 'but I do have a problem with you not showing me any sensitivity at all. You could've gone into another room and taken that call instead of asking me to keep quiet in my own fucking bedroom.'

Adrian paused as he looked at Matt. Then he said 'I'd better get dressed and get going.'

'Yes' said Matt, flatly. 'You wouldn't want your KFC to get cold.'

★

Sara brought Michelle Clarke in to take her fingerprints and a DNA sample. Mrs. Clarke protested but Sara said that it was no worse than what they'd asked of her husband who was still in custody. She'd learned from her experiences with Lady Eleanor Harding last year that the more you bring suspects into the station the more they seemed willing to tell the truth. It would seem elementary for a police officer to be able to deduce these things but Sara had always operated on the principle that she wasn't always right. It was her job to tease the answers out of everyone she needed to tell the truth and if that meant interviewing them in their own homes then that was better. But if it meant bringing them down to the station and putting on the whole official big shit thing then that was good too.

'Right, Mrs. Clarke,' said Sara as she walked into the interview room where Michelle Clarke was sitting. 'Let's talk for a few minutes.'

'Detective Inspector, I have three sons who will want feeding when they get home from school in a couple of hours time.'

'Well I won't keep you longer than necessary, Mrs. Clarke.'

'I don't even know why I'm here,' said Michelle, defiantly. 'You should be out there finding my mother's killer.'

'That's what we are doing, Mrs. Clarke,' said Sara.

'So you say,' Michelle replied. She bowed her head. If only she could turn the clock back and tell her mother that whatever had happened between her and Warren, they could talk about it. They could work things out. It was tearing away at her inside.

'Yes, Mrs. Clarke,' said Sara. 'I say.'

'Well at least can you give me an idea as to how long you're going to keep me here?'

'That depends on your answers to a few questions,' said Sara, 'and I must say, I'm surprised you haven't asked after your husband's welfare, Mrs. Clarke?'

'Are you going to charge him?'

'I don't know yet,' said Sara, 'we're still working on it.'

'I wish you luck.'

'Mrs. Clarke, you surely don't mean that?'

'My husband was sleeping with my mother, I don't owe him anything.'

'But you wouldn't want him falsely accused?'

Michelle shrugged her shoulders. 'Don't expect me to care about the duplicitous bastard.'

'I think that's understandable in the circumstances' said Sara. 'But I need to find your mother's killer. And I can't rule anyone out.'

'Anyone?'

'Including you, Mrs. Clarke.'

Michelle sat back in her chair. 'I was nowhere near my mother's house that night.'

'But you were angry with your mother over her affair with your husband and the fact that she'd cut you out of her will. That's a pretty toxic mix. Who knows what that might've led you to do?'

'Look, detective, I've made no secret of the fact that I was estranged from my mother when she died,' Michelle admitted as she fought back the tears, 'but to think that I could kill her is… well, not only absurd but deeply hurtful.'

'Do you believe your husband could've done it?'

'For what it's worth, no I don't.'

'How did you feel about your mother cutting you out of her will?'

'How do you think I felt? I was disgusted by it.'

'And when your husband told you the news did you attack him with a carving knife?'

Michelle shifted in her chair. 'He told you that?'

'I'm asking you, Mrs. Clarke' said Sara. 'Did you or

did you not attack your husband with a carving knife?'

'Yes, I did! I was angry, I was furious. Who could blame me?'

'Nobody' said Sara. 'Anybody would've been angry in your place.'

'But?'

'Mrs. Clarke, another set of prints were found in your mother's house. Were they yours?'

'No, they weren't mine!'

'Then do you know who they belong to?'

Michelle looked up at Sara and was about to say something but stopped herself.

'Mrs. Clarke?'

Michelle put her head in her hands and then reared it back up again. 'Oh Christ I'm no good at this.'

'No good at what, Mrs. Clarke?'

'I'm saying nothing more unless my solicitor is present.'

'Now why would you need a solicitor, Mrs. Clarke?' asked Sara, who could smell the blood.

'I said I'm saying nothing more unless my solicitor is present.'

Michelle Clarke adopted a visibly different demeanour now she was sitting there alongside her solicitor. Sara and Joe Alexander were on the other side of the table that filled the space between them. The solicitor didn't look much at Sara. He was young, maybe late twenties, a sharp enough dark blue suit but he looked as if he still wasn't at ease with these kind of adversarial situations. Well he'd better get used to it, thought Sara. It was his job after all. She'd had many a lad like him for breakfast and still been hungry afterwards. She'd had a rather physical session with Kieran last night. They'd gone at it so much they both nearly passed out and when she came to work this morning his cum was still dripping out of her vagina. They'd almost wrecked her bed but it was the session in the shower first thing that she'd particularly enjoyed. She was rather partial to doing it in unusual places. She loved doing it outside, in the back of a car, she liked to get it from behind whilst standing at her bedroom window looking out. She'd done it on a train, on a plane, in a pub car park, in the sand dunes at Blackpool. She'd lost count of all the men she'd had and all the different places she'd done it in and if that made her a slag in some people's eyes then she didn't care. If she was a man she'd be called a player. She had been thinking lately that she wanted more than just sex and conversation but Kieran was such a bloody good fuck that she couldn't help herself. And he was fun too. He made her laugh. She'd admit to thinking of him as special but she didn't know if she could let herself think anymore about him. What if he broke her heart just like Tim Norris had done all those years ago? She'd carved out a nice, independent life for herself. She'd have to be very sure about a man before she compromised all that.

Sara got the preliminaries over with by introducing the solicitor and detective sergeant Joe Alexander for the benefit of the tape.

'Now what is it you need to tell us, Michelle?' Sara asked.

'Last year,' Michelle began, 'we had some building work done on our house. We had the extension put on at the back and we had the attic converted into a study for our boys. Three desks, three computer terminals, various books to help them with their school work. They love it up there. Sometimes I have to drag them down screaming to have their dinner. Anyway, the firm we employed to carry out the work is run by a man called Nick Jackson. Nick is the same age as me and he was married when he was very young but he's been divorced for years. He has a daughter who's at Manchester University. We hit it off straight away and we were attracted to each other. I'd lost all respect for my husband and I didn't love him anymore. Nick is everything that my husband isn't.'

'So you were cheating on your husband when you found out that he was cheating on you?' said Sara.

Michelle jammed her finger on the table. 'With my mother! That makes it just that little bit different, don't you think?'

'It must've felt like the ultimate betrayal,' said Joe who could see tears falling down her cheeks but it was almost as if they didn't belong to her. She'd detached herself from any guilt over her own affair and was passing it all onto her husband for his affair with her mother. It made Joe wonder about his own relationship with Carol. What really went through Carol's mind about him and what they were getting up to? If the shit was to hit the fan would she blame him for it all as a means of excusing herself? She was the one who was married after all.

'And then there is the business with the money,' said Michelle. 'I knew Warren's business was in trouble. I knew we'd stretched ourselves too far but he's always been a bloody fool where money is concerned. The business is a good one and he's got a lot of regular customers. He just spent too much.'

'What are you trying to justify here, Mrs. Clarke?' Joe asked.

'I'm not trying to justify anything … '

'…it sounds like you are to me' said Joe.

'Look, my relationship with my husband had broken down to an extent that I never thought was possible,' said Michelle, 'I had nothing but contempt for him.'

'Whilst you were starting a relationship with someone else' added Joe.

'Yes, but these things are never that cut and dried, are they?'

'We're the ones who are asking the questions, Mrs. Clarke,' said Joe.

'Look, I've never been involved in anything like this before' said Michelle, earnestly.

'Like what, Mrs. Clarke?' Sara asked.

'Nick has been in the building trade for a long time and he knows people.'

'What do you mean?' Sara asked.

'I wanted to hurt my husband,' said Michelle. 'I wanted to teach him a lesson. Nick knows people who could do that.'

'So, are you saying to us that you arranged some kind of hit on your husband?' said Joe.

At that point the solicitor whispered a conversation with his client but Michelle brushed him aside.

'I knew he was going to see my mother that night,' said Michelle. 'I wanted them both to suffer. I agreed a fee of two hundred pounds.'

'To do what exactly?' Sara wanted to know.

'To beat him up,' said Michelle. 'I knew my mother would've left the back door open for him. There's an alleyway down the side of her house and the back can't be seen from the street. I wanted them to beat him up there.'

'Where your mother would be able to see what was happening?' asked Joe, incredulously.

Michelle put her hand over her mouth and looked up at the two detectives appealingly. She nodded her head.

'Did you meet with the men yourself?' asked Sara.

'No' said Michelle. 'Neil handed over the money on my behalf.'

'Mrs. Clarke, have you heard anything from the men since?'

'No,' said Michelle, composing herself as best she could, 'but Nick has. They told him in no uncertain terms that murder wasn't part of what they do.'

'And what do you deduce from that, Mrs. Clarke?' asked Sara.

'That those two men must've seen who did kill my mother,' said Michelle, her voice faltering, 'and it obviously scared them off. You see, the fee was two hundred pounds but the deal was that it was split in two. I gave them a hundred up front and the other hundred would be paid …'

'…would be paid when, Mrs. Clarke?' Sara pushed.

'On completion' said Michelle. 'Now Warren wasn't beaten up that night and I know he wasn't threatened by anyone. They must've got there early and seen everything.'

'Yes' said Sara. 'Unless they were the ones who murdered your mother and they were just covering up for themselves.'

'But they're small time according to Nick' said Michelle, 'they're rough around the edges and like a good fight but murder? They'd have had no reason to murder my mother.'

'Well can you think of any other reason why someone would murder her? She could've seen them and they panicked. It's happened before.'

Michelle broke down and wept. 'Oh my God!' she cried. 'Her death could be… I mean, if I hadn't arranged… it could be all down to me that she's dead!'

CHAPTER FOURTEEN

Angela had decided to tell Paddy about the murder of Rita Makin but first she was going to get through her latest session with him first. She was also going to tell him about Father Philip Evans and his offer of help in trying to trace what had happened to Paddy's mother and she would ask Paddy if he remembered a Canon Brendan O'Farrell or Father O'Farrell as he would have been known then. Although Canon O'Farrell had said that he hadn't been working at the church at the time when Paddy was left at its orphanage, Angela hadn't believed him. Something told her he was lying. And she'd like to find out why.

'So tell me about your life with Eileen and her boyfriend, Paddy?' Angela asked.

'Well like I said last time, Doc, I hadn't realised I was getting into a kind of threesome,' Paddy recalled.

'But it wasn't the kind of threesome that most of us know about?'

'Why, have you had one, Doc?'

'As a matter of fact, Paddy, no,' said Angela, smiling, 'but coming back to your past. What did Eileen's boyfriend get you to do?'

1974

Paddy had spotted the young lad whilst he was hanging on the corner of the street eating what looked like a vegemite sandwich. Paddy hated vegemite. It was like spreading your bread with cold black tar and it didn't taste much better. But a young lad like the one he was now walking towards would taste very good to Eileen's boyfriend, Glenn. He was probably a couple of years younger than Paddy so he'd be at the top end of Glenn's age range, but he was still within Glenn's strict limits.

'How's it going?' asked Paddy as he stopped once he was beside him.

The boy looked up suspiciously. 'Alright. Who wants to know?'

'I'm Paddy. What's yours?'

'I'm Davey. Are you at Allerton High? I haven't seen you there before?.'

'No' said Paddy. 'But I used to be.'

'I'm in year 10.'

'Year 10? So, fourteen, fifteen?'

'I'm fifteen in two weeks.'

'Oh beauty,' said Paddy. He'd virtually lost all trace of his English accent now. He sounded like a real meat pie Aussie. And that wasn't surprising seeing as he spent most of his time with Eileen and Glenn and they weren't exactly the brains of Melbourne. Paddy knew enough about stuff to appreciate that. He hardly even remembered his mother's face either. Except in those times in the middle of the night when the demons came flying at him and ripped his eyes out. If the bloody bitch walked back into his life now he'd probably turn and walk away. She'd done her damage. She could never even begin to take back the years that he was continuing to lose.

'Why are you talking to me?' Davey wanted to know.

Paddy tried to answer the highly suspicious look on Davey's face. 'Can't a bloke talk to another one anymore? I was just being friendly. Don't chuck a mental on me.'

'I won't,' said Davey, 'it's just that my Dad says I've got

to be careful what with all those boys going missing.'

'Your Dad's right, Davey' said Paddy, 'you've got to watch yourself with those perverts around.'

'My Dad says they should be bloody strung up,' said Davey who tried to inject his voice with as much grown up venom as he could.

'Your Dad's right,' said Paddy who couldn't help smirking at the irony of what this young idiot was saying. God, he wished he'd finish those bloody vegemite sandwiches. The sight of him tucking in and making his tongue and teeth temporarily dark was making him want to bloody puke. 'I couldn't argue with him.'

'My Dad's a policeman,' Davey announced, 'I reckon I'll join him in the force when I leave school.'

'You've got it all planned out then?'

'Yeah, mate,' said Davey, 'and my Dad reckons that the state of Victoria force is the best in the whole bloody country too.'

'Does he now?'

'Yeah,' said Davey, 'He's going to help me when the time comes. Says it'll make him proud to see me put on the same uniform as him and help to keep the mongrels off the bloody streets.'

'That's good, mate,' said Paddy.

'He also says it's a great way to get the chicks.'

'Is that right? Well that's good too then, mate.'

Paddy wondered what his own father would've wanted for him. It certainly wouldn't have been to see him as a procurer for a child killer. But what would his father have wanted? He must've had a father. Everybody has to have had one. But he couldn't remember anything about him. What could've happened to him? Did his mother dump him somewhere too?

'Anyway,' said Davey who'd finished his sandwiches

and picked up his school bag, 'I'd better get going. Bell will be going in five minutes for this arvo's lessons. I've got geography. I bloody hate geography. Who wants to know where anywhere else is when you live in Australia is what my Dad says. Anyway, see ya later.'

'Wait, I'll walk on with you, I'm going that way,' said Paddy who looked up and saw that the car was in place. After the row of shops they'd just been standing near there was nothing on their side of the road except for a park for the next half a mile. On the other side was just some plain unused land. There weren't many houses in the immediate vicinity. Nothing that gave Paddy too much of a concern.

'What do you do?'

'Oh I work for a butcher,' said Paddy.

'Really?'

'Yeah, I take the meat for slaughter.'

'Where do you do that?'

'On the other side of the city' said Paddy, 'I'm only over this side visiting my folks.'

It was then that Glenn pulled up alongside them in his car and wound the window down. 'Excuse me? Can you blokes tell me where Crosby Street is, please?'

'Crosby Street?' Paddy questioned. 'I don't think I know. What about you, Davey? Do you know where Crosby Street is, mate?'

'Yeah, I know where it is,' said Davey.

'Do you want to tell the gentleman?'

★

'So you made your victims disappear in broad daylight?' Angela probed.

'We became quite good at it.' said Paddy, 'We'd pick the right spot and when the kids were offering the direction we'd asked for, Eileen would reach through from the back and hit them with a cloth over their mouth and nose that was doused in chloroform.'

'And then what happened?'

'We'd take them back to Glenn's place,' said Paddy 'He had this small place out in the country near the Essendon airfield. His Aunt had left it him. I don't think she intended him to use it to torture kids.'

'Torture?'

'He'd start off by strapping them to an iron bed frame' said Paddy. 'Do you really want me to explain the rest?'

'No' said Angela. 'I'll read your manuscript when I'm feeling brave. But how did it affect you, Paddy? Did you take part?'

'No!' Paddy emphasised. 'I adamantly denied that at the trial and it was true, Doc. Yes, I procured the kids and I made it happen for that bastard, Glenn. But do I wish it hadn't happened? Of course I bloody do. Am I ashamed of myself? That doesn't even come close. But I was trying to survive, Doc. I was doing what I always had to do and I was trying to survive.'

'Seven children were tortured and killed, Paddy.'

'Yes, I bloody know, Doc, I was there!'

It was rare for Angela to see Paddy rattled but she was seeing it now. Usually he was so controlled and spoke of the facts without much emotion. But now she could see it in his eyes. He regretted everything about what had happened to those children. But was that enough? The parents of the victims would say they all should've been hanged for their crimes.

'And did they take all that into account at the trial, Paddy?'

Paddy looked up scowling. 'The trial? That was a bloody joke. Australia hadn't hanged anybody since 1967.

They hadn't hanged a woman since 1951 and she'd had to be sedated so they could carry out the sentence. There was this move towards abolishing the death penalty altogether, once and for all, but we gave them reason to think again. The whole nation wanted our blood.'

'Can you blame them?'

'There's no soft soap with you, is there, Doc? Well no, I couldn't, truth be told. If I'd been in their position I'd have wanted the same.'

'How had you been caught?'

'A young lad called Dean Watkins got away when we were trying to carry him from the car into Glenn's place. Eileen hadn't used enough chloroform. I don't know how it happened exactly but he broke free and ran.'

'He probably still feels very lucky.'

'Yeah, he probably does,' said Paddy, thoughtfully, 'but that's how it all unravelled. Anyway, the trial went on and we were all spared the death penalty. Public opinion couldn't overturn the prevailing political winds. Eileen and Glenn got sent down for thirty years. They both ended up dying in prison. That was poetic justice some would say. I got five years.'

'They were quite lenient with you,' said Angela, 'compared to what they handed down to Eileen and Glenn. Did they say why that was?'

'I know why that was, Doc.'

'So tell me.'

'Andy Cook turned up' said Paddy.

'Andy Cook? But I thought he'd perished at the same time as Father Michael?'

'So did I,' said Paddy, 'but he hadn't. He'd been rescued. He took pity on me because he knew what I'd been through at the children's home and he forgave me for what I'd done to him. He made the court understand what had gone into making me the shit that I was. That was how I got off with such a light sentence.'

'And did they go right back to your childhood?'

'All the way.'

'Did they find your mother?'

'Yes,' said Paddy, 'and it was the one chance she'd had since she'd dumped me to try and be a mother to me. But she refused. She refused to fly out to Australia and confirm even that I was her son.'

'Oh Paddy,' said Angela as she watched the tears begin to fall down Paddy's cheeks. 'You must've been crushed?'

'I was, Doc,' said Paddy as he wiped his face, 'I was, but at least by not coming she did me a favour.'

'How do you make that out?'

'Well it meant that the court had more sympathy with me' said Paddy. 'So as they say, it's an ill wind that blows nobody any good.'

'So you know your mother's name?'

'No, Doc.' said Paddy, 'They only told me that they'd been in touch with her and what they called "the results of that communication".'

'Well Paddy, I'm not sure if this is the appropriate time to tell you but I've got some bad news about someone I know you cared about a great deal.'

'Who?'

'Rita Makin, Paddy' said Angela. 'I'm sorry, Paddy, but she's dead.'

'Dead? What, recently?'

'Yes' said Angela.

'Doc, something tells me I'm not going to like this?'

'She was murdered, Paddy' said Angela. ' And it wasn't a random act. It seems that somebody had set out to kill her.'

CHAPTER FIFTEEN

'Are you happy, dear brother?' asked Susie.

Matt paused with a piece of chicken with bamboo shoots caught in mid-air in his chopsticks. 'Yes'.

'Well do you think that message could get through to your face?'

'Shut up you cheeky cow.'

Matt was sitting with his sister Susie and her fiancé Angus in the Rice Bowl Chinese restaurant in Manchester's Cross Street. It was Saturday and the three of them were having lunch together.

'Matt, you've had a face as long as a wet weekend in Blackpool since we met up. Is there something wrong?'

'Sorry' said Matt.

'Hey, it's okay, mate,' said Angus. 'We just want to help if we can.'

Matt laid down his chopsticks one either side of the bowl he was eating from. He told them all about Wendy and her breast cancer diagnosis. It brought him close to tears.

'That's so unfair' said Susie, holding her brother's hand, 'I know how much she means to you.'

'It isn't fair,' said Matt. 'I mean, what has Wendy done to offend the Gods? She met a man and fell in love, she married him and together they had two beautiful children. And her reward? He can't stay faithful and she gets cancer which means she won't see either of her two boys grow up. You're right, it isn't fair.'

'Can't they do anything?' asked Angus.

'They've done all they can,' said Matt, 'It's all over and I feel so helpless. I helped her through the divorce. I helped them both through the divorce. But I can't lessen the tragedy of her illness. I can't lessen the implications of that.'

'It's only natural to feel like this when it's someone close, mate.' said Angus, 'My best mate at school died of leukaemia when I was twelve. I felt helpless then too. I didn't get over it for weeks.'

'You didn't tell me that,' said Susie.

'Well it's not something you just drop into conversation when you're falling in love, baby,' said Angus.

Susie turned back to Matt. 'He's been flying with his American friend Mason again. That's why he keeps calling me baby. It'll wear off in a day or so.'

Matt smiled. 'Well I think it's quite sweet,' he said.

'Well you would' said Susie. 'Anyway, what's going to happen to the boys?'

'That's what's breaking Wendy's heart,' said Matt, 'their intended stepmother shows no sign of wanting to show them any maternal instincts.'

'He'll dump them on you' said Susie.

'Susie!'

'Well he will! He'll go along with whatever that money grabbing tramp wants and the boys will spend their time effectively being brought up by their Uncle Matt.'

'I'd gladly do it,' said Matt, tearfully, 'for Wendy's sake.'

'Oh Matt you are so weak where that man is concerned.'

'I said I'd do it for Wendy,' said Matt, firmly, 'you're out of order, Susie. One of my closest and dearest friends is dying and I'm going to do whatever I can to lessen her worries.'

'I think you should listen to your brother, Susie,' said Angus.

Susie swung her face around on Angus but didn't say anything. That's one of the things Matt liked about Angus. He was the first of his sister's boyfriends who could shut her up when she was giving it out. She seemed to be respecting him for it too. This was good, thought Matt. She wasn't going to always wear the trousers with this one.

'Okay,' said Susie, who then squeezed Matt's hand. 'Sorry.'

'Do you mind repeating that because I so seldom hear it.'

Angus started laughing and Susie couldn't help but join in.

'I'm not coming out with you two again if you're going to gang up on me.'

'Well, let's eat,' said Matt at last, 'I'm sure Angus doesn't want to hear all this shit anyway.'

Angus raised his hands. 'Hey, I want you to be happy just as much as your sister, mate' he said, 'I'm just not as blunt.'

They spent the next few minutes enjoying into their food. Angus had gone for the Peking duck and was busy pulling flesh off the bones and wrapping it n pancakes. Susie had gone for sizzling prawns with fried crispy noodles and Matt himself was carrying on with his chicken with bamboo shoots and fried rice. .

'And let's order some more wine,' said Matt, 'when are you flying next, Angus?'

'Not until Monday afternoon' said Angus.

'So you're alright for one or two.'

'Oh yeah.'

'So,' said Matt who now wanted to change the subject.

'Did you see Desperate Housewives the other night? I love that show. It has just the right mix of light and shade and I love the characters.'

'No, we didn't,' said Susie, holding Angus's hand, 'we don't get to watch much telly.'

'Well that's the difference between your life and mine, Susie,' said Matt, 'you've got Angus and I've got the TV.'

'Well that reminds me of something, actually, Matt, darling,' said Susie, 'Angus works with a lot of gay men and…'

'…oh no, I'm not being set up,' said Matt.

'But if I flew with someone who I thought you might be interested in?' said Angus. 'I'd be more than happy to get you guys together.'

'You'd do that for me?'

'Of course I would,' said Angus, 'we're going to be family and that's what you do.'

'Go on, Matt,' said Susie, rubbing his arm. 'I know you hate living alone. Say you'll give it a try just for me?'

Matt thought about it and edged towards acceptance. He didn't have anything against a blind date as such and as long as Angus kept to what he knew Matt liked in a man then, why not?

'Nobody effeminate' Matt warned. 'I want a man, not a Queen.'

'Absolutely not,' said Angus, 'any degree of camp and I won't even entertain him.'

'So you'll do it, Matt?' asked Susie, excitedly, 'I mean, you'll go along with it?'

'Yes' said Matt who could do with some fun to pepper all the darkness. 'But I'm not promising anything.'

Just at that moment when his mood was lifted Matt looked up and saw what he really didn't need to see. The Rice Bowl was in a basement with steps down from the street. He, Susie and Angus were sitting at a table where Matt had a view of the bottom of the stairs where people stopped to wait to be shown to a table. There was a fish tank to the left which was of great interest to any children and a bar behind it which was of more interest to their parents.

And there, waiting to be greeted by one of the Rice Bowl's staff, was Adrian, standing with a woman and three children who Matt took to be his wife and family. The doctor in Matt noticed that Adrian's wife looked somewhat pale and a little pre-occupied and then Matt locked eyes with Adrian who looked away pretty quickly. The situation was excruciating for Matt. He carried on a normal conversation with Susie and Angus, talking about their upcoming wedding, listening to Susie complaining about her and Matt's Mum because of how much of a pain she was being about the church service, and all the time Adrian was sitting just a few metres away. He looked happy. The family man talking to and laughing with his kids, exchanging knowing looks with his wife that spoke of a deep tenderness between them. It was all making Matt feel as guilty as Hell for having infringed on it all.

'Excuse me,' said Matt as he pushed his chair back and stood up. 'I need the toilet.'

There was a doorway opposite the bar that led to the toilets. Matt stepped through another door into the gents and unzipped his fly before pissing into the stainless steel urinal. Then he zipped himself back up again and turned to the wash basins. He'd just finished drying his hands when the door opened and Adrian came in. He was in a pair of jeans and a white t-shirt. His furry arms looked so strong like they always did. He hadn't shaved. Matt tried his best but he couldn't stop the rise of desire inside him.

'I don't suppose you'd just pay the bill and leave,

would you?' Adrian asked.

Matt was furious at the audacity of Adrian's request. 'Why should I?'

'Because I find it difficult you sitting there when I'm here with my family' said Adrian. 'I don't want my wife to be humiliated.'

'Adrian, the only people who know the truth are you and me. Now I can handle it and you're just going to have to do the same.'

'Are you still mad at me about the other night?'

'No, Adrian. Believe it or not I'm a grown up and I get over things.'

'That's me told.'

They looked at each other the way people do when there's conflict that then turns to smiles when they realise how absurd they're being.

'Let's not stop having fun, Matt' said Adrian.

'Well I don't want to stop.'

'I'll try and be a bit more sensitive,' said Adrian 'I'll do my best.'

'That's all I can ask' said Matt.

'I'll call you Monday and see when you're going to be free next week?'

'Sure' said Matt. 'I really wish I didn't fancy the fucking bollocks off you.'

'Well, who can blame you? You're only human.'

Matt smiled. 'You're a cheeky bastard.'

'Who is it you're with out there?'

'My sister and her fiancé.'

'They seem like nice people.'

'They are,' said Matt, 'they're one of those couples who really are meant for each other.'

'I'm sorry I came on a bit strong when I first came in' said Adrian.

'Well let's forget about all that now. Now go on, get back to your family and enjoy the rest of your meal.'

'Yes, Doctor' said Adrian who then sneaked a kiss with Matt before walking out. Matt followed him a few seconds later thinking how lucky they were that nobody had come in and disturbed them. He liked Adrian. He liked him very much. But where it mattered, deep inside his heart, Matt also knew that what he felt for Adrian was still nothing like how he felt about Charlie.

'Look, why don't we pay up and go on somewhere else where we can get magnificently pissed?' he said to Susie and Angus. 'I'm really in the mood for it.'

'Sounds good' said Angus. 'Susie?'

'Oh yes, I'm up for it,' said Susie. 'But it's my turn to go to the toilet now so you'll have to hang on.'

'We'll settle the bill whilst you're gone' said Angus.

Susie got up and stepped through the door to the corridor where the ladies was located a few metres before the gents. Matt and Angus chatted whilst Matt tried not to look across at Adrian.

'Matt!' Susie shouted from the door to the corridor.

Matt looked up. 'What's wrong?'

'There's a woman in here who's collapsed!'

Matt ran through to the ladies where the woman in question was Adrian's wife, Penny. The manager of the restaurant plus half the waiting staff came rushing in after him but Adrian pushed through to the front. Matt told everyone except Susie, Adrian, and the restaurant manager to go back. Penny Bradshaw was lying unconscious in front of the wash basins and Matt began his examination after telling Susie to call for an ambulance. He looked upon her as just another casualty. The personal connotations suddenly meant nothing. He was a doctor and he just wanted to treat her and make sure she was alright. Adrian got down on his knees and held his wife's hand.

It only took a few minutes for Matt to do his work and make Penny as comfortable as he could whilst they waited for the ambulance. Matt then stood up and walked over to the basins to wash his hands. Adrian jumped up next to him.

'Well?' asked Adrian. 'What do you think is wrong with her?'

'She had a miscarriage, Adrian' said Matt, 'And she passed out.'

'A miscarriage?'

'Yes' said Matt, 'I'm sorry. Has she had one before?'

'No' said Adrian, 'No, she hasn't.'

'Well then it must be a bit of a shock,' said Matt, 'I'm really sorry, Adrian.'

'A shock?' said Adrian who looked down at his wife who was dozing in and out of an uncomfortable sleep. ' Matt, I didn't even know she was pregnant.'

★

Matt was typing some notes about a patient into the computer on his desk when Joan, the receptionist rang through to say that a Miss Natasha Bowles wanted to see him. He didn't know what the hell she wanted but he did have a ten minute gap before his next patient so he told Joan to send Miss Bowles down to his consulting room.

'Hello, Matt,' said Natasha as she came in. She was dressed in a long fifties style light green skirt with a white blouse tucked in and a dark pink cardigan over her shoulders. Her stiletto shoes were also pink and had rather high heels. He'd heard her coming down the corridor for several seconds before she'd knocked on his door. Her hair was broadly blond and it flowed over her shoulders. Her make-up was, as always, impeccable and her nails were painted in the deepest red. She looked every inch the air stewardess. She couldn't be anything else in all that discount price looking affected chic.

'Natasha,' said Matt, 'I can't imagine why you've come to see me.'

'Oh Matt, darling, that's not much of a welcome, and I chose some of my pink things to put on especially for you.'

'Sorry, is that supposed to mean something?'

'I see,' she said testily, 'may I sit down?'

'No, because you won't be stopping' said Matt. ' I've got a patient in five minutes.'

'Charles won't like it if he hears you've been less than friendly towards me.'

Matt threw his head back and laughed. 'You sound like a child.'

'You've never liked me.'

'Yes, you're right, I never have. Now, why are you here?'

'I want you to get out of Charles' life.'

'I beg your pardon?'

'I don't want him being close to a gay man.'

'Well, Charlie and I…'

'…his name is Charles!'

'I've known him as Charlie for twenty years and that's how I'll always know him!'

Natasha pursed her lips and stuck her chin out. 'You will get out of Charles's life.'

Matt was in no mood for this bullshit from Little Miss Gold digger. His friendship with Charlie had been somewhat strained of late but that was largely due to Natasha's influence on his friend's thinking. He stood up and watched her breathe in. She knew she was no match for him but she was so stupid that she'd thought she could just walk in here and get him to agree to break up his oldest and most meaningful friendship.

'You must be very insecure of your man,' said Matt, smirking.

'What do you mean?'

'Well if you don't want him to be best friends with a gay man then that speaks volumes about your perceptions of your own womanhood,' said Matt. He watched the reaction in her eyes. She had no idea what he was talking about. 'Do you think I spend my life thinking of ways to bring him onto my side of the road?'

'Don't be disgusting.'

'Ooh sorry, did I strike a nerve? Are you going to lock him up every day so that pretty boys and pretty girls won't flirt with him?'

'I give Charles everything he needs,' said Natasha, defiantly, 'he will always remain faithful to me unlike his first wife. Ooh sorry, she's a friend of yours isn't she.'

'You're not worth the ground she could spit on.'

Natasha giggled. 'Ooh sorry, did I strike a nerve?'

'What do you want, Natasha?'

'For you to stay out of his life,' said Natasha, 'you won't object to him selling his share of this practice, you won't object to him re-negotiating his divorce settlement, and you won't object to whatever I decide we do with his brats.'

'What do you mean by that? They're my godchildren!'

'Yes, well they'll be going away to boarding school once I'm in charge.'

'But Wendy wouldn't want that,' said Matt.

'Really? Well that's a shame isn't it because poor, pitiful Wendy won't be able to have a say. And that's because she'll be dead!'

Matt slapped her face hard, so hard that she had to step back. She rubbed her face as she brought her head back up. Matt could well see a look of triumph in her eyes and he could kick himself for having lost control.

'Thank you,' said Natasha, 'you've just given me every reason to get Charles just where I want him.'

★

Canon Brendan O'Farrell walked into the presbytery study just as Father Philip Evans was finishing a phone call.

'Who were you talking to there, Phillip? Did I hear you say the name of Angela? It wasn't Angela Barker the psychotherapist now, was it?'

'Now why would you think that, Brendan?'

'Because I overheard another of your phone conversations yesterday when it was quite clearly Angela Barker you were speaking to because you also mentioned the name of Sean Patrick O'Brien. Now do you mind telling me what's going on?'

'Alright, Brendan,' said Phillip, stretching out his legs and sitting back in his chair. 'I decided that she deserves our help with Mr. O'Brien.'

'On what basis?'

'On a purely Christian basis, Brendan. Now I know you said all records were destroyed in a fire but there must be something that can be done for her? I want to try and see what that is.'

'After I'd already dealt with the matter you decided to wade in yourself?'

'Yes, Brendan,' said Phillip, 'because I believe we owe a responsibility to those children who we sent across the world on a pack of lies. You said as much yourself,

Brendan.'

'You're meddling in things you don't understand, Phillip,' warned Brendan.

'Well then enlighten me, Brendan,' said Phillip who'd never seen Brendan look as grave as he did right now. 'What's wrong with us helping Angela to help Sean Patrick?'

'I've already given you an answer to that, Phillip.'

'Except that no, you haven't, Brendan' said Phillip. 'No disrespect but I've listened to you preaching the language of liberation and proper hope and I've been greatly inspired by it. I'd go so far as to say that your example and the views you put across in our conversations will help to make me not only a better priest but also a better man. You recognise the reality of modern life for so many of our flock and I think that's laudable in a man as senior as you in the church. But then along comes a woman working with someone who clearly could've been damaged by what the church did to him all those years ago and you won't help her? Why, Brendan? I just don't get it.'

'I'll only give God an answer to that one, Phillip,' said Brendan.

'Brendan, Sean Patrick O'Brien will be released in a few weeks time,' said Phillip. He couldn't understand Brendan's attitude towards all this. Did he have something to hide? He'd barely be able to believe it of someone like Brendan if he did because it must be something pretty awful for him to act the way he is. Brendan was one of the good guys. Or so Phillip had thought.

'And your point is, Phillip?'

'Well what are you going to do if he comes knocking on the door himself looking for answers? What are you going to say to him then?'

Matt was sitting in the staff room at the surgery eating a chicken and avocado sandwich for lunch. He'd made it himself and brought it from home because shop bought sandwiches were a nightmare for him. He detested mayonnaise, ketchup, pickle, mustard and all the other unnecessary crap they put on pre-packed sandwiches. And why did they always mix tuna with bloody mayo? Why couldn't they mix it with a little olive oil and some black pepper? That's what he did with it when he wanted to make a tuna sandwich. He was with the French when it came to cuisine. It should be kept simple and uncomplicated so as not to confuse the pallet with too many unnecessary additional flavours.

He'd just got to the leader section of the Independent when Charlie came in and slammed the door shut behind him. Matt decided to ignore the display of tantrum and stood up and walked over to the kettle.

'I was just about to make myself some tea,' said Matt without looking at his friend. 'Do you want one?'

'No' answered Charlie, flatly.

'What's wrong with you?'

'Like you don't know?'

'If you expect me to apologise for slapping Natasha then you'll have to wait for a cold day in Hell, Charlie.'

Charlie marched up to Matt and grabbed his arm. He pulled him around so they were facing each other. Matt was startled by the move but then they both paused. They stood there, up close and almost personal, staring each other down.

'You've got to give it up, Matt' said Charlie.

'Give what up?' asked Matt who felt strangely calm despite Charlie's obvious fury. His small light green eyes were narrowed and his short light brown hair framed an anxious face. Were those beads of sweat that Matt could see on his forehead?'

'This way you have of interfering in my bloody life! For the last twenty years every time I've turned you've always been there with your looks and your comments and lately your downright hostility.'

'Well that's rich coming from you at this moment.'

'And your remarks that you think are so fucking clever. Well they're not clever and neither are you. You're just sad. And you can't bare it because I'm happy.'

'Is that what you call it?'

'And what would you know? Thirty-eight years old and you've never got past half a dozen dates with a man before he's got fed up with you.'

'That wasn't called for, Charlie.'

'No, but it hit home. I can see that. Oh but let's not leave out all the married men who've used your body to satisfy their curiosity. They're the only ones who stick around because they're getting everything and you're getting fuck all.'

Mark swallowed hard. ' Have you finished?'

'You're so trapped in your fucked up little excuse for a life that you can't bare it that I've been able to find happiness twice in my life.'

'Do you know what Natasha is planning to do with the boys?'

'She's planning to love them like they were her own.'

Matt smirked as he sensed getting the upper hand. 'Is that what she told you?'

'That's what she told me and I believe her so take that fucking look off your face.'

'I'm not the sad one here, my friend,' said Matt, 'she's planning on sending them to boarding school. She's got it all mapped out. She'll make up some cock and bull story about how distressed she gets watching them grieve for their mother and then she'll come up with what she sees as the perfect solution. Then she'll sell it to you and you'll buy it because you won't want to let her down again after putting all the other changes she wants to make to your life on hold. She'll use Wendy's death to get the boys as far away from you as possible so she can have you all to herself.'

'You're lying.'

'You mean she hasn't told you about her little plan? Well, well, well. Seems like that happiness you're so boastful about doesn't always come with the truth attached.'

Charlie lifted his hand and placed it on Matt's face. Matt was aware of his heart beginning to pound away. The pace of his breathing increased and he felt himself flush. Suddenly Charlie was only a thin line away and this was the moment he'd waited twenty years for.

And then they were kissing. Not just affectionate pecks but deep throat tongue exploration type of kissing. Matt's hands went inside Charlie's jacket and around his back. He could feel Charlie's kisses behind his ears and on his neck and groaned out loud with pleasure. Then all of a sudden, just as the fire was burning nicely, Charlie stopped. He clutched the lapels of Matt's open necked shirt and was catching his breath.

'What's wrong?' asked Matt.

'I can't' Charlie spluttered.

'You can't do this to me, Charlie,' said Matt. 'I've been waiting a lifetime for this to happen.'

Charlie was almost in tears and couldn't lift his head to look at Matt. 'I'm sorry' he said. 'But I can't.'

'Charlie, please don't go' Matt pleaded.

Charlie then stepped back further before turning and

leaving the room, leaving a confused and devastated Matt standing there.

CHAPTER SIXTEEN

Sara Hoyland and Joe Alexander interviewed Nick Jackson at the station and he confirmed that he'd been Michelle Clarke's lover for over a year and that, on her behalf, he'd approached two men who he'd known in the building trade as being the ones to approach if he needed their particular talents.

'How easy did you find it to break the law, Mr. Jackson?' asked Joe. He hadn't known what to think about Nick Jackson when he'd first come in and he still didn't as Jackson sat there not giving much away other than the words that came out of his mouth. He was certainly dressed in the nouveau riche attire of the working class lad made good. The collar of his light blue polo shirt was turned up, his blue jeans looked suitably expensive and both garments were neatly pressed. Finishing off the ensemble were a pair of trainers that, predictably, looked like they'd come from the top end of the market. Joe couldn't help but put himself in Jackson's position, although their situations weren't exactly the same. Carol's husband deserved to have some violent act perpetrated against him but although Joe would like to initiate that, he knew he couldn't in case a paper trail led back to him and his job. Carol had been really showing the strain lately but all Joe could do was love her as best he could and, though it really wasn't easy, not apply any pressure on her. But that was difficult when he loved her so much.

'I did it for Michelle,' said Jackson, 'that idiot she's married to doesn't appreciate her.'

'So you arranged to have him beaten up,' said Sara, incredulously. 'Tell me, are Relate recommending that as a therapy these days?'

Jackson looked up and snarled. 'I don't suppose you'll solve any cases with that kind of sarcasm, Detective.'

Sara banged her hand on the table. 'Just remember why you're in here, Mr. Jackson, and let's have less of the backchat if you don't mind. Now you arranged for two men to have an innocent man beaten up. You're in a lot of serious trouble, Mr. Jackson, but you can mitigate the consequences of your actions if you co-operate.'

Jackson looked serious but Joe thought he could see traces of some kind of capitulation in his eyes. Jackson rubbed his chin. 'What would that involve?'

'Well you could start by giving us the names and addresses of the two men you hired,' said Sara who didn't have one iota of sympathy for the arrogant little prick. He and Michelle Clarke were made for each other.

Jackson paused and then gave the names and addresses of Declan and Mick McDermott.

'But you'll be wasting your time going there to find them,' said Jackson.

'Why is that?' asked Sara. 'Have you given us the wrong address?'

'No,' said Jackson, 'because after what they saw they legged it to Ireland. Apparently, seeing a woman having her throat cut isn't a pleasant experience.'

★

Matt walked down the stairs in his house and could still feel Adrian inside him. Adrian was a big boy and he could always feel him for several hours after he'd been around. After Charlie had played out his little drama the other day, Matt didn't know if he really wanted to carry on seeing

Adrian. If he thought there was even the slightest chance with Charlie then nobody else would matter. But he had no idea how it would play out and in the meantime he wasn't going to cut off his nose to spite his face by turning Adrian down. He liked the policeman. He liked having him in his bed and for a moment or two it had made him feel better.

'Have you got everything?' Matt asked. Adrian was already standing in the hallway ready to go.

'I'm really sorry I can't stay,' said Adrian who pulled Matt to him and put his hands together in the small of Matt's back. 'But I really can't.'

'KFC bargain night again?' asked Matt cheekily who was stark naked in contrast to Adrian who was back in his suit, shirt and tie.

Adrian smiled. 'No, my Mum is coming around to have dinner with us and also, Penny is still a bit fragile after the miscarriage. I'm a naughty boy for taking this time out really.'

'Did you really not know she was pregnant?' Matt asked, his hands gently rubbing Adrian's shoulders through the cover of his shirt and jacket. He wished Adrian hadn't got up and put his clothes back on as soon as he'd brought Matt off. Giving Adrian a pearl necklace through the thick hairs on his chest was sexually satisfying but Matt wouldn't have minded a bit of intimacy afterwards. He wanted to tell somebody about what had happened with Charlie the other day and how Charlie had been with him since but then he wondered if Adrian would be the right person to tell all of that too. It might come a bit too close to home.

'No, I didn't,' said Adrian. 'We'd talked about it and I'd said I didn't want another one but let me tell you, Matt, women rule the world with their wombs. Half the time they never discuss with their man if they want to have a child. They just decide they want one and go ahead and get themselves pregnant. I'll be honest, it makes a lot of men feel completely powerless.'

'And how are things between the two of you?'

'We're okay,' said Adrian, 'we need to talk about it but it's not the right time yet. I've learned enough from my male lover to know when it's time to be sensitive.'

'I'll make a new man out of you yet' said Matt who thought it was cruelly ironic that he'd influenced Adrian to be sensitive with everyone but Matt himself.

'You will but look, thanks for everything in the restaurant. Penny keeps saying how lovely you were to her.'

'That was Matt the doctor' said Matt. 'I was just doing my job, sir.'

Adrian kissed Matt's forehead. 'Well I'm grateful' he said. He then kissed Matt again.

'If you keep doing that I'll be dragging you back upstairs.'

'Then I'd better go.'

'You'll be back soon?'

'You can bet your life on it.'

At that moment they were both shaken by the brick that came flying through one of the glass panels in Matt's front door and landed heavily on the floor just a metre or so from where they were standing.

'What the fuck!' Adrian exclaimed.

They were still holding onto each other when Natasha appeared in the gap left by the broken glass. 'I hope you're satisfied, Schofield! Because of you I've been dumped by Charles and now you're going to pay… she stopped dead in her tracks when she saw Matt with her brother-in-law

Adrian. Then she started to laugh '…oh thank you, God. What a fucking result!'

Adrian went chasing after her. She had a pink velour tracksuit on and her mascara was running down the cheeks of her face. Her hair was tied back. She had a sledgehammer in her hand and was poised ready to do damage to Matt's car.

'Don't come any closer' she warned.

'Natasha, it's not what you think' said Adrian.

'Oh beauty! That stupid cliché has just cost your lover his headlights.'

Natasha then smashed both of Matt's headlights.

'Natasha, please…' Adrian pleaded. His whole world could come crashing down on him if he wasn't careful. He may have to let her take her vengeance out on Matt if he could agree to her not saying anything to Penny about why he was there.

'…how long has it been going on?'

'About six months.'

'And does my sister know?'

'No, Natasha, she doesn't.'

That earned Matt a massive dent in the bonnet of his car after Natasha had brought her sledgehammer down on it.

'Well she will be pleased when I tell her.'

'No, Natasha, please don't do that' Adrian pleaded, '[please don't do that to her.'

'Me do that to her? You're the one who's been sleeping with another man behind her back. You fucking disgust me!'

'I know and I understand, Natasha' said Adrian who was scared shitless about what this bitch of his sister-in-law would do. How could he explain to Penny about Matt? She'd never be able to understand it. Christ, this was a fucking nightmare!

'Liar!' screamed Natasha who then smashed the windscreen on Matt's car. She was determined to destroy as much of it as she could. 'You're a liar! And so is that bastard inside who's destroyed my life!'

A crowd of Matt's neighbours were gathering around to watch the show. Adrian noticed but he had to ignore their stares. He had to stay focused on Natasha and what she might do next. He stepped closer to her and held out his hand.

'Natasha, please give the sledgehammer to me.'

'Why? I haven't stopped having fun yet?'

'You really don't want to do this, Natasha.'

'Oh yes I flaming well do! So what's it all about, this Brokeback Mountain thing you've got going on? I must admit, I'd never have expected it of you. Oh no, I thought you were just another boring straight man who didn't have any guts.'

'He seduced me, Natasha, I'd never done anything like this before … '

'…and with what did he seduce you? I mean, does he give better head than Penny does? Is that it?'

'Natasha, there's no need for talk like that.'

'Well what is it then because I can't work it out!'

Matt had got himself dressed and came as quietly as he could out of his back door. He'd heard everything that had been said. Natasha was so engrossed in her argument with Adrian that she didn't even notice Matt creeping up behind her. She was about to send her sledgehammer crashing through another of his car windows when he lunged forward and grabbed her. She screamed. She struggled but Matt was intent on stopping her doing anymore damage and he managed to wrestle her down to the ground.

'Put the sledgehammer down!' he commanded.

'Fuck you!'

'I said put it down!'

'Get off me!'

'I will once you've put the sledgehammer down.'

She thrashed around all over the place trying to break free but Matt's grip was too firm. Eventually she dropped the sledgehammer. It fell onto the driveway next to his car and he looked up appealingly at Adrian for him to pick it up and take it away.

'Well don't just stand there!' cried Matt as he continued to struggle with a determined Natasha. Adrian looked like he was in the presence of some dangerous animal that he didn't know how to handle. 'Pick the bloody thing up, Adrian!'

Adrian picked up the sledgehammer and moved it to a safe distance several metres away. He didn't know whether to just go or stay in case he might be needed. He decided to stay.

'Get off me you home wrecking bastard!' screamed Natasha.

Matt almost laughed at that. Was it the best she could do? Maybe under the circumstances he shouldn't expect more in the way of wit from the brain dead trolley dolly.

'Now you listen to me,' he said, firmly as he tightened his grip around her. He looked over to Adrian who was still doing nothing except to just stand there. 'You don't walk into my life and start calling the shots. Make sure you remember that. Charlie dumped you because you're a selfish, manipulative little bitch who tried to use the fatal illness of his first wife and the mother of his children to get your own way. You're scum, Natasha. You're nothing but gold digging scum and now Charlie has finally woken up to that. Now you get off my property and expect a very large repair bill tomorrow.'

Matt loosened his grip around Natasha. She looked around at him but realised her little performance was all over as she stood up and sloped off back to her car. She got in and drove off. Matt got himself back onto his feet and walked back towards his front door, stopping when he got to Adrian.

'Matt, I don't know what to say.'

'Call yourself a police officer? She could've knocked down my fucking house and you'd have stood there.'

'I didn't know what to do!' pleaded Adrian, rather feebly. 'She's my sister-in-law for God's sake.'

'Oh just go home now, Adrian! And don't come around here again.'

★

Angus Carleton drove out of the staff car park that was to the east of Terminal 2 at Manchester airport. It had been a difficult flight back from the Greek island of Corfu. The weather had been absolutely shit from Switzerland onwards and hadn't let up until they were halfway across England and about to make their approach into Manchester. The passengers had all complained because he and the Captain had told the cabin crew to suspend the service for half an hour whilst they went through a rather nasty and unpredictable area of turbulence. It seemed like the mass of the travelling public didn't mind crew risking life and limb as long as they got their tax free goods.

His car was a dark blue Renault Megane that his parents had helped him buy when he first qualified as a pilot. His mother and her long-time boyfriend Malcolm were coming up from Surrey this weekend to spend it with him and Susie and the four of them were going out to a rather posh restaurant in Prestbury with Susie's parents. They were also going to go to Susie's brother Matt's place for Sunday brunch. Angus' Mum and Malcolm liked Matt. But then everybody liked Matt. It was such a shame, thought Angus, that Matt couldn't find anybody to love him as well as like him. He was still working on trying to find him a beau but all the stewards he worked with, although great fun, were all a bit too fabulous and Angus knew that would put Matt off. Either that or they were pretentious, snooty little bastards who pursed their lips at anybody they deemed to be beneath them, which often turned out to be the entire world except themselves. That would certainly put Matt off. His future brother-in-law was definitely a substance over style man. He didn't care what you did or where you came from. It was about who you were now that mattered to him.

Angus had taken his tie off and undone the top two buttons of his shirt. He'd also removed the epaulettes and his name badge from his shirt. He wanted to pop into Tesco on the way home and he thought that one of the naffest things ever was when he saw someone in uniform doing their bloody shopping. Okay, so you work at the airport. That's great! It just doesn't need to be rubbed into people's noses as they reach for a stone baked pizza. You're not a celebrity. You just do a job.

He drove his car along the side roads that took him through the more salubrious parts of South Manchester where footballers and people like his fiancée Susie lived, and now where he lived too. Some of the Captains at work were amazed when he told them where he lived. They thought it was an area for them with their established careers and not for co-pilots like Angus who were barely on the first rung of the ladder to greatness. So then they assumed that his family must have money and he soon put them straight on that. His parents aren't poor but he wouldn't call them rich either. They'd just taken care of what they had and been careful. So eventually Angus told them that he was marrying someone who owned a highly successful company and he'd moved into their house. So by that they assumed it was a man and that Angus was gay. It made him laugh. What century did these bastards live in? Someone was highly successful in business so they must be a man. And when he suggested that when he and Susie started a family that he might put his career on hold and stay at home to raise the kids whilst Susie carried on with the business, they virtually lynched him. Flying aeroplanes wasn't just a living to some of these guys. It was also a means to get away from their God awful wives. Angus had met some of them and they could be even more socially ignorant than their bloody husbands! And God, some of them had let themselves go. It all went to prove what some of the gay boys at work often said. 'There's nothing as plain as a Captain's wife and nothing as desperate as a Captain's mistress.' Well he and Susie were going to create their own little world where they were as far removed from all that shit as possible, even if they were living in the same private lane with the right kind of Cheshire address.

He got what he wanted from Tesco and loaded his shopping bags into the back of his car. He then drove home and unpacked everything. He went upstairs and had a shower and got changed. He was starting to feel tired now. He'd been up since four but thank God he didn't have to be at work tomorrow until ten in the morning. After several early starts the last few days he'd be glad of the opportunity to have a lie in. Unless of course Susie decided to use and abuse his body in which case he wouldn't object however knackered he felt.

He looked at his watch and saw that it was half past. He was due to meet Susie for a meeting with Canon O'Farrell at the church in an hour but he didn't have to leave just yet so he decided to make himself a cup of tea and sit down with those bits of the paper that he hadn't been able to get through on the flight deck. The meeting was intended to go through the service and for him to listen to the Canon giving him another disguised lecture on the word of the Catholic Church. He didn't mind though. It made Susie happy because it made her Mum happy so that was fine and Canon O'Farrell wasn't a bad old boy. Angus thought he was quite human for a priest really.

He filled up the kettle and flicked the switch on just as he heard a knock at the front door. When he opened it he was surprised to see who was standing there.

'Hi! What are you doing here?'

Susie was standing outside the church waiting for Angus. The place held a lot of memories for her. It was where both Susie and her brother Matt has been baptised, where they'd each received confirmation, and where Canon O'Farrell was going to marry her and Angus in just over a week's time. She was so excited when she thought about it all, like a little girl waiting for Christmas. Angus was so perfect for her. A few years younger but very much the man, strong, unwilling to take any crap from her, but sensitive, kind, and warm hearted too. She got on great with his Mum and Dad and his two sisters. Everybody in the whole extended family on both sides got on. She'd landed on her feet. She knew that and she got down on her knees and prayed thanks to God every day but only when Angus wasn't looking. Prayer was a bit like vomiting. She preferred not to have an audience for either.

But where was Angus?

'Don't you be worrying yourself now, Susie dear,' said Brendan O'Farrell as he joined her at the end of the path to the presbytery door, 'I'd rather your man be late today than on your wedding day.'

Susie smiled. 'Brendan, you've known me since the day I was born. You know I don't like to be late for anything.'

'Well come on in,' said Brendan, leading her by the arm, 'My housekeeper, I think you know her, does a very acceptable afternoon tea with home made scones, jam and cream and the lot.'

Susie laughed at the look on Brendan's face as he talked about her Mum as if she didn't know her. 'I'm supposed to be on a diet, Brendan, or I'll never fit into my wedding dress. That's why I've not been back to Mum and Dad's for anything to eat lately because, as you well know, Mum is such a feeder.'

'Well indulge this old man for just one afternoon,' said Brendan with that familiar twinkle in his eye. 'Do you think you could manage that?'

'Well, seeing as it's you,' replied Susie before casting a concerned glance over her shoulder. Angus was fifteen minutes late and there was still no sign of him. What the hell was he doing?

Susan's mother Ann had made the scones and tea and left them out for the pair of them. Although Ann was great friends with Brendan, this was a kind of official talk that priests have with their members of their congregation and so for that reason she decided to go home before

Susie arrived. She didn't want to interfere and she knew she wouldn't be able to help herself if she stayed.

A while later Susie was enjoying every morsel of her mother's home made scones and regretting what they must be doing to her waistline. But that was nothing compared to the mounting anxiety she felt over Angus. He was never late. That's one of the things they had in common. He was so used to having to abide by schedules at work that he transferred the same attitude to the rest of his life. And if he said four o'clock then normally he meant four o'clock. So why was it now heading towards a quarter to five and still no word?

'Oh Brendan, you don't think he's had an accident, do you?'

'I'm sure he hasn't,' said Brendan in his best reassuring voice although he was starting to worry himself now too. 'There'll be a perfectly logical explanation, Susie. Have you tried the airport to see if his flight was delayed?'

'Do you know, I never thought about that,' said Susie as she pressed the button on her mobile. Angus had programmed in the airport information number just in case she needed it. She pressed in his flight number but when the automated voice came back with her information her face dropped.

'According to that his flight landed seven minutes early,' said Susie.

'Well try his mobile again,' said Brendan now trying to hide his anxiety.

Susie dialled Brendan's mobile from her phone once again and it went straight through to voicemail.

'No good,' she said, anxiously. She dropped the hand that was holding the phone down to her lap. 'It's the same as before.'

'And your home landline?'

Susie dialled her home number but that went to voicemail too.

'I'm going home!' said Susie quivered. 'Something's happened.'

'Now Susie all that will have happened is that he'll have fallen asleep,' said Brendan. 'The man will be tired keeping all those unsocial hours and you're putting two and two together because it's getting nearer the big day and you're getting nervous.'

'Well, we'll see. Thanks, Brendan.'

'Will you phone me when you get there?'

'Sure,' said Susie, attempting a smile. 'I will.'

'Give the man chance to explain himself.'

'Oh I will, Brendan' said Susie. 'After I've torn a strip off him."

Just under half an hour later Susie got home and saw that Angus' car was there. If he had fallen asleep she will not be very bloody impressed. She marched up to her front door but saw that it was slightly ajar. She pushed it open and tried to switch the light on but it wouldn't work. It was getting dark outside and there were shadows everywhere. That's when she got scared. She swallowed hard. Something wasn't right.

'Angus!' she called out. 'Angus!'

She found him slumped in one of the armchairs in the living room. He was covered in blood. His eyes and mouth were both wide open. His throat had been cut.

Susie stopped, momentarily frozen by shock, before she ran out of the house screaming.

CHAPTER SEVENTEEN

'Paddy?' said Angela, who wasn't getting much out of him

today. 'I can't talk to myself.'

'Can I go to the funeral, Doc?'

'Rita's funeral?'

'Yeah,' said Paddy, 'and will you come with me?'

'I can only ask the prison governor, Paddy, and see what he says.' said Angela. ' I promise you I'll do that much.'

'And you will come with me?'

Angela smiled. 'If you want me to then I'd be glad to come with you, Paddy.'

'Thanks, Doc,' said Paddy who then brightened a little. 'So I reckon you want to know what happened after I came out of prison the first time?'

'Yes, and the fact that Andy Cook was alive and testified on your behalf. That must've come as quite a surprise?'

'It was and the daft bugger was waiting for me when I got out on Christmas Eve 1978. He'd been coming to see me all the time I'd been in there and if it wasn't for him, Doc, I'd have had nobody at visiting time.'

'What did he do the day you came out of prison? Did he take you back to his place?'

'Yeah' said Paddy. 'He was married by then to a girl called Jolene. Pretty thing she was with long auburn hair and a small, around mouth. They didn't have much. Just a small unit, sorry, flat, a mile or so outside the city. But they opened it up to me and told me to treat it as my own.'

'You and Andy must've got quite close?'

'Oh we did, Doc,' said Paddy. 'I told him everything. We used to talk for hours. We'd go out to the pub or to the tote...'

'... the tote?'

'Sorry again,' said Paddy, 'that's the Aussie word for the bookies. Then we'd get back and Jolene would have the dinner on the table for us. It was a bit chauvinistic I suppose, looking back, but it seemed to work for the three of us, Doc. Jolene seemed quite happy anyway to be looking after two blokes instead of just one. But it wasn't all about that. The three of us would go out too. And Jolene had her friends who she used to go out with.'

'What did you do for money?'

'I got a job driving a truck. I went all over the state and into the neighbouring states of New South Wales and South Australia. It was the first time I actually started to enjoy being in Australia. I had the freedom of the open road and I loved it. They were the happiest days of my life, Doc, and if I could wave a magic wand then that's where I'd go back to.'

'So what happened?'

'I fucked it all up.'

'How did you?'

'I had an affair with Jolene and Andy didn't like it,' said Paddy. 'Not surprisingly, I admit. She was a beautiful girl, Doc. I never thought I had a right to be with her, you know? I never thought I was good enough. But I thought she loved me. I got that wrong.'

'How do you mean you got it wrong? You were having an affair with her'

Paddy realised what he'd said. He'd have to be more careful. 'Yeah, she loved me, Doc, of course she loved me. She wouldn't have had an affair with me if she didn't, I realise that now like I realised it then. Yeah, Doc. Yeah, she loved me.'

Angela wondered what that was all about.

'How long did the affair last for?'

'We'd been going at it for six months when she told me she was pregnant. That was the real knife in Andy's back. More so even than the actual affair.'

'Why was that?'

'Because Andy was infertile, Doc. Something to do with the accident all those years before.'

'An accident that you'd caused.'

'Yeah, Christ, it was such a bloody mess.'

'So Jolene knew that the baby was yours even though I expect she was sleeping with Andy at the same time?'

'That's about it, yeah, Doc' said Paddy.

'No wonder Andy wasn't pleased.'

'He said I'd betrayed him which I had,' said Paddy. 'He said I'd chucked everything he'd done for me back in his face, which I had. Andy kicked both me and Jolene out. We got ourselves a unit in a suburb called Redfern and did our best to get on with things. We had a baby on the way. We both had jobs but it wasn't easy once Jolene had to go and hire lawyers and stuff.'

'And then what happened?'

'Andy came looking for us one night,' said Paddy rubbing his chin between his thumb and his forefinger, 'and it turned pretty ugly.'

CHAPTER EIGHTEEN

Superintendent John Hargreaves hurried into the squad room looking for Sara. The press were baying at the gates of headquarters. Two members of the public had lost their lives in brutal attacks and they wanted answers.

'DCI Hoyland? What have we got?'

'Sir, they were executed. In my opinion, both Rita Makin and Angus Carleton were executed by the same individual.'

'But ma'am?' questioned Joe Alexander. 'What could be the possible link between a woman in her sixties who used to work in a flower shop and a young man who was just starting out on his career as a pilot and came from the other end of the country?'

'You're going by the prints, Sara?' said Hargreaves.

'Yes, sir,' said Sara. 'The same set of unidentifiable prints found at both murder scenes.'

'The rest of it does seem far fetched though,' said Hargreaves, 'for the reasons Joe stated.'

'Yes, I know, sir,' Sara replied as she ran her hands through her long, blond hair and caught Hargreaves watching her. He'd been looking at her a lot like that lately. It was beginning to annoy her. 'But the method was also the same in both murders and the rest is just screaming out at us. No forced entry which suggests to me that the victims knew their assailant. These weren't random attacks, sir. Our friend knew who he was going for and there's something that connects these two people that the murderer is using as justification for his actions. We're going to find what that is. That's unless the McDermott brothers come up with the answer first.'

'How do you mean, Sara?' said Hargreaves.

'Sir, I'm convinced that the McDermott brothers not only saw Rita Makin's killer but he was also familiar to them in some way. Otherwise, why abscond to another country? Why not just give us a description of whoever it was they saw?'

'They're not big time are they,' said Hargreaves.

'Not at all, sir' said Sara. 'By all accounts they fancied themselves as gangsters but the action hasn't followed the words. They haven't done anything to touch our radar apart from a couple of speeding tickets.'

'What's the latest on them, ma'am?' asked Joe.

'They've got relatives in County Clare who we know they've been in contact with. But nobody knows exactly where they are. I'm in daily contact with our colleagues in the Garda and they're on the hunt for them. I think it's vital that the Garda find the McDermott brothers because I'm certain they'll lead us to the individual who murdered both victims.'

'And who's to say there isn't going to be more?' said Joe.

'That's what I'm afraid of, Joe' said Sara.

'So what's being done to find this link in the absence of a statement from the McDermott brothers?' Hargreaves knew he needed quick answers, the last thing he needed was a city on red alert because there was a killer on the loose.

'DS Bradshaw went to see Felicia McDermott this morning, sir,' said Sara before turning to Adrian. 'DS Bradshaw?'

Adrian was lost in his own world; wondering when the shit was going to hit the fan at home. His sister-in-law Natasha was poison and she'd take great pleasure in telling his wife Penny about his relationship with Matt. She'd love every minute of sticking the knife in. It had been two days now and she hadn't made her move yet. Why didn't she get her evil deed over and done with? Matt had already been in touch to tell him that he wasn't going to press any charges against Natasha as long as she paid for the damage to his car. That at least was something.

'DS Bradshaw?' Sara repeated. 'Sorry, are we boring you?'

'Ma'am?' said Adrian.

'Mrs. McDermott? What did she tell you if anything?'

'Sorry, ma'am. Felicia McDermott is adamant that neither of her two sons gave any hint as to the identity of Rita Makin's murderer before they left for Ireland.'

'Did you press her, DS Bradshaw?'

'Of course, ma'am' said Adrian defensively, 'this is an important case.'

'I'm so glad you recognise that fact, DS Bradshaw,' replied Sara with a sarcasm that wasn't lost on Superintendent Hargreaves who shot her a knowing look.

'My apologies, ma'am,'

Adrian was suitably chastened but his mind wasn't on the job and he knew it. The ball (his balls?) were entirely in Natasha's court and that's what scared him the most. Penny had noticed that he hadn't slept much these past couple of nights.

'DS Bradshaw, I need everybody to be focused on this. You do appreciate that?'

'Yes, ma'am, yes, of course I do,' said Adrian who was now feeling a bit picked on. 'I'm sorry if I gave you the wrong impression but I've given you my assurances and, with all due respect, ma'am, that should be enough.'

A momentary chill came over the room but Sara was determined to brush it aside.

'Warren Clarke has said he doesn't intend to press any charges against his wife Michelle and her lover, Nick Jackson, for attempting to have him beaten up,' said Sara breaking the tension., 'but we've still had to send the case to the DPP and I hope they still get charged despite the good grace of Warren Clarke. They were collateral as far as the wider case is concerned though. A crime within a crime you might say.'

'Yes and I don't think it's productive to spend anymore time on those characters,' Hargreaves agreed, 'we need to move on and find the actual killer of Rita Makin and Angus Carleton. And I agree with you, DCI Hoyland that it certainly looks like the same assailant committed both crimes.'

'Sir,' said Sara, 'And despite the sensitivities, the family of both Angus Carleton and his fiancée, Susie Schofield will need to be pressed hard when being interviewed. Something is there for us to find out somewhere.'

Natasha didn't put on any make-up, which was unusual for her because normally she considered it as a necessity. She may as well stop breathing as leave the house without her face on. But she needed to play for maximum effect when it came to her sister Penny and that's why she'd 'dressed down' in plain light blue jeans, a dark green cardigan and a plain white t-shirt. She'd put on a pair of white flat shoes that she couldn't remember ever buying because she'd never buy anything as awful as those and from her overall appearance today nobody would know that she was the same immaculately made up stewardess who would greet her first class passengers on Friday as they departed for Los Angeles with the best smile she could muster.

She'd never been this far east of Manchester before. This was nearly Derbyshire or even Yorkshire for God's sake. Now there were many rich folks in Yorkshire and she'd maybe have to get herself over there now that her darling boy Charles had been such a bastard. Or maybe she'd fall back on one of the many pilots at work who were desperate to get into her knickers. She could do with a change and they all lived in the depths of Surrey where she'd surely meet the right kind of friends. A couple of them were okay looking and she could always fake it at the right moments. Then she could push out a brat or two and settle into high tax brand domesticity a million miles away from her penurious upbringing. Not that it was that bad but she didn't go to private school and her father was desperately working class, a fact she didn't tell anybody about at work. But for now there would also be the sympathy factor that came from having been dumped by a celebrity doctor. She'd get plenty of mileage out of that for quite a while.

She wasn't sorry to say that she'd never been out to her sister's house in Saddleworth before. The estate stank of ordinariness. They were probably all just a generation away from a semi in one of Manchester's more faceless suburbs. At least Saddleworth had the appearance of aspiration and was different because of all the bloody hills around and about. If she was a more giving kind of person she'd admit to it all being rather picturesque. But she wasn't so she didn't, not even to herself.

'Mum told me about Charles,' said Penny as she walked her sister through to the kitchen. 'I'm sorry.'

'He said some awful things, Penny.' Natasha began taking a paper tissue out of her handbag to wipe away some tears she'd managed to force out, 'I can't repeat most of them. But they hurt, Penny. They really hurt.'

Instinctively Penny threw her arms around her sister even though she knew she'd get bugger all back in the way of emotional support. She still hadn't talked to Adrian about the miscarriage and she was dreading it. She'd gone behind his back and let herself get pregnant even though he'd said he didn't want another baby.

'What did Charles say?'

'Didn't you hear me? I said I can't repeat most of them.'

Penny wanted to slap her. 'Hey now, look, Natasha, you can get out now if all you're going to do is have a go at me because I've got troubles of my own and I'm not in the mood to fight you.'

'Oh you'll get over it,' said Natasha, dismissively.

'I beg your pardon?'

'Well you've already got three but then you've always been a greedy cow.'

'You never cease to amaze me, Natasha, with your insensitivity.'

'Well if you stopped thinking that everything is all about you just for five seconds of your life then you might not forget about the plight of other people!'

'Oh that's rich coming from Little Miss I Want Everybody's Attention!.'

'Well can you blame me? I come here because I need my sister and all she does is get into a row with me.'

'Natasha, did you know this is the first time you've visited me here and we've been in this house for four years now?'

'There you go again!' Natasha exclaimed. 'Bringing it all back to you!'

Penny breathed in deep as she took the verbal onslaught from her sister who hadn't asked her at all about her miscarriage. But then that was why Natasha was Natasha.

'I'll make us some coffee' said Penny.

'I don't drink instant.'

Penny paused and closed her eyes. 'I have a coffee machine' she said. 'It makes very good coffee as you'll soon see.'

Penny put on a pot of coffee and tried to keep her patience. Why had Natasha come around? What was on her agenda?

'Alright,' said Penny. 'You haven't come around here to offer your condolences over my miscarriage or to see how I'm feeling after it and, quite frankly, if you try and act like you're the only one who's going through it then so help me, I'll slap you. I know you don't love me, Natasha and I know you don't even like me. And I don't believe you need me in any way, shape or form after what's happened with Charles. So what is it? You haven't got Mum here to help you stick the knife in today so come on, what are you here for?'

'My God, I never realised you were so paranoid.'

'Only where you're concerned,' said Penny, 'because you see, you'll always choose the most underhand way of dealing with anything. I pity the man who marries you. He'll need to be looking over his shoulder the whole time. In fact, I'll bet you've already got some other poor bloke lined up to play your little games. He doesn't know what he's in for.'

'I'm sure you'd take great delight in telling him.'

'Oh I'm sure I would because I'm tired of not throwing it back at you, Natasha,' Penny replied now thoroughly enjoying getting it all off her chest. 'You've got away with being vile and nasty to me for too long. But not anymore.'

'I see,' said Natasha sitting back in her chair at Penny's kitchen table with a smirk, 'have you finished?'

'For the time being.'

'I must say it makes a change to see you with a spine, sister dearest,' said Natasha. 'I'm quite impressed'

'Why are you here, Natasha?'

'Where's Adrian?' Natasha was going to enjoy this.

Penny was taken aback by the question. 'He's at work like he always is.'

'Are you sure about that?'

'What are you talking about?'

'Did you know your husband has been sleeping with someone else?'

Penny crossed the space between them and slapped her sister across the face. 'You lying little bitch.'

Natasha rubbed her face and the smirk returned. 'And I know who it is.'

'Well if that's the case what's her name?' Penny demanded.

'Oh it's not a woman,' said Natasha who watched the pain of confusion rip across her sister's face. 'It's a man. Remember that nice doctor who was there when your foetus did a runner? Well it's him. Doctor Matt Schofield. I can give you his address if you like only let me be there when you confront him. I could do with a good laugh.'

★

Ann Schofield was shaking as she tried to pour the morning tea for Brendan and Father Phillip.

'Come on now, Ann' said Phillip as he got up from the table to help her, 'sit yourself down. I'll finish things off.'

'But you're just back from your study trip, Father, and I know you boys don't eat enough when you get your heads and your hearts into the books.'

'Ann' said Phillip, 'you've had a terrible shock. Now please sit down and let me wait on you for a change.'

Ann smiled. 'Alright' she said, 'if you insist.'

'Phillip is right' said Brendan as Ann joined him at the table and he patted her hand. 'Listen to the young man. He can be wise for his years.'

Phillip smiled cheekily. 'Oh well thank you, Brendan, that's really made my day'

'Well don't let it go to your head or you'll be doing every early morning Mass for the next month.'

'I'll keep well buttoned, Brendan,' said Phillip. 'You know how I hate early mornings.'

Brendan then turned to Ann. 'So, my dear. How are you holding up?'

'I'm not, Brendan,' Ann admitted before breaking down in tears. 'My little girl Susie is so distraught she spends most of the time under sedation. Our Matt is taking care of her at the moment. Bill has had to go back to work and take over the running of the business until Susie is well again. And I'll never forget the look of pain on the faces of Angus' mother and father. The funeral will be down near to where his mother lives, a place called Leatherhead, I think. His father lives out in Hong Kong. I just hope Susie is well enough. She's always been strong. I've never seen her like this.'

'Have the police any clues as to who did this evil thing, Ann?' asked Phillip.

'They seem to think it's the same individual who killed poor Rita Makin.'

'Why is that?' Brendan wanted to know. 'I don't understand.'

'Apparently the… the method was exactly the same and the police believe they were targeted.'

'But why?' wondered Phillip aloud, 'They didn't even know each other as far as I know.'

'The police are looking into everything,' Ann answered, 'all of our family and friends.'

'Seems like a wise move,' Phillip commented, 'they've got to look wherever they can.'

'Yes, they're coming here this morning,' added Brendan.

'Oh that's right,' Phillip remembered, 'you told me. About eleven you said? I'll be here.'

'Good' said Brendan. 'Thank you, Phillip.

'But if they were targeted then do they think that others are at risk?' Phillip wondered.

'It could be,' Ann was just as confused as the priests, 'but why would anybody target them? Rita would never hurt anybody and neither would Angus. He'd have made such a good husband for our Susie. I don't think she'll ever get over it, Father Phillip.'

At that moment Brendan felt a chill go through his soul.

★

'Are you religious, Joe?' Sara Hoyland asked as they pulled up several metres from the church where Rita Makin's funeral was about to take place.

'No, Sara, not particularly. I'm the usual weddings, funerals, christenings type of bloke. And you?'

'No, the same as you really. I don't need the church to give me a moral code. I've got my own conscience to tell me the difference between right and wrong.'

'You won't be kneeling and making the sign of the cross before taking your seat inside then?'

'I don't think so, no Joe. Will you be?'

'It wouldn't be the getting down on my knees that would be the problem, Sara,' Joe laughed, 'it would be the getting back up again.'

'You're not that overweight,' Sara laughed, 'there are many down at the station who are much heavier than you.'

'I know. I want to lose weight though.'

'So why don't you?'

'Now's not the time, Sara, I'm under enough pressure as it is.'

'Joe, I'd noticed you'd been a bit preoccupied lately, you know you can always talk to me as a friend?'

'I do and I appreciate that, but not today. At least not until we're in the pub.'

'We'll be lucky to get there before it's pretty late tonight,' said Sara. 'Not now we've got the Angus Carleton case as well as this one. Perhaps it's a good thing that neither of us have got anybody to go home too.'

'I thought you were seeing Kieran Quinn?'

'I'm seeing him, yes' said Sara, 'but we're not living together. What about you and whoever is giving you the long face?'

'She lives with somebody else.'

'Ah, the love triangle.'

'Yeah, something like that.'

'Don't let yourself get hurt, Joe, you're a good man and I wouldn't like to see that.'

'Thanks,' Joe smiled, 'but I think it's too late for that, Sara. Can I ask you something?'

'Sure, go ahead.'

'Would you stay with a man who hit you?'

'The short answer to that is no but I've met enough victims of domestic violence to know it's not always as simple as that, Joe. Is that what the problem is? Your lover is being physically abused by her husband?'

'Yes'

'And you can't understand why she won't give up all that to come and live with you?'

'That's about the size of it, yeah.'

'Well then you've maybe just got to give her time, how long has she been married to this guy?'

'Fifteen years,' Joe answered, 'they've got two kids.'

'Does she have a job?'

'No.'

'Well there you go, it's the security, Joe. She needs to feel as financially secure for her and the kids with you as she does with him.'

Joe shook his head. ' So is that what it comes down to? She knows I'm okay financially and that I'm not likely to take to gambling in Las Vegas or something.'

'Yes but she needs to be sure and when she is that's when she'll fall irretrievably for your ample charms, Joe.'

Joe turned over what Sara had said as they fell into step with the rest of the mourners on their way into church. He'd never understand women. If all Carol was waiting for was to feel that he could provide for her and the children then she should know that she's got nothing to worry about on that score. He didn't know what else he could do.

'I wonder if the murderer is here,' Joe whispered.

'I think he probably is, he's somewhere around,' Sara answered under her breath.

'Remind me who the prisoner is, Sara?' said Joe looking up ahead at a man handcuffed to a prison officer on one side and with a woman in her mid-thirties on the other.

'Sean Patrick O'Brien,' said Sara, 'been in Strangeways over twenty years but he's up for parole shortly and it's felt that he'll get it.'

'Why is he here?'

'He was in a children's home when he was a child and Rita Makin was his carer. She took over the motherly role just after his own mother had dumped him there.'

'It was very generous of the family to let him be here' said Joe, 'everybody is looking twice at him especially when they see how close his arm is to that thinly disguised prison officer.'

Sara smiled. 'I know. Pretty obvious, isn't it. As for the family, I think they must've thought that they didn't have much of a moral leg to stand on after what they've been up to with and against each other.'

'Well Rita Makin must've made quite an impression on the young Sean Patrick for him to remember her all these years on.'

'Yes but then they were parted when he was forcibly migrated to Australia.'

'Oh yeah I saw a documentary on the television about that once. Didn't make me feel very proud to be British, I must say.'

'No, I know what you mean. He was horribly abused down there by almost every adult male he came into contact with. Then he escaped one day but that didn't end his misery. He had the bad luck to be taken in by one of Australia's most notorious paedophiles.'

'And it all started with his mother abandoning him.'

'Yes but we don't know the circumstances she was in and the Catholic church have got a lot to answer for too. They worked in collusion with the government of the day and they both made money out of these unfortunate kids.'

'But he must've come back from Australia?'

'Oh he did' said Sara. 'When he was an adult but he didn't stay out of trouble for long.'

'What was he sent down for?'

'He murdered his girlfriend' said Sara, 'in front of her toddler son.'

CHAPTER NINETEEN

Sara and Joe introduced themselves to the prison officer who was accompanying Paddy O'Brien. Then Angela held out her hand to them.

'I'm Angela Barker,' said Angela, 'I've been working with Paddy.'

'She's been sorting my head out and she's worked bloody miracles,' said Paddy, looking at Angela. 'So much about my stupid life has come into perspective since I started talking with her.'

Sara could've sworn she saw Angela blush. Maybe she had a little crush on her patient? They seemed close but then counsellor and patient often become so if they strike up the right connection, which these two obviously had and that made Sara make a mental note to go and see Angela. She wanted to find out what Sean Patrick O'Brien had been telling her. If he'd said a lot about Rita Makin, enough for the prison governor to let him out for her funeral, then he may have something to say that would help the case. It was a long shot considering he'd known her so long ago but it may be worth a try.

'Keep communication to a minimum, O'Brien,' warned the prison officer, 'it won't do you any good if you disobey so soon before the parole hearing.'

'Yes, I hear you, sir.' said Paddy, 'Now I'm here to mourn if you don't mind.'

Sara wondered if the prison officers' intervention had been completely necessary but she said nothing. There is a code amongst people in their respective positions that no criticism is made in front of prisoners. It would be very easy for some corrupt officer to use that kind of behaviour to undermine a colleague. Sara was sure that some of them do but she wasn't going to add herself to that particular list.

Once the funeral Mass was finished inside, the congregation followed the coffin out into the church yard. Sara noted that Nick Jackson, Michelle Clarke's lover, wasn't there and she thought he'd done the right thing. His presence wouldn't have been appropriate. But Michelle wasn't crying. Oh she looked bewildered and there were even traces of grief in her eyes but she spent her time holding the hand of her eldest son who looked about fifteen. In fact, Sara thought that Michelle's three boys looked more upset about their Grandmother's demise than Michelle did. Warren Clarke naturally, under the circumstances, was trying to remain stoic but Sara could tell the pain he was going through. So he'd fallen in love with his mother-in-law? It didn't make him villain of the year.

O'Brien had been told that he could stand by the graveside once everyone else had dispersed, so as to spare the feelings of his fellow mourners. Angela, and of course, his prison guard, stood there with him as he looked down into the grave. Sara and Joe mingled with people as they walked to their cars. Sara wasn't convinced that they would get anything out of it. The killer of Rita Makin wasn't going to be amongst this crowd of lower middle-class South Manchester folk who'd just finished building their extensions and were now voting Conservative. But this was what you had to do in a murder enquiry. Waste your time by doing things that were against your instincts but which tick all the right investigation theory boxes.

Once the last of the mourners had gone, Joe told Sara that he'd gained absolutely nothing in the way of potentially useful knowledge about the identity of Rita Makin's killer.

'Me neither, Joe' replied Sara who turned and looked towards where O'Brien was standing with his entourage by the graveside.

'At least we know it wasn't him,' said Joe.

'No' said Sara as they started to walk towards them, 'but you never know where he might fit into it all.'

'You like to go really out there with your theories, Sara, don't you.'

'It's what's underneath the obvious that ends up solving the case in my experience, Joe. Look how intricate the Lady Eleanor Harding case was last year? We had to dig pretty deep on that one and I think this is the same.'

'You could be right' Joe admitted.

'Well look, don't you think it's strange that a man who hasn't seen Rita Makin since he was five years old wants to be at her funeral? Okay, I can accept that she must've made a pretty big impression on him at a time when he needed it but even so. Stick with me, Joe. We'll get there.'

'Yeah, but look at this guy, Sara. Two people have been murdered whilst he's been in gaol. So are you thinking he's working with someone on the outside?'

'Maybe,' said Sara, 'or maybe not.'

When they got close up to O'Brien, Sara noticed something that made her stop and touch Joe's arm.

'Joe' she whispered, gesturing in the direction she wanted his eyes to follow. She took her mobile out of her pocket. 'I'll call for back up.'

'I wouldn't do that if I was you, copper' said Paddy as Sara started to turn her back to the others to make the call. ' Unless you want to witness an execution. Now hand over your mobile phones. Both of you.'

Sara and Joe had no choice but to comply with Paddy's request. They had to watch whilst he threw their mobiles to the ground and crushed them both to pieces under his foot. The graveyard was massive, stretching half a mile across a hill with trees at the top and they were in the middle of it close to the church. This was lucky, thought Paddy. He didn't have far to go to get away.

'O'Brien,' Joe began 'you know this is crazy.'

'What I know, copper, is that you have to shut up and I'll deal with you both later.'

★

Penny got around to the station where her husband

Adrian was based and asked the sergeant on reception if he was in. Five minutes later they were sitting in Adrian's car in the space he'd driven into that morning.

'I just want to know if it's true' said Penny. Her elbow was resting on the window frame and her thumb nail was scratching her chin.

Adrian sat back and rested his head against the back of his seat. He sighed heavily. 'What is it you want me to tell you, Penny?'

'The truth, Adrian!'

'Like you told me the truth about being pregnant?'

'That is not the same thing, Adrian, and you know it,' Penny shouted, her voice heavy with emotion. 'Do you know what it felt like, Adrian? Do you know what it felt like for my own sister to tell me that my husband has been sleeping with another man?'

'Don't make it sound so…'

'… what, dirty? Oh sorry, did I devalue your little love nest?'

'Penny, please don't do this.'

'Do what?'

'What happened with Matt is nothing to do with what I have with you.' He placed his hand on his wife's shoulder but she brushed it off. 'If you don't believe anything else then please believe that. I know you're angry, Penny, and I understand that.'

'That's big of you.'

'But I have told you the truth, Penny' said Adrian. 'I've never lied to you.'

'How do you make that out?'

'I've never been unfaithful to you, Penny.'

'Well you'll forgive me for not being able to accept that' said Penny, astonished at her husband's attempted duplicity. 'So what did you think you were doing?'

'I don't know.'

'Not good enough, Adrian.'

'Well I don't know, Penny! I'd never had feelings for a man before and I've never had them since.'

'So it was about feelings then?' said Penny. 'It wasn't just about sex?'

'No, it wasn't just about sex but I've had a hard time admitting that.'

'And how did it start?'

'It was just one night when it just felt like the right thing to do.'

'The right thing to do? For God's sake, Adrian, you're talking about a homosexual affair! '

'No, he's a mate who I have sex with, Penny'

'Oh listen to yourself. Adrian. Do you have sex with all your mates?'

'I've told you, Penny, no! I don't know why I wanted it to happen with Matt. I just don't know.'

'Have you been careful?'

'I've never used more condoms in my entire life.'

'Oh spare me all the gory details!' Penny cried, 'You've always needed a lot of sex and I've always been happy to give it to you. You can't say we haven't had a healthy sex life.'

'No, I can't say that and I wouldn't say that, Penny' Adrian admitted, 'I told you it's nothing to do with our relationship. It's to do with another side of me that I didn't know existed. Matt brought it out.'

'Do you want to leave me?'

'No, Penny ....'

'...at least just for a while to see if you can work out who it is you want?'

'Penny, I know who I want. I want you and I always

will.'

'But I don't give you enough to prevent you from looking elsewhere?'

'With a woman, yes! I'd never sleep with another woman, Penny.'

'Then I should thank heavens for small mercies,' said Penny, as tears fell down her cheeks. 'That day in the restaurant when I had my miscarriage? You sat there knowing that he was a few metres away. Both of you knew what a fool you were making of me. That's really getting to me, Adrian.'

'I asked him to leave.'

'You did what?'

'I asked him to leave the restaurant precisely because I didn't want you to be made a fool of, even though Matt is not the kind of man who would think like that.'

'Oh I'm sure he's a saint once you get to know him.'

'It was pure chance that he was there that day but I'm glad he was because it meant that he took care of you. And whatever you may think of him, Penny, he is a good doctor. When he was our assigned GP at the station I saw evidence of that many times.'

'Is that... when it all started?'

'Yes' said Adrian. 'Yes, it was.'

'You know I've always feared that you'd leave me' said Penny. 'I knew that a big, handsome bloke like you would have his offers and that one time in a moment of weakness you'd maybe succumb to some dolly bird's charm. I never thought, I mean it never even crossed my mind that it would be another man.'

'Penny, I...'

'... no, let me finish, please, Adrian' Penny interrupted, holding up her hand to silence him. 'You've always known what it's been like for me with my parents and

Natasha. They've stabbed away at my confidence all these years, telling me you'd go off with someone else because I wasn't worth staying with for a lifetime. And yet when I was by your side I felt ten feet tall. I thought I was the luckiest girl in the world when I met you and found that someone as handsome and strong as you really wanted to be with me...'

'...please, Penny...'

'... and through all these years I've loved you more and more as time went on. I should've told you about the pregnancy and I'm sorry.'

' It doesn't matter about that now.'

'But now you hit me with this and I don't know what to do. If it was a woman I could fight her getting her claws into you. But another man is like trying to fight the unknown. Adrian, I really don't know what to do or what to think.'

'I'm begging you, Penny,' Adrian pleaded, 'I'm begging you to believe that something happened between Matt and I that I can't explain but which has nothing, and I mean nothing, to do with us and our family. Now look, can we talk later?'

'When you get home?'

'Where else would I go?'

'Alright' said Penny, who didn't want to close the door on her marriage despite how distressed she was feeling. She'd always said to her friends that if she'd discovered that Adrian had slept with another woman once, as long as it was only once, she wouldn't necessarily consider it as grounds for a major crisis. But to find out that your husband has been sleeping with another man, and on more than one occasion, really was something very different. No matter what Adrian said, he was sufficiently attracted to the difference a man can give him to go with

Matt Schofield and to keep on going back.

'You're not going to throw me out?'

'No, Adrian, I'm not,' said Penny. 'But I do need to try and understand better than I'm doing now. I accept what's happened and I hear everything you're saying…'

'… but it's not enough?'

'Not yet' said Penny, 'I feel like I've got to get to know you all over again.'

'I'm not any different now to how I've always been, Penny.'

'You can easily say that, Adrian, but I need to feel it. Do you understand? I need to feel what you're saying. I don't know how I'm going to work through this, Adrian, but I owe it to the kids to try. I owe it to you and to our marriage. I need time, Adrian. Don't rush me.'

'I won't,' said Adrian, 'and thank you. I thought I was going to lose you and that terrified me.'

'But what would you say if you thought you were going to lose Matt, Adrian? Would that terrify you too? Or have I got to think about opening up this marriage to the three of us? It would be like a custody arrangement. I have custody of you but you go and see him on set days.'

Adrian picked up his wife's hand. 'I'm sorry, Penny. You're my life and my world and I'm desperately sorry that I've hurt you. I don't know what else to say.'

★

Paddy pressed the end of the barrel of his gun further into the side of his prison guard who was trying to convince him that he should stop what he was trying to do.

'You will do as you're told, big man, or else your kids will be growing up with only a memory of their father.'

'Don't be an idiot, O'Brien' said the guard, 'you know you'll never get away with it. It's completely pointless and you're up for parole soon. Why put that at risk?'

'You don't ask me any questions and you don't speak to me unless I speak to you,' Paddy growled, 'do you understand?'

The prison guard didn't answer.

'I said do you understand?' Paddy repeated.

'Yes, O'Brien, I understand.'

'Right, so make one wrong move and you'll die. Now give me the key to the handcuffs.'

The guard did as he was told and in a matter of seconds Paddy had unlocked his side of the cuffs and fastened them to the guard's side so that the guard's hands were now cuffed together behind his back.

'Don't forget' said Paddy. 'Do as you're told and you'll live.'

'Paddy, please!' Angela begged. She couldn't believe what she was witnessing or how easily she'd been duped by her patient. 'What the hell are you doing? I got you out today because I trusted you. I thought we'd invested a lot of genuine emotion into our relationship.'

Paddy was genuinely sorry about the effect of what all this was having on the Doc but he had no choice. If he was to sort things out once and for all then this was the only way to do it. He had to try and stop the killings before anybody else copped it.

'We have, Doc, we have.'

'But how can you say that and then do something like this? You've let me down, Paddy. After all these weeks you've let me down but it isn't too late to put it right.'

'Oh I'm going to put it right, Doc, just not in the way everybody here would expect,' said Paddy. He then grabbed the prison officers' arm. ' Now where's your car, Doc?'

'My car?'

'Yes, where is it?'

'Well it's the red BMW just outside the gates,' said Angela who by now was absolutely terrified at the thought of whatever Paddy was planning .

'Lead me to it.'

'O'Brien!' Sara pleaded, 'Put the gun down and we'll talk this over. You know you're not going to get very far and even if you do, this won't all end well.'

'Shut your pretty little mouth, copper!'

'I'll bet you've been planning this for months, O'Brien,' said Sara.

'Ten out of ten, copper.'

'We can still help you, O'Brien,' said Joe who could see the looks on the faces of Angela and the prison officer. Fear didn't even come close.

'Don't make me laugh, fat bloke,' said Paddy who nodded in the direction of the church. 'Now all of you get in there.'

'What on earth is going on?' Brendan demanded as he came back from seeing the last of the mourners on their way. Then he exchanged a look with Paddy and in that instant they both knew.

'Give me the key to the church, Father'

'What in the name of God...'

'...I said give me the key to the church, Father! And don't mess me about.'

Brendan handed the key over and then Paddy ordered Brendan, Sara, and Joe to get inside the church.

'And don't even think about trying anything' Paddy warned, 'you know I've killed before and I'll kill again.'

'Just tell me why you're doing this' said Sara.

'You'll find out soon enough.'

'But I want to know now!'

'Yeah, well, we don't always get what we want.'

Once they were all inside the church, Paddy told Angela to lock them in. She did as she was told but her hand was shaking so much she almost couldn't turn the key in the lock. Eventually she managed.

'Right, let's get moving.'

Paddy marched the prison officer down the path to the church gate with Angela following anxiously behind them. Once they got to Angela's car he told her to open the boot. He then told the prison office to get in and closed it down on him.

'For God's sake, Paddy, the man won't be able to breathe!'

'Yes he will, Doc' said Paddy, looking around. 'Now get in. We're going for a drive.'

'Where to?'

'I don't know yet but I'll tell you which way to go.'

'Paddy, please' Angela pleaded tearfully. 'Let me go home to my husband.'

'I will, Doc, I promise you will. I've no problem with you.'

They got into the car and Angela began to drive off.

'Paddy, I...'

'...now let's get one thing straight, Doc. My name isn't Paddy or Sean Patrick O'Brien. It's Andrew John Cook. Andy Cook.'

CHAPTER TWENTY

When Penny got around to Matt Schofield's house and knocked on the door she suddenly didn't know what on earth she was going to say. How do you start off a conversation with the man who you've found out has been sleeping with your husband? Do you threaten to scratch his eyes out? Penny allowed herself a small smile. She wouldn't be as crass as that with a woman who'd slept with Adrian so she wasn't going to be like that with Matt Schofield. It was getting dark. She knocked again. His car was in the drive so he must be in. He must've had it repaired pretty quickly because there was no sign of the damage that she knew her sister had inflicted on it. She didn't know which was more twisted. The petty little dramas of her sister or the reality of the situation she now found herself in. She could hear someone inside running about but she was about to give up and leave when the door opened and Matt Schofield was standing there, tucking his shirt into his trousers.

'Sorry' he said. 'I've just come out of the shower.'

'Well if I've called at a bad time?'

'No,' said Matt, looking back into Penny's appealing eyes. She was a good-looking woman without being flash. Her shoulder length auburn hair was soft and she didn't need a lot of make up to bring out the prettiness of her oval shaped face. She had on a flowery print dress in different shades of green and a medium length cream coloured single breasted raincoat. 'Did you knock before?'

'Only a few seconds ago.'

'It's just that I thought I heard something downstairs when I was in the shower,' said Matt. 'Just before you knocked. Oh well, listen Penny, sorry, please come in.'

Matt led Penny through to his kitchen where he switched on the kettle. All of a sudden he was nervous. He'd taken something from this woman. Something that she believed wasn't his to take. And he hadn't had any conscience about it.

'Would you like tea or coffee?'

'Tea, please,' Penny slid her bag off her shoulders,

'could I sit down?'

'Of course.' Matt pointed at a chair she was standing behind. 'I'm in a bit of a flux because, well you know what happened to my sister's fiancé?'

'Yes,' said Penny. 'I'm so sorry. She must be in a terrible state.'

'She is. She still needs to be sedated a lot of the time. She found him, you see. The poor soul can't get that image out of her mind.'

'I can imagine what that must be like' said Penny.

'I'm on my way over there now to look after her. My parents are exhausted. Well, all three of us are.'

He turned back to the kettle and made the tea in a pot. He placed a couple of mugs on the table along with some milk and sugar. Then he sat down opposite her at the table and waited for the tea to brew. He hated this tendency these days to just throw a bag in a mug and make tea that way. Tea had to be made in a pot or not at all.

'I don't want to like you, Matt.'

'No, well I can understand that.'

'But my sister Natasha hates you so that must mean you're not that bad a bloke.'

Matt managed a half smile. 'Natasha and I never got on from the word go.'

'Natasha has got a big collection of people she doesn't get on with.'

'I take it you the two of you don't get on?'

'Never have, we're just not the same kind of people.'

'It's different with my sister and I. We've always been close.'

'She'll need you now more than ever'

Matt smiled. 'Yes, and I'll be there for her. But Penny, as sad and as savage as recent events in my sister's life have been, I'm sure you didn't come to talk about them.'

Penny blushed. 'No, you're right. I wanted to be angry with you. Well not just angry. I wanted to be bloody furious with you. But I'm not. I had a long talk with Adrian earlier and I'm angry with him but not you.'

'Why?'

'Because he betrayed his loyalty to me. You didn't. He did. You didn't owe me anything. At least that's how I'm trying to rationalise things.'

'He didn't betray his loyalty to you, Penny, there's a distinction to be made. If you like, you and I found different parts of him.'

'Yes I know he tried to explain all of that himself but I don't know…'

'But that's what it amounts to, Penny.'

'Yes, but I didn't know there was this different side to him, Matt. And it's hard to take.'

'I know and I understand, believe me.'

'Do you want to share him?'

'No' said Matt. 'I don't.'

'Would you have carried on seeing him if I hadn't found out?'

'I don't know' said Matt, thinking of Charlie. 'I really don't know.'

'And are you going to fight for him?'

'No, Penny. I'm going to back off and leave you to sort things out. I've no interest in breaking up anybody's marriage.'

'But will you miss him?'

Matt suddenly felt emotional. 'Yes' he admitted. 'I'm not going to lie to you. Yes, I will miss him.'

'Are you in love with him?'

'I thought I wasn't' said Matt clearing his throat. He didn't want to break down in front of her but everything seemed to be in such a mess. 'But I think I must be a little bit. Life's a bit complicated for me at the moment though.'

'Then I'm sorry,' said Penny who felt strangely magnanimous towards her husband's lover, 'I know how easy it is to fall in love with him.'

'This is all very grown up, Penny.'

'That's because we're both grown up people' said Penny. 'I've always left the big dramas to Natasha. But it's not me. All I wanted to know was whether or not I've still got a relationship with Adrian to save.'

'Which you most definitely have.'

'And I wanted to know what you were planning to do' said Penny. 'And you've answered that in a more generous way than I could've expected.'

'I've given you the truth.'

'It's going to be hard though, Matt. As you say, we're being very grown up but there are certain things I can't get out of my head. Like when I imagine the two of you together and yet he says he's not even a little bit gay.'

'I think Adrian is essentially straight but he had this side to him that was curious about other men. I just happened to be the one who turned the key in the lock if you like.'

'Do you think some other man in the future could do that too?'

Matt looked at Penny and knew what it was she wanted him to say. So he decided to give it to her even though it wasn't what he felt.

'No, I don't think so,' he lied, 'and that's not my ego talking. I just think he took a once in a lifetime chance and I think he'll put it all quietly away now.'

'Thank you.'

Matt tried to smile but it wouldn't come and then he

was saved by his mobile ringing. It was sitting on the table and he picked it up to look at the caller id display. He saw that it was Angus' parents. He said 'excuse me' to Penny then he answered.

'Hello, Margaret? …of course you can but would you mind if I called you back in a minute or so? …it's just that I've got somebody with me …no, that's fine. Speak to you in a minute.'

'Sorry about that, that's the mother of my sister's fiancé. Her family seem to think that because I'm a doctor that I can somehow be some kind of counsellor too so when they need to talk they ring me. I don't mind though. They're good people and they've lost their son in such awful circumstances.'

'I'll go,' said Penny making to get up.

'No, stay' said Matt. 'Please. I'd like to carry on talking for a little while if that's okay with you?'

'Well, yes' said Penny. 'If you want to.'

'Help yourself to some tea' said Matt as he stood up. 'It should've brewed by now. I'll go and make this call upstairs and I'll be down in a few minutes.'

It was about ten minutes later when Matt finished his call and went back downstairs. He turned into the hall that led to the kitchen and immediately noticed up that his back door was open. Maybe Penny wanted some fresh air? He'd heard her chair scraping against the tiles on his kitchen floor and thought she might be getting up to walk around a bit. Then he looked down and saw a trickle of blood seeping through the doorway into the hall. He stopped. He felt sick. He proceeded slowly and as the macabre scene was revealed he brought his hand up to his mouth. Penny was still in the chair she'd been sitting on when he went upstairs. But she was dead. There was blood all over the place. Her eyes and mouth were both wide open.

Her throat had been cut.

Matt slid down the wall and began to shake.

★

'My father was a good deal older than my mother, Doc,' said Andy Cook. 'He was just past sixty when he married her. He was the good old boy from the pub who'd invested more emotion in his beer than in any human relationships. She was the tart with a heart who'd never found what she'd always really wanted which was true love. And she still hadn't found it with my father but it was as close as she was ever going to get, I suppose. Then I came along and that seemed to please them both. Mum doted on me and Dad was a really proud father, you know. He took me everywhere.'

Angela was finding it hard to take her eyes off the gun in Andy Cook's hand. She was listening to him but she was also reproaching herself. How could she have been so stupid? She'd been in the profession for all these years and yet he'd so easily duped her into believing he was Sean Patrick O'Brien. But then he'd fooled everybody. The authorities in Australia, the authorities here. How had he got away with it? And why? He'd got her to drive out to a pretty remote spot on the hills between Macclesfield and Buxton, where the Cheshire plains met the Derbyshire Peaks. If the circumstances were different she could almost imagine herself enjoying it all. As it was they were a long way out of town and she felt vulnerable. They'd driven down a track that was off the main road and nobody would notice them if they weren't specifically looking this way. He'd assured her that she was going to be okay but the 9/11 hijackers had told that to the passengers on the planes that they flew into the World Trade Centre, hadn't they?. And if Andy Cook had been capable of impersonating another man all this time, including doing a long stretch in prison under that name, then what else could he be capable of? Then she kept thinking about the poor prison guard handcuffed in the boot. What must be going through his mind?

'I take it there's some rain to come on this story?' she said, trying to keep the trembling out of her voice.

'Oh yeah, Doc, you could say that. I was just a bit past twelve years old. In fact, it hadn't been long since my birthday. Anyway, my Dad dropped dead with a massive heart attack. They tried to revive him apparently but it was no bloody good. He'd gone. My Mum and I were heart broken, absolutely cut to pieces with grief. Then about a year later, just when we were starting to come to terms with it, my world got ripped apart again. My Mum was knocked down by a bastard hit and run driver.' He started to cry. 'They said I had to be a big, brave boy because Mum wouldn't be coming home.'

'And that's when they put you in the children's home?'

'Yeah' said Andy. He wiped his mouth and face with the back of his hand.

'Weren't there any family members who could take care of you?'

'Mum had lost touch with all her folks years before. A couple of them came to the funeral but they didn't ask what was going to be happening to me. I had an Uncle on my father's side up in Brisbane but he was in his late seventies and didn't want the responsibility of taking on a nephew he didn't know. So yeah, I got sent into the fun palace.'

It never ceased to amaze Angela the depth of tragedy that some people have to get themselves through in life but she also had to remember that she was being held against her will by a man who was unpredictable.

'Andy, is everything you've told me about Sean Patrick just a fabrication?'

'No, Doc, I wouldn't lie to you,' said Andy, indignantly.

'But he must've thought you'd died when you went over the cliff that time?'

Andy sighed deeply and turned his eyes to the hills all around. 'He did, Doc, and so did I. I broke both legs and both arms in that fall and cut half the side of my face open. But some people nearby ran and stopped me from going into the sea. They called the rescue teams and I went into hospital for the best part of a year.'

'That's where the scar came from,' said Angela, 'and that slight limp you have.'

'That's right, Doc.'

'It was obvious but I didn't know enough to put two and two together'

'I've not been fair to you, Doc' said Andy. 'But I had my reasons.'

'Did they know in the hospital that you were from the children's home?'

'Yeah, but, luckily for me, the nurse who took care of me had been in the home and knew what went on in there. He got me sent to a different home once I'd been released from hospital. One where he knew I wouldn't be abused.'

'But then you had to leave?'

'As soon as I was sixteen,' said Andy, 'I got through. I got a job in a builders yard keeping stock of everything. Then one day I heard on the news about Paddy O'Brien getting mixed up with those evil paedophiles and I just felt sorry for him. I went to see him and said I'd testify for him.'

'I'll bet he was surprised to see you?'

'Oh yes,' said Andy, laughing. 'He really did think he'd seen a ghost which to him he had because he thought I was dead. But we struck it up pretty close. I visited him in gaol and when he came out I gave him the spare room at the unit I shared with my girlfriend Jolene. He'd been living there a good while before I found out he was having an affair with her.'

'Well I've already heard it from his angle,' said Angela who could've laughed at the absurdity of what she'd just said. 'But what was your reaction?'

'I chucked a proper mental' said Andy. 'I could've lost my life because of O'Brien and yet I'd forgiven him and taken him into my home when he had nowhere to go. I saw us both as victims of this pile of shit we call life. And yet he repays me by carrying on with the girl I loved.'

Angela was having to focus hard on what Andy was telling her. 'Sorry, Andy, it's just that when you were being Paddy I heard all this from a different perspective and I'm getting a bit vague in places. Where did you get Paddy's story from and when and why did you take on his identity?'

'Paddy's story I got from the manuscript I gave you' said Andy. 'When he stayed with me he really opened up and told me everything. I wrote it all down.'

'Why did you do that?'

'I don't know. I just had the feeling it might come in useful one day.'

'So where is Paddy now, Andy?'

'Well see, he and Jolene moved into their own place and had a kid. I heard from various sources that they were really happy and I couldn't stand it. I was miserable. I was mightily pissed off! I went over there one night and Paddy and I got into a fight. He chased me down the street but I managed to get behind a corner. I reached out for him as he came past and threw him against the wall. I heard his neck break.'

'You'd killed him.'

'Yes' said Andy. 'I'd killed him. But I was buggered if I was going to do time for the bastard. It was dark and the area wasn't so good so there wasn't much in the way of street lighting. I managed to get the body onto the beach which was only a few metres away. The tide was in and I threw him into the water. He might've ended up in New Zealand or even South America for all I cared. But it was the next day that I got my really big break.'

'Why, what happened?'

'Well an English guy came to my flat, the one I'd shared with Jolene and then also with Paddy the traitor, and said he was looking for Paddy. I asked him what he wanted him for and he said that he was married to Paddy's mother, the one who'd dumped him in the orphanage when he was a little bloke, and that a few months previously Paddy had written to the church where the orphanage had been and because he was about to become a father, he wanted to try and trace his mother to make amends with her.'

'The orphanage was knocked down a few years ago' said Angela. 'There are flats there now.'

'Yeah, I know' said Andy. 'But the church received the letter and they passed it on to Paddy's mother who worked there apparently. She'd shown it to her husband who was now standing in front of me. He was on a business trip to Australia and had decided to look Paddy up to tell him that there was never going to be any reconciliation, that his mother had two other children now, a boy and a girl, and when he started talking cash that's when I saw my opportunity. I said that I was Paddy and the bloke offered me twenty grand to never contact his wife again. I agreed. He brought the cash around the next day and I never saw him again. I went straight around to Jolene's and said to her that we could use the money to start again by heading to England and set up home there. I planned to extort more cash out of the family, Doc. That was the only reason I wanted to leave Australia. I said that she owed it to her son, Paddy's son, to get as much out of the family as we could, given the way they'd treated him. I mean, what kind of bastard pays off the first son of his wife to stay away? And what kind of mother could've gone along with that? I fancied I had a bit of the moral high ground on that part of the sordid little tale, Doc. Anyway, I knew some people who could get me a false passport as Sean Patrick O'Brien.'

'But what about the fight you'd had with Paddy? You'd killed him'

'What about it? It was never reported so if anybody had asked we were going to say that Andy Cook had just walked out and we didn't know where the fuck he was.'

'So Jolene agreed to your plan?'

'Yeah, she did, eventually' said Andy, his voice drifting a bit. 'It was a beautiful summer's afternoon on February 21, 1982 when we took a Qantas jet out of Kingsford Smith airport in Sydney headed for London and stopping at Singapore and Bahrain on the way. We thought we'd hit the jet set and the little bloke loved being on the big plane. I didn't know that would be the last time I'd ever see my homeland.'

'My God' said Angela, 'but what did Jolene say about what you'd done to Paddy?'

'I never told her what had really happened' said Andy. 'I told her that he'd said to me that he was feeling trapped and was pissing off for good. She just assumed he'd run away and she wouldn't see him again.'

'So what went wrong?'

'We managed to get another ten grand out of the family' said Andy. 'But we found it hard to settle to tell you the truth. I got bad tempered and spent a lot of the cash on beer. Then Jolene kicked me in the balls again. She had an affair with one of our neighbours. I saw red. I mean, this time I really saw red. I'd moved halfway around the world for her and her son. I hadn't had to share the money with her, especially after what she'd done against me with Paddy. I could've just kept it all to myself but I didn't. I was too bloody soft where that woman was concerned. We had a flaming argument and I hit her. Then I kept on hitting her harder and harder until she was dead.'

Angela winced at the description of such violence. 'What happened to the child?'

'He got taken into care' said Andy. 'I don't know what happened to him after that. But I think that he's the one who's carrying out these murders, Doc.'

'What makes you say that?'

'He's started off on the periphery, going for Rita Makin and then Angus Carleton. I think his next strike will be against one of the family members themselves. He wants revenge for his father, Doc. I'm perhaps the only one who can try and stop him.'

'Why have you risked everything to do that, Andy? You could've gone back to Australia after you'd been paroled and started again. It wouldn't have been too late.'

'Would you believe an attack of conscience?'

'Try me?'

'I want to do right by Paddy's son,' said Andy. 'I left him without a mother or father. I killed them both.'

Angela let her head fall back on the headrest of her

seat. She was reeling with everything she'd been told.

'It's quite a story, hey, Doc?'

Angela sat up straight and rubbed her forehead with her fingers.

'What happens now, Andy?'

'Doc, I want you to get out of the car. Then I'm going to drive off. I want you to give me just fifteen minutes and then you can call someone and get them to come and get you.'

'But what about the prison guard?'

'I'll take care of him, don't worry.'

'Don't hurt him, Andy' she implored, 'just don't hurt him.'

'I won't, Doc' said Andy. 'You have my word on that'

'So the manuscript was written by you from all of what Paddy had told you.'

'That's it, Doc, yeah.'

'But you've left one thing out?'

'What's that?'

'The name of the family who paid you off?' said Angela. 'Or at least thought they were paying Sean Patrick O'Brien off.'

'It's Schofield, Doc' said Andy. 'Bill Schofield is the bastard who came to see me, well came to see Paddy, and his wife Ann is Paddy's mother.'

★

Brendan O'Farrell came back to the presbytery from giving his statement to the police and wasn't feeling well disposed towards Father Phillip.

'Have you been in touch with Angela Barker since her ordeal?' Brendan asked.

'Yes, briefly, Brendan' said Phillip, 'she's as well as can be expected.'

'I warned you not to meddle in this business, Phillip' said Brendan, 'I warned you not to get involved but oh no, you have to go riding in like the proverbial Knight in shining armour. And look what you've done! You could've got us all killed and now there's two potential killers out there on the loose.'

'Brendan! I don't deserve to be attacked in this way! I was helping Angela because I felt the church had an obligation to do so and because you wouldn't.'

'Despite whatever I said?'

'Well you tell me, Brendan? I asked you before why you didn't want to help Angela Barker and you wouldn't tell me. Therefore, all I can think is that you've got something to hide.'

'How dare you speak to me like that! Just remember who it is you're talking to!'

'Oh I see,' said Phillip, smirking, 'your respect for me only survives as long as I don't seriously challenge your views? Is that it?'

'Who knows what Sean Patrick O'Brien is planning to do next.'

'Yes, Brendan, and people could die because you didn't co-operate with Angela Barker and her counselling of Sean Patrick O'Brien right from the start. One of us is going to end up on the side of the angels, Brendan. And one of us isn't. What I've done is easily squared with my conscience. Can you say the same?'

CHAPTER TWENTY-ONE

Sara and Joe arrived at the offices of Schofield Caravan Parks and asked to be taken through to see Bill Schofield.

'Mr. Schofield' said Sara after they'd been shown into

his office.

'Have you found the mad men who're targeting my family?'

'No' said Sara. 'But of course, that's why we're here.'

'Well what do you think I can tell you?'

'Information which can tell us how we got to this point, Mr. Schofield.'

Bill sat down heavily in the chair behind his desk. He then gestured for Sara and Joe to sit in the chairs in front that faced him. He'd always feared that this day would come. That's why he'd hardly slept these past few nights.

'You look like you know why we're here, Mr. Schofield' said Joe.

'Where did you get the idea that I can help you?'

'We told you that Sean Patrick O'Brien had absconded from Rita Makin's funeral?'

'Yes and it's been all over the news.'

'Well it seems that the man known as Sean Patrick O'Brien was in fact another man,' said Sara. 'His name is Andrew James Cook, or Andy Cook. He was an associate of O'Brien's down in Australia.'

Bill was shocked at this latest revelation. 'But I recognised him' he said, 'from the photo in the papers I recognised him as the man I met all those years ago. A lot older of course but there was no mistaking him because of that scar on his face.'

'Andy Cook made quite a confession to the psychologist, Angela Barker,' said Sara. 'That's why we're here.'

'I'd better not tell you what I'd do to him if I got hold of him.'

Sara forced a smile. Objectivity was all very well if you wanted to be everybody's Girl Guide and help old ladies across the street. But subjectivity was much more fun and she just didn't like this supercilious little twat. He wouldn't last a second with Andy Cook but even men like Bill Schofield had to let you know that they thought themselves as hard.

'So what happened to O'Brien?'

'Andy Cook has confessed to the murder of Sean Patrick over thirty years ago,' said Sara. 'Just before you met him.'

'Mr. Schofield?' said Joe. 'Can you confirm that you visited Australia in early 1982?'

'You know that I did,' said Bill, sighing heavily. This was like the bottom falling out of his world. He'd been duped out of thirty grand. 'Do I need to consult my solicitor?'

'We're not charging you with anything, Mr. Schofield,' said Sara, feigning surprise at his question. 'We'd just like you to help us with our enquiries.'

'Look, I'm a man who will do anything to protect his family and that's what I did.'

'And part of that was in Australia thirty years ago?'

'It wasn't the primary reason I went there.'

'And what was the primary reason, sir?'

'Well as you know, detective, I built up a business from scratch that's now worth a considerable amount of money but back then we were only just enjoying the first fruits of success. We weren't into organising our customers. They organised themselves around what we could provide for them. It was the start of the public wanting more choice and more control over their holidays. We seemed to tap into all that. It was the freedom and the fact that we were providing, and still do provide, excellent value for money for families who prefer a more independent minded holiday. My daughter has some big plans for taking the business forward in the future.'

'But back to Australia in 1982, Mr. Schofield?' interrupted Joe who was growing impatient. They weren't fucking business journalists.

'I was there to look at the way the Australians had developed their caravan parks and to see about buying some static mobile homes which at the time were going for a steal out there, even with the transportation and import costs.'

'But you decided to look up Sean Patrick O'Brien whilst you were there?' said Joe.

Bill remembered well the day almost thirty years ago when he'd ventured into a part of Sydney that, after asking around as casually as he could, he had been told wasn't the most salubrious part of town. But he'd needed to go there because he'd had to protect what he and Ann were building together.

'He'd sent Ann, my wife, a letter' Bill snarled, 'with a picture of her grandson, would you believe. Talk about emotional blackmail.'

'Wasn't he entitled to try and trace his mother?' Joe wanted to know.

'When she left him at the orphanage she'd left specific instructions that she didn't want to be contacted at any time,' said Bill, in measured tones.

'Was that her idea or yours, Mr. Schofield?' Joe asked.

'We both agreed.' said Bill, firmly, 'Both of us. Anyway, it had been a lifetime since she'd last seen him and to try and contact her after all those years was a complete imposition.'

'He hadn't exactly had an easy time of it' said Sara. 'From the account given to us by Angela Barker. Cook gave her a highly detailed manuscript of O'Brien's life, all of which was told to Cook by O'Brien. Both sexual and physical abuse, living on the run at fourteen, being lured into working for one of Australia's most notorious paedophiles and underneath it all the memory of having been dumped by his mother at an orphanage. I'm not one for making excuses for people, Mr. Schofield, but I'd say that was enough to send anyone off balance. Wouldn't you?'

'We couldn't help that' said Bill. He thumped the table with his fist. 'Damn it, why should we feel responsible?'

'Because your wife left him at the children's home when you could've taken him in as part of your family' said Sara. 'He could've had a much different life to the one he endured and if you had have taken him in then we may not be sitting here now and three people might not be dead.'

'I don't raise other men's children,' Bill emphasised, his emotions rising. She was right and he knew that. He'd been living with the rights and wrongs of his decision for the last thirty years. 'I made that clear to Ann right from the start.'

'You made her choose' said Joe.

'Yes, and she chose me' said Bill. 'Then life moved on. Look, my conscience is clear.'

'I don't see how it could be,' said Sara. 'You may not have committed any crime in the legal sense but you and Mrs. Schofield are both morally guilty as far as I can see.'

'He was a bastard child, not a beautiful one like our two' said Bill. 'Look, he wasn't trying to make contact with his mother for any kind of emotional reason. He sent her that picture of his kid so that he could get money out of us.'

'How can you be so sure of that?'

'Because I know that sort' Bill emphasised.

'That sort?'

'The sort who try to extort money from those of us

who've worked hard for what we've got.'

'He was your wife's son' said Sara. 'Didn't that make a difference?'

'Not to me it didn't, no.'

'Mr. Schofield, how do you feel now that you know the man you met in Australia and gave that money to wasn't O'Brien but Andrew John Cook?'

'Cheated.'

'And his confession to the murder of O'Brien, your wife's son?'

'That leaves me cold to be frank.'

'Money was extorted from you' said Sara, unable to believe the continuing show of callousness by the man. 'Not by O'Brien but by Cook who was pretending to be O'Brien.'

'I'm sure O'Brien would've taken the money had he been able to.'

'Did you have any contact with Andy Cook once he'd arrived in this country?'

'Yes' said Bill. 'When Cook, who I thought was O'Brien, contacted me and asked for more money I had a private investigator check him out. He was stupid enough to give me his home address after I'd falsely agreed to give him more cash in return for him letting me know where he lived so I could hand it over to him personally. I also wanted to know whether or not there was in fact a child.'

'And when you found out there was did it make any difference?' asked Sara.

'No' said Bill.

'Why doesn't that surprise me?'

'The private investigator came up with quite a file on O'Brien, Cook, whoever the devil he is. All sorts to do with where he drank, where they shopped with the money I'd given them, who their friends were. That's when I got the idea.'

'The idea?'

'It was me who told him that his tart was having it off with some other bloke.'

Sara and Joe looked at each other in astonishment. 'And why did you do that, Mr. Schofield?'

'To cause trouble! To cause him the kind of trouble that would get him out of our lives. And it succeeded.'

Sara raised her voice with agitation. 'Only by Jolene MacKenzie losing her life and her child being orphaned in a strange country!'

'I wasn't to know that would happen!'

'Do you know what happened to the child?'

'He grew up I expect.'

'And that's all you've got to say?'

'Detectives, I'm watching every member of my family go through a living hell right now,' said Bill, 'and I've got to live with the fact that it could all be my fault. So forgive me for not getting concerned over a child that means nothing to me.'

★

It had raised Superintendent Hargreaves' eyebrows when Sara told him she was going to the morgue with Adrian Bradshaw when he had to take the clothes he wanted them to bury his wife Penny in. But she was going and if the superintendent had any real issues with it then he'd have to take them up with her when she got back.

'Are you sure you're up to this, Adrian?'

'She's my wife, Sara' said Adrian, heavily. 'I have to be up to it.'

Sara's heart broke for him. He looked so utterly dejected and the shadows around his eyes seemed to be blocking out the light from his entire face. He managed to hand over the clothes and glance again at her porcelain face and the jagged red line underneath her chin before he broke down and Sara took him out into the corridor and sat him down. She sat beside him and gave him the time to let it all out and then try and regain his composure. He was leaning forward with his head down between his legs. He was breathing heavily as if there was a machine inside him that was starting to go wrong.

'We'll get him, Adrian' said Sara. 'We will get him.'

'What have you got so far, Sara?' he asked.

'Do you really want to hear all about that just now?'

'I need to know, Sara,' he said, defiantly. 'I really need to know what's going on.'

Sara breathed in deeply. 'Alright' she said. 'I don't think Penny was the target. I think it was Matt Schofield. He heard what he thought was someone downstairs when he was having a shower a few minutes before Penny called around. He also said that when he was in his bedroom making a call he definitely heard something going on downstairs. Then he went down and found his back door open.'

'And my wife' said Adrian. 'My God, why?'

'Adrian, were Penny and Matt Schofield friends?'

'No' said Adrian. 'I was friends with Matt. You know, this is all Penny's sister Natasha's fault. Penny always felt that her parents didn't love her. She always thought that Natasha was the favourite. And Natasha can be a nasty piece of work. She told Penny that I was more than just friends with Matt and Penny must've gone around to confront him about it.'

'And are you more than just friends with Matt Schofield, Adrian?' asked Sara, believing that Adrian wasn't telling her the whole truth.

Adrian swung around, ' No! Sara, I'm straight. One

hundred percent straight!'

'Okay' said Sara who didn't believe a word of Adrian's fervent denial. A simple no would've sufficed. Some people were absolutely gay, some were absolutely straight. But Sara now viewed Adrian as one of those men who was mostly straight. She wasn't so small minded that she didn't believe it was possible for a straight man and a gay man to be just friends. Of course it was possible and of course it did happen. But she didn't believe that Adrian's wife would've gone around to see Matt Schofield if she hadn't been suspicious that her sister's allegations were true. 'It was perhaps the wrong time to ask you that question and I'm sorry.'

'Whenever you ask me, the answer will still be the same'

'Why did Penny believe that her parents didn't love her?'

'Because they could be pretty nasty to her just like Natasha could be,' said Adrian. 'They even told her that she wasn't good enough for me. Can you believe that? She was a saint compared to me. And yet she kept on hoping that things would get better. She was always optimistic despite some of the awful things they said. But she would always have had me. I would never have left her.' He leaned forward with his hands clasped back together. 'I just can't believe she's gone, Sara. I just don't know what I'm going to do.'

'How are the kids doing?'

'They're broken hearted,' said Adrian, bringing his hand to his mouth, 'she was such a good mother. My Mum is with them at the moment.'

'Well you'd better get back to them' said Sara. It was obvious the poor bastard was in a right state. He needed his family just as much as they needed him. 'They're really going to need their Dad now.'

'I know' said Adrian, his voice faltering. 'But I'll never be as good as Penny.'

Sara leaned forward with her hand on Adrian's back. 'You'll be the Dad that they need, Adrian. Just like you've always been.'

Without turning around Adrian placed his hand on Sara's.

'Now take as much time off as you need, Adrian' said Sara. 'I mean that. Don't come back to work until you feel really ready. I'll sort everything out with the Superintendent. Don't worry about anything.'

★

Susie got herself showered and changed for the first time in three days. She at least wanted to start making an effort on the outside, although whenever she thought of her darling Angus she had to drag herself back from square one. For as long as she lived she'd never forget his face. She dropped down to the floor and held her head in her hands. This was supposed to be the time of all her dreams coming true. She was going to build a life together with Angus. They were going to have a family. They were going to dream the same dreams and see them all come true. But instead of all that she felt like she'd been buried alive. If he'd died in an accident or developed some kind of illness that claimed his life she could've somehow made sense of it. Accidents and illness are things that happen because of external factors or because of a body that becomes diseased. But her life with Angus had been snatched away by an act of evil. The act of someone who'd deliberately singled her beloved out for execution.

Her thoughts were drifting in and out of here and

there when she realised there was a horrendous amount of shouting going on downstairs. She went down tentatively, not knowing what the hell she might be walking in on and when she went into the living room she found her parents and her brother Matt bawling each other out like she'd never seen them do before.

'Will you lot tell me what the hell is going on here?' she shouted.

Susie and her brother Matt sat side by side on one of the leather sofas in their parents' living room. They'd sought each other's closeness when their parents' said that there was something about their family they needed to tell them about. They'd always done it when they were children. If one of them had been in trouble then they'd stick together against the common enemy. They both knew though that this time it was going to be a great deal more serious than who'd broken a window during a game of football.

Ann Schofield was visibly shaking as she played around with a paper tissue in her fingers. She looked up at her husband Bill who was standing with his back to her, staring out of the window.

'It's time you both knew,' said Ann.

'Knew what, Mum?' asked Susie.

Ann sucked in a breath and tried to draw inspiration from somewhere. She tried to go deep into her faith but all it was telling her was that the truth had to come out.

'When I was a young girl,' she began, 'I fell pregnant. Nothing remarkable about that you might say but this was the late fifties and girls like me from nice, Catholic families didn't get pregnant. And if they did then there were always consequences to be paid. I had my son. I called him Sean Patrick.'

Susie was shocked. 'So Matt and I have a brother?'

'A half brother' her father corrected without turning around. 'He was only ever your half brother.'

'Why do you talk about him as if he was part of the past?' Susie persisted.

'Because he was murdered by the man who's been pretending to be him ever since,' said Bill. 'Andy Cook. He was part of the past, Susie. And that's where he should've stayed.'

'I want the whole story' said Matt.

'And so do I' said Susie. 'Go on, Mum?'

'Your grandmother never forgave me for what I did,' said Ann, her eyes filling with tears as she recalled her mother's disapproval that carried on right up until the day she died. 'She loved the two of you dearly but she never forgot that you weren't her only grandchildren and that I'd sent the other one away.'

Susie shook her head and ran her hands through her hair.

'And then he was sent to Australia as an orphan. Except he wasn't an orphan. He had a mother.'

'And you're saying, Dad, that Andy Cook has been claiming to be our brother Sean Patrick for all these years? Why?'

'To get money out of the family,' said Bill.

'Andy Cook?' Susie exclaimed. ' Isn't he on the run?'

'Yes' said Ann. 'The police say they have no idea where he is.'

'He can't have committed the murders but... are there any other members of the family that Matt and I don't know about?'

'Apparently,' said Ann, 'Sean Patrick had a son. He was taken into care after his mother was murdered by Andy Cook, or Sean Patrick as he was claiming to be.'

'They don't know yet what happened to the child'

said Ann. 'My grandchild.'

'But he could've grown up with a pretty big sense of grievance?' said Susie. She was joining it all up in her head and it didn't paint a pretty picture. 'It could've led him to carry out desperate acts of revenge.'

'Susie, please let me explain before you start ripping into me,' said Ann, 'it isn't easy for me to tell all this to the two of you.'

'Well, we're listening,' said Susie, 'but it had better be good.'

'I lived at your grandmother's house with Sean Patrick for the first couple of years of his life. But your grandmother lived in a council house, as you know, and the council were threatening her with eviction because of the overcrowding. They said that Sean Patrick had to have a room of his own and that it wasn't appropriate for him to be sleeping in the same room as me or your grandmother. He wasn't an infant anymore. He was a child and all the rules changed.' She looked up and noted the apprehensive looks on their faces. She also noted that her husband of almost forty years was still staring out of the window. 'So they gave me a flat of my own. I never took to it. Every sound at night made me think there was someone trying to get in. Some people are not disposed to living on their own and I'm one of them.'

'But you weren't alone' said Susie. 'You had your son.'

'But that's not the same!' Ann insisted. 'It's not the same as living with another adult.'

'But lots of women out there live on their own with their kids,' Susie continued.

'Well I couldn't be one of them,' said Ann. 'Then I met your father. Things weren't all bad. I had some hope in my life.'

'You also had a son,' said Susie. 'What was the matter?

Did he get in the way?'

'It wasn't like that' said Ann.

'Oh so what was it like you sanctimonious cow!'

'Susie!' Bill roared. 'Don't speak to your mother like that!'

Matt leapt to his feet to defend his sister. 'You take one more step closer to her, Dad, and I will flatten you.'

'All of you, please!' Ann cried.

'Oh no, you're going to get yours now!' said Susie. 'All these years you've threatened us with your precious God! All these years you've done everything you could to make us feel guilty for the smallest, most inconsequential piece of nonsense. The Catholic guilt trip. It comes gold plated,' she turned to her father. 'Did you make her do it? '

'I thought it best that we started out with a clean break,' Bill spluttered to his daughter. The look in her eyes was crushing him. She looked like she held him in complete contempt.

'But you dumped a child!' Susie emphasised, enraged at her mother's disclosures.

'But he wasn't mine and I didn't want him as part of our family,' said Bill.

Susie slapped her father across the face. 'Matt and I had a brother who we didn't get to know because of your… I was going to say selfishness but it doesn't seem strong enough a word.'

'Susie,' said Ann, standing up and moving next to Bill. 'Please don't hate us!'

'Hate you? If I find that my Angus died because of something you started years ago then you will have to forget you have a daughter, just like you forgot you had a son.'

'That goes for me too,' said Matt. 'We have a nephew who we don't know what happened to and a brother who died in God knows what kind of circumstances. All my life, Mum, you've made me feel bad about myself because I'm gay and in your eyes that goes against what God wishes. Well when I die I'll be able to look St. Peter in the eye with a clear conscience whereas you, well you'll be standing in line with all the other hypocrites. You disgust me.' He then turned to his father. 'Both of you do.'

★

Sara was about to go into a briefing at the station when her mobile rang. It was Manchester Social Services whom she'd asked to look into what had happened to the child that had witnessed his mother, Jolene MacKenzie, being killed by Andy Cook.

'We have found some significant information for you,' said the young female voice who identified herself as Danielle.

'Yes?' said Sara.

'Well, after his mother was murdered he did get taken into care as you might expect and seeing as his father had been a British citizen it was decided he should stay here in this country.'

'Were there no relatives of Jolene's in Australia he could've gone back to?' asked Sara.

'Apparently not' said Danielle who was reading from a computer screen on her desk. 'A couple of years later he was adopted by a couple in North Wales.'

'Do we have a name?' Sara asked.

'Yes,' said Danielle, 'it was Evans. And his new parents called him Philip.'

'Phillip Evans?'

'Yeah' said Danielle. 'And now here's the thing. His parents were quite religious, very strong Catholics. I suppose you could say he was pushed but he became a priest.'

The penny dropped inside Sara like an atom bomb. 'Don't tell me. Father Phillip Evans currently attached to the Holy Saints church in Salford?'

'Yes,' said Danielle. 'That's him'

'Thank you,' said Sara, 'I now have my prime suspect.'

CHAPTER TWENTY-TWO

Sara woke up early the next morning and decided to go straight into the office. It was barely past six but the building wasn't empty. A police station of that size never is. There are always suspects in cells and diligent police officers like Sara driven by their hunches to the point of distraction and insomnia. No sightings had been reported overnight of either Andy Cook or Father Phillip Evans who, not surprisingly, had now disappeared. A full scale manhunt was now underway for them both.

Sara's lover Kieran was on front desk duty and he called Sara to say that a Matt Schofield was there and wanted to speak to her. After they'd finished with the business of the call they whispered a couple things to each other that they shouldn't and then hung up. Sara smiled at the phone. Kieran was such a filthy bugger and what he'd said to her had nothing to do with 'sweet nothings'. She'd also noticed him getting a bit moody though lately and she had no idea what that was all about.

She went downstairs and took Matt Schofield into an interview room just off the front desk area. She couldn't help looking at her watch. It was just before eight o'clock.

'Detective Hoyland,' said Matt. 'I'm sorry to bother you so early but I'm on my way to morning surgery.'

'Oh no that's alright,' said Sara.

'It's just that I noticed you looking at your watch,' said Matt. 'I didn't even think you'd be here this early.'

'Well we've got a lot of work on at the moment.'

'Yes, I can imagine,' said Matt, 'and I don't want to take up too much of your time.'

'It's okay, really. What can I do for you?'

'I wanted to talk to you about what Andy Cook told you about the man I now know was my brother, Sean Patrick O'Brien, the man Cook has been impersonating these past years. I know you're in the middle of an investigation but I just wondered if you could give me any information on him and his life. You see, detective, my sister and I need to try and get a hold on our brother and what happened to him.'

'It was pretty tragic' said Sara.

'Well I guessed that.'

'Look, the psychotherapist Angela Barker was given a detailed manuscript by Andy Cook about your brother's life. He wrote it from what your brother told him back in Australia and was going to turn it into a book. I can't give you the original but I can make a copy and give that to you.'

'That would be very generous, thank you' said Matt.

'I warn you though that it's not a feel good read, your brother was forcibly migrated to Australia as a child.'

'After my mother dumped him there and forgot about him.'

'Those are the facts, yes,' said Sara.

'But they don't end there, do they' said Matt. 'You're looking for Father Phillip Evans because you suspect him to be the killer. And he's my nephew.'

'Yes,' said Sara, 'I'm sorry.'

'It's not me who needs the sympathy, detective' said Matt, 'and it's certainly not my parents.'

'Okay' said Sara. 'But look Matt, seeing as I'm going to be doing you a favour, can you do me one in return?'

'I'll try' said Matt.

'Matt, are you or were you, in a relationship with Adrian Bradshaw?'

Matt paused and in doing so realised he'd given her the truthful answer. He hadn't wanted to lie but he didn't know for sure what Adrian might've said. He'd tried contacting him countless times since Penny was murdered but Adrian hadn't returned any of his calls. And he was worried about him.

'I expect he's denying it?' Matt enquired.

'Well normally I wouldn't talk about the private lives of my officers but these aren't normal circumstances' said Sara. ' So yes, he does deny it.'

'I thought he would' said Matt. 'Not that I blame him under the circumstances.'

'A bit disrespectful to you though.'

'I went into it with my eyes wide open,' said Matt. 'Have you ever had an affair with a married man?'

'Yes' said Sara. 'It was a long time ago and my heart was broken. It taught me a valuable lesson.'

'Yeah, well' said Matt, 'learning that particular lesson is still on my 'to do' list.'

'He blames his wife finding out on all on the mischief making of his sister-in-law Natasha' said Sara, 'he says she told his wife there was something going on just to spite her.'

'Well Natasha is a downright bitch so that would fit.'

'You have experience of that?'

Matt felt he had no choice then but to tell her about when Natasha had been over to his house and smashed his car up. 'That's when she found out about Adrian and me because Adrian was there at the time.'

'I see,' said Sara. She was furious that Adrian hadn't told her about the incident outside Matt Schofield's house. She'd have to tackle him about it later. 'You didn't report it?'

'Natasha promised to pay for the damage and she has done,' said Matt. 'I decided to leave it there for the sake of Adrian's wife.'

'But Natasha told her anyway and that's why Penny came around to see you.'

'Yes' said Matt, 'but when I think about it, it's a wonder Penny didn't find out before she did considering that we were sort of friends by proxy. Her sister was going out with my best friend Charlie and …I was seeing her husband.'

'Oh what a tangled web, eh?'

'You might say that,' said Matt. 'It might even be funny if people hadn't been murdered.'

'How long have you been seeing Adrian?'

'About six months.'

'How did you and Penny Bradshaw get on by the way?'

'Quite well to tell you the truth,' said Matt, 'she seemed like she was a bright, intelligent woman. I liked her to be honest. If circumstances had been different we might even have been friends. It was odd really.'

'Considering you'd been seeing her husband?'

'No' said Matt, thinking back. 'It was like I felt a strange kind of closeness to her. I don't know why. And I was absolutely honest with her about Adrian. She deserved that much.'

'Has Adrian been in touch with you since?'

'No' said Matt. 'No, he hasn't. I've tried calling him but he's not returning any of my calls. He probably blames me. I seduced him in the first place, you see, and if I hadn't, if I'd just left well alone… but there was a strong attraction right from the start. I became a bit smitten.'

'Did Adrian tell you about Penny's difficult relationship with her parents?'

'Yeah he did' said Matt. 'He said that they were always putting her down even though she'd never given them any trouble compared to Natasha who was clearly the favoured one. But then judging by what I've found out about my own parents lately, I've no right to judge anyone. The weight of what's been happening is pretty heavy for my sister and I at the moment, detective.'

'I don't doubt that. But Matt, I'm concerned about you going back to work.'

'Why?'

'Because you're exposed there' said Sara. 'Until we catch Andy Cook and Phillip Evans everybody in your family is at risk.'

'I have to get back to work, detective,' said Matt. 'For the sake of my sanity and besides, Phillip Evans is family. I'm not going to make myself scared of him.'

'Matt, we can be pretty certain that he was going to kill you when he came to your house.'

'Yes, I know' said Matt. 'But I've got patients to see and my partner in the surgery has got his own problems too.'

'And are you still staying at your parents house?'

'No' said Matt. 'My sister Susie and I have checked into a hotel. We had a huge row with our parents and we couldn't face going back to our houses knowing what had happened in them.'

'Which hotel are you staying at?'

'The Malmaison near Piccadilly Station.'

'Under your own names?'

'Yes' said Matt. 'Although Schofield isn't a name I'm

particularly proud of at the moment.'

'Well look, I'll go and make that copy for you but I warn you, it doesn't make for very pleasant reading.'

'I thought as much.'

'And keep in touch. For your own sake.'

Matt drove down to the surgery and after he'd parked his car he started reading the copy of the manuscript detective Hoyland had given him. He got so deeply into it that when the practice nurse knocked on his car window as she was passing, he nearly jumped out of his skin. He then walked with her into the building and just after he got to his consulting room he received a visitor. It was Charlie. Matt looked up at him and burst into tears.

'Hey' said Charlie. He pulled up a chair and put his arm around Matt. 'This is not like you. You're the strong one who carries the rest of us on his shoulders.'

'Everything is such a bloody mess.' Matt pleaded. 'The police have given me a copy of a manuscript that details everything my brother Sean Patrick went through. And my own nephew, a nephew I never knew I had, just like I never knew I had a brother, is wanted for murder. How did we get here, Charlie? How did my mother, egged on by my father, leave her little boy to his fate?'

'I don't know, mate' said Charlie. 'I wish I did.'

'My brother had a hell of a life after my mother dumped him,' said Matt who'd read several pages of the copy of Andy Cook's manuscript. 'How could she do that? How could she leave him and forget about him?'

'I really don't know, Matt,' said Charlie. 'Knowing your mother it doesn't make any sense at all.'

'How's Wendy doing?'

'She's poorly.'

'Very poorly?'

'Yeah' said Charlie, softly.

'And the boys?'

'They don't like to let me out of their sight.'

'I can imagine.'

'They've been asking for their uncle Matt.'

'I'm sorry I've not been to see them,' said Matt.

'Hey look, I understand' said Charlie, rubbing Matt's back. 'You've had a lot on your plate.'

'You always did understand me, Charlie.'

'Yes and I always will,' said Charlie.

Charlie placed his fingertip under Matt's chin and lifted up his face. He looked into his eyes and touched Matt's lips with the end of his thumb. Then he kissed him. Then Matt kissed Charlie and before they knew it they'd spent several minutes engaged in the kissing of a love that had never been alive before.

'What was all that about?' asked Matt, tentatively.

'What you've always known to be true.'

★

Ann and Bill Schofield received a call from Brendan asking them to meet him down at the church. When they got there Bill pulled up right outside the main gate. They were both in a state of emotional distress and it showed on both their faces. Their children hated them and were refusing to speak to them. They were both praying to God but neither of them knew how they were ever going to put this right. They got out of the car and walked slowly down the path to the main door of the church. They looked around. The police had said they were watching both their house and the church so they must be around somewhere.

'Did Brendan say we had to go inside the church to meet him?' asked Bill.

'Yes' said Ann. She felt herself shaking as she had been for days.

They went inside the church and it was strangely quiet. It often was when there were no services taking place but this was different somehow. Then Ann looked up to the front and saw a massive black cloth draped between the two main pillars and blocking the view of the altar. It made the church seem dark because it was also blocking the light coming through the stained glass windows behind. What was that all about? Her natural instinct was to go up and take it down but she was stopped in her tracks by the sound of the door locking behind them. They both turned around and saw Phillip Evans standing there with a gun in his hand pointing at them. Ann gasped and Bill lifted up his hands.

'Now then son there's no need for this,' said Bill. 'Put the gun down.'

'I decide what happens here!' said Phillip. 'Now go to the front of the church.'

Neither Ann nor Bill could move. They were frozen with terror.

'Do it!' Phillip bellowed. 'Now!'

They held each other's hand as they stepped forward. Ann stumbled and Bill picked her up. Evans came up behind and pushed the gun in Ann's back.

'Move it!'

'You keep your hands off her!' Bill demanded.

His defence of his wife earned Bill a sharp blow across the face with the butt of Phillip's gun. Bill stumbled backwards and Ann went to help him but Phillip lifted her up and dragged her up the aisle and threw her down onto the front pew. Bill's face was bleeding as Phillip commanded him to come and sit by his wife. Ann and Bill huddled together like frightened children.

'And if either of you make a move or do anything stupid then it'll be the last thing you do.'

'Why have you brought us here?' Bill demanded. 'If it's just to kill us then get it over with!'

'Oh but we're going to have some fun first' said Evans, swaggering about, enjoying his captives expressions of fear and trepidation.

'I can't believe who you've turned out to be' said Ann. 'And I know that a lot of things have been done that are wrong. But we can put things right. We can pay for you to get out of here and we won't say a word about this.'

'Oh you think that a wad of cash will put things right, Grandma? I watched my mother being murdered by Andy Cook. I didn't know then what had happened to my father, a man who was there one day and gone the next. I didn't know that Cook had killed him.'

'But you've made something of your life, son' said Bill.

Phillip threw his head back and laughed. 'I've made something out of my life? I was adopted by a family for whom religion meant torture. My father took his belt to me every single night to beat what he called the devil out of me. Every single night! I can't cry anymore about anything because I cried so much when I was little. So don't tell me I've made something of my life.'

'I'm sorry,' Ann pleaded, 'but we're flesh and blood.'

'Yes, I am Grandma. I'm Sean Patrick's son. I'm your grandson. And the line of suffering began when you dumped my father at that orphanage. You've got to pay, Grandma. You've got to pay for what you did.'

Bill lunged forward at Evans who pushed the gun in his face.

'Another move like that from you old man and I'll re-arrange this dog ugly face of yours. I mean, how could you Grandma? How did you do it? Or did you just lie back, open your legs and think about all the nice money Billy boy was going to make with his business? Did the nice house and the comfortable lifestyle help you forget about what you'd done to my father?'

Ann cried out and wept.

'I'm warning you!' said Bill. 'You can see what a state she's in.'

'And she deserves to be in pain! She never gave a second thought to the pain that my father and then I had to endure.'

'If I'd known who you were then I would've tried to put things right,' Ann pleaded.

'And what would you have done? Thrown some more potatoes on for dinner? You're a complete inadequate, Grandma! You can dish it out but you can't take it. That's not a sign of how strong you are. It's a sign of how pathetically weak you are!'

'I said I'm warning you!' Bill roared.

'You're in no position to warn me, old man, and I'm getting a little tired and tetchy at your constant interruptions. Now button it. Unless of course, you want to die now? No, I didn't think so. So shut it!'

'What are you going to do to us?' asked Ann, tearfully.

'Well it's quite simple, Grandma. I had to watch Andy Cook murder my mother in front of my eyes. And now you're going to watch someone you love die in front of your eyes.'

Evans pulled back the black cloth to reveal Brendan. A noose of thick rope was suspended from the ceiling and tied around his neck. He had some tape over his mouth and his hands were tied together behind his back. His feet were also bound and he was standing on a stool that Ann recognised as being from the presbytery.

'As soon as I kick this stool away, old Brendan here will finally find out what really does happen after a person dies. I know how close you've always been. How do you feel about that, Bill?'

'Don't be disgusting.'

'Please!' Ann begged. She could hardly speak through a mixture of horror and tears. 'Please stop this! I know I should never have left your father at the orphanage but I didn't have any choice. And don't blame Bill. I wanted to make a fresh start as much as he did.'

'By dumping your child?'

'I know I shouldn't have done it but I didn't know what was going to happen,' Ann pleaded, 'surely you can see that?'

'He suffered years of agony because of what you did.' said Evans. 'Years of crying out for his Mummy whilst sick priests and monks ripped his childhood away from him with their cocks. Years of having to get fucked every night just so they'd leave him alone during the day.'

Ann fell to her knees, her face contorted with anguish and pain. 'I know I did wrong but let me put things right with you,' Ann pleaded, 'please let me do that.'

'How the fuck are you going to do that?' Evans shouted. 'How are you going to make up for me never getting a bedtime story? How are you going to make up for me getting my father's belt every night? The Evans family were so upright, decent, honest, religious people. They were considered pillars of their local church and community. But behind closed doors they were twisted, sick bastards.'

'I'm sorry, I'm so sorry.'

'Sorry? Sorry just isn't fucking good enough, Grandma! You're a completely selfish bitch both then and now! But finally I'm in control on behalf of me and my father. Rita Makin had to die because she was the second mother figure in his life to let him down. She said she'd always take care of him but when the going got tough she was nowhere for him. Then I went for Angus so that your spoilt brat of a daughter would feel something of the pain and the misery that my father and I went through. Then if that stupid bitch Penny Bradshaw hadn't got in the way it would be my Uncle Matt's funeral you were organising. But instead, Matt and Susie will have to organise yours.' He turned to Brendan. 'Any last requests before I make you dangle, Granddad?' He reached up and pulled the tape from Brendan's mouth so he could speak.

Brendan called out. 'Ann! Don't worry, my love, this will all be over soon, it'll all be fine, you'll see, Ann, you'll see, my love. Pray for them, Ann. Pray for the souls of our son and our grandson.'

'Oh boring!' Evans declared before putting the tape back across Brendan's mouth and holding the leg of the stool whilst Ann looked on in absolute horror. 'I've listened to you, Brendan, talk about justice and I've admired you for it. I've learned from you and I've respected you. But you're grandma's best mate. So you have to die.'

'Please don't do this to us!' Ann cried out. 'It's not too late.'

'Why don't you save your breath until you really need it you duplicitous bitch!'

They both turned their attentions to Bill when they heard him gasping for breath.

'I thought he'd been a bit quiet' said Evans, 'looks to me like he's having a heart attack. Must be all the stress, eh?'

Ann moved towards him but Evans stopped her. He grabbed her by the hair and pulled her head around so that she could see her husband. She was sobbing but it was doing no good.

'Shall we put him out of his misery?' he asked as they watched Bill collapse in excruciating pain. 'I mean, that's what they do with animals so why not?' He then shot Bill right in the chest, killing him instantly. Ann screamed and was inconsolable when Evans swung her around again to look at Brendan whose horrified eyes mirrored her own. 'Now when they used to hang people in gaol they'd put a bag over their head out of dignity for the prisoner and to save the distress of anyone watching. But I'm not going to do that. I remember having to watch Andy Cook killing Mummy and that was all part of a line of evil that you started, Grandma. So you're going to have to watch now as I settle the score.'

Evans then pulled the stool from underneath Brendan. His body dropped and his face began to lose its colour when a shot rang out from the back of the church that broke the rope and sent Brendan crashing to the floor. Evans released his grip on Ann and turned to see where the shot had come from. Then two more shots were fired and Evans was dead.

Andy Cook stepped forward, his gun still smoking, and asked Ann if she was okay. She was shaking so badly that she couldn't properly reply before the doors of the church burst open and armed police came rushing in, followed by Sara and Joe.

CHAPTER TWENTY-THREE

Adrian went around to see Penny's parents to tell them that he'd made all the funeral arrangements. He'd had to wait for the body to be released after the post mortem which was standard in a murder case and now that the

DNA on her body had been matched with that of Phillip Evans they could now conclude that he murdered her.

'What time on Friday?' Penny's mother, Sylvia, asked.

'Eleven o'clock,' said Adrian who still felt wretched. He didn't know how he was keeping it all together but he was managing somehow. Thank God for his own family. His mother, his brothers and his sister had rallied around him and without them he didn't know what he would have done.

'Oh no, we can't do eleven' said Sylvia.

Adrian breathed in deep to quell his mounting irritation. 'I'm not talking about a hairdressers appointment here, Sylvia. This is your daughter's funeral for God's sake.'

'But Friday is the morning we do the shopping.'

'Damn the bloody shopping!'

'We like our routines in this house, Adrian' Sylvia emphasised. 'I've nothing against you, Adrian. I think you deserve a medal to have put up with Penny for all these years.'

Adrian was astonished at the woman's insensitivity. 'Sylvia, your daughter was murdered! And you're still laying into her?'

'Like I said, I've nothing against you,' said Sylvia. 'Despite the fact that your friend wrecked my poor Natasha's life. She's in bits because of it. She's gone to Barbados to recuperate. Well you know, they get cheap staff tickets when they work on the airline and she needed to get away after what had happened.'

'What had happened? She got dumped, Sylvia. Your other daughter got murdered! It's not quite the same thing, wouldn't you say? So are you telling me that Penny's sister won't be at the funeral either?'

'Well no because, like I told you, she's gone to Barbados

to try and mend her broken heart. Me and her Dad gave her some money to spend whilst she's there because I understand it can be a bit expensive. Well, exclusive places like that often can be, can't they.'

'Are you interested in how your grandchildren are doing at all?'

'Well I expect you're taking care of them.'

'Sylvia, they're your flesh and blood and they've just lost their mother in horrific circumstances.'

'Well that's it, you see,' said Sylvia, 'they're not my flesh and blood.'

'What are you talking about?.'

'Sit down, Adrian,' said Sylvia, who gestured for Adrian to sit in the armchair that was facing her own. 'You may as well know. Penny was adopted. We thought we could never have any children but just after we adopted her I fell pregnant with our Natasha. We couldn't love Penny like we loved Natasha, you see. We always felt like she'd got in the way if you see what I mean.'

'She was a human being, Sylvia.'

'Yes, and she was someone else's daughter,' said Sylvia, 'she wasn't mine.'

'You never told her.'

'No' said Sylvia, 'we couldn't have coped with all the upset it would've caused.'

'So you made her feel worthless instead' said Adrian.

'We bought her and we couldn't send her back.'

'What do you mean you bought her?' Adrian demanded. 'Haven't you pissed on her memory enough?'

'We bought her from the church' said Sylvia, ignoring Adrian's obvious anger. 'We had to scrape it all together but we were desperate for a child because we didn't think we could have one normally. It was a priest called Brendan O'Farrell, the one who nearly died in that incident with the other priest this week. He said that he knew her birth mother personally and that she'd grow up to be a good person.'

'And she did' said Adrian. 'The best.'

'Alright, I'll give you that,' Sylvia admitted, 'but I just couldn't bond with her once I'd had my own daughter.'

'But Sylvia, you were so rotten to her. You said some evil things that I know hurt her very deeply.'

'Look, enough of the lecturing from you' said Sylvia, fighting back. 'You're the one who's got to live with the fact that you were sleeping with another man behind Penny's back. I'd say that was more than just pissing on her memory as you put it.'

★

Adrian called Matt and went around to the Malmaison hotel to see him.

'I'm so pleased you called' said Matt after he'd led Adrian into his room and closed the door. 'I've been worried about you, Adrian.'

'I'm going through a living hell' said Adrian, looking around the room.

'I know the feeling.'

'I'm sorry about your father.'

'Yeah, well,' said Matt, 'it's complicated. Do you want something to drink? I've got a bottle of red open.'

'Okay' said Adrian who then looked through to the room next door. 'Who's through there?'

'My sister' said Matt. 'We wanted to be able to keep an eye on each other whilst certain killers were at large. She's downstairs in the hotel restaurant having something to eat with a friend. We won't be disturbed.'

'I haven't come around here for sex, Matt.'

'I didn't mean that,' said Matt who then handed

Adrian his glass of wine. 'And if you had then you'd have gone away disappointed. I'm not exactly in the mood.'

'I usually only have to click my fingers to get you in the mood.'

'These aren't usual times.'

'You're not kidding there,' said Adrian, 'I've found out that Penny was adopted.'

'Really?'

'Yeah' said Adrian. 'Her parents bought her off your man Brendan O'Farrell.'

'You're joking'

'No, I'm not,' said Adrian who then took a gulp of his wine. 'That's why they were so rotten with her all her life because she got in the way when their natural daughter came along.'

'Poor Penny.'

'Yeah. Matt, tell me what she was like in those final moments?'

'What she was like?'

'Well she'd come around because Natasha had spilled the beans about me and you. Was she angry? Upset? What was she like? I mean, did the two of you compare notes on my performance? Did you tell her that you give better head than she did?'

'Alright' said Matt, putting his glass of wine down. 'If you want to have a go at me then be my guest. If you want to use me as a whipping boy then do it.'

'You should've left me alone' said Adrian. 'You shouldn't have come on to me that night. My wife died knowing what had been going on between us. I'm finding that hard to cope with.'

'Your wife was a highly dignified, intelligent woman.' said Matt. 'Yes, we talked about you and yes, she asked me how I felt about you. But you would've worked it all out,

Adrian. She was all set to do that with you.'

'But she never got a chance, did she! Because she got what was meant for you!'

'Adrian, I think you'd better leave'

Adrian put his glass down and lunged at Matt, pinning him up against the wall with his hands around his throat.

'Is this going to make you feel better, Adrian?' Matt gasped, 'Is killing me going to clear away all those ghosts inside? Do you think you'll be cleansed if I'm not around anymore to remind you of what you enjoyed every second of?'

'Shut up!'

'I'm sorry about Penny,' said Matt as he tried to push Adrian away but he was too strong for him. He could feel Adrian's fingers tighten around his throat but he wasn't going to give in that easily.

'Sorry, are you? Well if I'd never have got together with you then she would still be alive! Can you live with that? Can you?'

'It's not my fault that she's dead.'

'Oh yes it is! You've destroyed my life.'

'Alright, think that if it makes you feel any better about your gutless self! What am I looking at? I'm looking at a man who can't be honest with himself let alone his wife!'

Adrian stared into Matt's eyes and suddenly realised what he was doing. He loosened his grip around Matt's neck and stepped back.

'I'm sorry about everything, Adrian' said Matt whose own hand was now on his neck rubbing it. 'It's hard for you to believe that, I know, but I'm not to blame.'

Adrian took Matt in his arms and held him tight without saying a word. Matt could feel Adrian's tears drip onto the back of his neck and he wanted to say something but he couldn't.

Then Adrian left.

A MONTH LATER

'It's so beautiful here' said Susie who was standing arm in arm with Matt on the Northern beaches of Sydney, Australia looking out at the Pacific.

'I'd never tire of looking at that view' said Matt.

'You could move out here?' said Susie. 'We both could.'

'No, I couldn't, Susie.'

'Oh yeah' said Susie. 'I'd forgotten you've got unfinished business back home. That's what a place like this does to you. It makes you forget.'

Matt squeezed his sister's arm as she rested her head on his shoulder. 'I know, mate. But you know what I promised Wendy before she died. I promised I'd take care of the boys and make sure they were happy. I can't walk out on that promise, Susie, and I wouldn't want to.'

'The boys aren't the problem.'

'Not today, Susie.'

'What time did Gary and Ollie say they were picking us up?'

'They said to be outside the hotel at twelve.'

Susie looked at her watch. 'It's after eleven. We'd best get a move on.'

In all the mess that had been left by the actions of their parents, Matt and Susie had grown even closer than they ever were before. They leaned on each other to get through the days when the pain seemed unbearable but one thing they'd decided to do was to come out to Australia and arrange for a plaque to be put on the cliff edge where Andy Cook said he'd thrown their brother

Sean Patrick into the sea. Whilst they'd been there they'd looked into their brother's tragic history from his arrival in Australia to his placement in the boys' home and his year on the run that led to his entanglement with the paedophile monster. They also focused on when he was with Jolene and on how happy he'd been during that time, especially when their little boy had come along. What a tragic waste it had been for that little boy to have been so badly abused himself that he'd grown up to be so full of anger and resentment that he sought revenge on the family who'd started it all. Phillip Evans had killed and then he'd ended up dead himself. Neither Matt nor Susie had been able to get over the enormous sadness of what had been inflicted on their family, especially with the knowledge that their own parents were ultimately responsible for everything that had happened.

Matt's friends Gary and Ollie, who lived in Sydney, had arranged for the plaque to be made and placed along with others dedicated to loved ones lost over the same piece of cliff edge. They drove Matt and Susie to the spot and Susie broke down when she saw the plaque. Matt held her tight and Gary and Ollie stood back to let them have their private moment.

'…TO SEAN PATRICK, THE BROTHER WE NEVER KNEW BUT WHO WILL REMAIN IN OUR HEARTS FOREVER. WITH LOVE ALWAYS FROM MATT AND SUSIE …'

'He wasn't perfect.' said Matt.
'He never got the chance to be.' said Susie.
'And none of us are anyway.'
'He just needed someone to care about him' said Susie. 'If that had happened then we wouldn't be here

now.'

★

It's a long flight back from Australia but Matt and Susie felt strangely perky as they waited for their connecting flight to Manchester at Heathrow's Terminal 5.

'I'm sure jet lag is going to hit me like a train anytime' said Susie.

'I know' said Matt. 'We should feel more tired than we do seeing as we spent most of the flight enjoying the wines and the movies.'

'And you were flirting with that steward, Calum, on the Singapore to London leg of our Qantas flight,' Susie teased.

'Well he was easy on the eye,' said Matt, 'easy on my eye anyway.'

'I still can't get over the size of that plane' said Susie. 'A double-decker Airbus that stays in the sky all that time with all those people on board. I think the whole science of flying is amazing. I used to talk about it a lot with Angus. He would've been flying those big jets eventually.'

'Did being on the plane make you think about him a lot?'

'Sometimes' Susie admitted. 'Like when the pilot made his announcements. He'll always be there, Matt. Deep down in my heart he'll always be there.'

'I know' said Matt, squeezing his sister's hand. 'And I'm always there for when it gets unbearable.'

Susie smiled affectionately at her brother who'd been a rock for her lately.

'And did you know that the wings of that Airbus 380 are built in Chester?.'

'Are they?'

'And the engines are made in Derby.'

'But I thought it was a European aircraft?'

'It is, Susie' said Matt. 'And Britain is part of Europe in case you'd forgotten. That's why all those jobs are in Chester and Derby and not some other part of the world.'

'Point taken.' said Susie, 'You know, it's not fair. I could've had two big brothers to boss around.'

'Yeah, well, that's where Sean Patrick got off lightly.'

★

Matt and Susie had rented a house together in Swinton whilst they sold their respective properties. Neither of them could imagine living in their own houses again after what had happened inside them and Susie hadn't even been able to go back to her house. Susie planned to get some kind of penthouse apartment in Manchester city centre and Matt hadn't yet decided what he was going to do. Susie was keen to get back to running the business. She had thought of selling up but she didn't know what else she would do. And she wasn't the sort to sit around idly counting her money.

They'd been home an hour and were unpacking cases and filling the washing machine when Charlie called around.

'Well nothing personal, Charlie,' said Susie, 'but I'm going up to bed to try and get this jet lag licked. I want to go into the office tomorrow and pick up the reins again. Besides, you boys probably need to talk about stuff so I'll leave you to it.'

'She's back to her old self' said Charlie after Susie had gone upstairs and he sat with Matt at the kitchen table, each with a mug of tea.

Matt smiled. 'Some of the time, yes, but don't be fooled. She's still hurting badly and she'll miss Angus forever.'

'I don't know how I'd deal with my loved one being murdered.'

'Well, we've lost our father in the midst of it all of course but Susie and I have become incredibly close these past few weeks.'

'You and Susie against the world?'

'More or less, yeah… we've needed each other.'

'You really have'

'How are you bearing up? You sounded cheerful enough in your emails. On the surface at least.'

'Ah well that's the point,' said Charlie, 'underneath it's not quite such a pretty picture.'

'I didn't think so.' said Matt. 'It's only been a few weeks though, Charlie. That's not very long.'

'No' said Charlie, looking down at the table.

'What is it?'

'Matt, I've always known that I've been in love with two people in my life. Wendy and you. I've denied it. I've run away from it emotionally but it's true and I don't see any point in denying it any longer.'

'What are you saying, Charlie?'

'Look, can we go and sit down in the living room? Just to be more comfortable.'

They moved into the living room and sat down beside each other on the sofa. Matt could feel his heart beating as he waited for Charlie to continue.

'Matt, I want you to move in with me and the boys.'

'You do?'

'Yes, I do, and I know they'd love it,' said Charlie who could feel himself shaking as he formed his next words in his head. 'But when I say I want you to move in, I mean I want you to move into my bedroom too. When we kissed the other day… well I haven't been able to forget about it. It was as if I'd finally let go and then I got to thinking how bad could it be if we got together? We both want it.'

Matt took hold of Charlie's hand. 'Are you sure you do, Charlie? You know how I've always felt about you but I can't have you messing with my head. That would finish me off on top of everything else just lately.'

Charlie caressed the side of Matt's face with his hand. 'That's why I'm being absolutely honest with you,' he said. 'Matt, I don't know yet how I'm going to handle the physical side of things and you're going to have to be patient with me. But I do know that I love you and I want to give us the best I've got.'

'Then we'd better pick the boys up from school together and tell them,' said Matt.

'They'll be absolutely thrilled.'

'Not half as much as I am,' said Matt, 'you've got your fears but we'll sort through them. We'll be a family. The four of us.'

'It's going to be a bit of a shock for some people.'

'We'll be sensitive,' said Matt, 'but they'll have to deal with it in the end.'

They kissed to seal the deal and then they wrapped their arms around each other and went for the full-on tongues down throats like they'd done before in the surgery. Charlie hadn't felt this happy for a long time and he just hoped he wouldn't let Matt down.

'How do you feel?' asked Matt.

'Excited,' said Charlie, 'and nervous. It is the right thing to do though, Matt. I know that much. I just hope that I can live up to what you deserve.'

'Don't worry about that' said Matt, 'just relax and the rest will follow.'

'I am sure about this, Matt' said Charlie, 'I really am.'

'I'm going to make you so happy' said Matt, tearfully.

'That's going to work both ways' said Charlie who was equally unable to stop the tears from flowing.

Susie had stopped on the top of the landing to listen in. She was delighted. Her big brother was going to get his man finally and nobody could be happier for him then she was. She went halfway down the stairs and paused.

'Charlie, just one thing?' she said.

'What?' asked a startled Charlie, still embraced with Matt.

'My brother has been waiting for this moment for twenty years,' said Susie, leaning on the banister and looking down on them. 'And I know there were times when he never thought it would happen.'

'What are you saying?'

'That you might have bought a bottle of champagne to celebrate!'

Matt burst out laughing. 'You were listening?'

'Too right!' said Susie, 'So, the champagne?'

Charlie was laughing now too. 'It's in the car. I'll go and get it.'

'And I'm taking you all out to dinner tonight' said Susie. 'I think I need to get to know the boys a little better now that I'm their Aunty.'

CHAPTER TWENTY-FOUR

Superintendent John Hargreaves and Sara were sitting in Sara's office and having a good laugh at the news that the McDermott brothers were claiming incapacity benefit. It seems they couldn't go to work because they'd been traumatised at having seen the murder of Rita Makin take place. This was from the brothers who'd been trying to set themselves up as the local lads who could "see to things" for you. Sara said she didn't doubt that it wasn't a pleasant experience to watch someone being murdered by someone who is known to you, but they'd been on the front page of the Manchester Evening News as Phillip Evans 'forgotten' victims. What a joke.

'I'm glad we can find a laugh from this case,' said Hargreaves, 'it's been so bloody awful.'

'I know, sir' said Sara, 'it's not been the easiest. But at least now that Andy Cook has been sent down for ten years for the murder of Phillip Evans, some justice can be seen to be done.'

'Some people might say that Evans was a victim' said Sara. 'And Andy Cook too in his own way. But it all started with the policies of the government of the day and the Catholic Church. None of us can be proud.'

'Forcibly transporting children halfway around the world was a pretty nasty business,' said Hargreaves.

'And telling them they were orphans when they weren't.' said Sara. ' However long I stay in this job it'll never cease to amaze me how people think that their actions will never have a consequence.'

'Like Ann Schofield?'

'Yeah,' said Sara who was painfully aware of the personal territory she was stepping on. She just had to hope that the son she gave up for adoption is happy and with a family who love him. She told herself that the difference was that he was still a newborn baby when he left her arms. Sean Patrick O'Brien was a five year-old child capable of comprehending the kind of emotional damage that would stay with him forever and lead to him making all the wrong kind of decisions.

'And how could Bill Schofield have made Ann make that choice?' said Hargreaves. 'I'm not a perfect man but that wouldn't even cross my mind if I was in a similar situation.'

'No' said Sara, thinking back to when she'd backed off from making Tim Norris choose between her and his then fiancé Helen. She wouldn't have had to give away Tim's baby if she had told him about it but she still thinks she made the right decision. She'd have been second best to Helen in Tim's heart, they'd have split up eventually and she'd have been left a single mother. What she did made sure that they all had the chance to be happy. 'I know what you mean, sir.'

'But your instincts were sound once again in this case, Sara.' said Hargreaves. 'You said fairly early on that they were executions that were taking place and you were right. Well done.'

'Well thank you, sir, but I just wish we could've got there sooner.'

'No matter. We got there in the end and it wasn't easy with no obvious link at the start.'

'You can say that again, sir.' said Sara. 'Now there is one other thing I need to talk to you about.'

'Okay?'

'Adrian Bradshaw was having a sexual relationship with Matt Schofield. Adrian is denying it but Matt Schofield confirmed it and I've no reason to believe that he was lying. Besides, it all fits with why Penny Bradshaw was at Matt Schofield's house.'

'I see' said Hargreaves. 'Well I could understand in normal circumstances why he's denying it, Sara, but although his desire to keep his relationship with Matt Schofield private wouldn't have had any bearing on the case we've just concluded, it does sound warning bells in my head for the future. He's a widower living with a pretty big secret and those things combined could affect his professional judgement.'

'I don't want to take him out of the squad, sir' said Sara, 'he's a good officer.'

'I agree but you'll need to keep your eye on him, Sara, I'm in no position to judge on infidelity, as you know. And neither have I got a problem with anyone being gay.'

'Me neither, sir. I've no patience with any degree of homophobia.'

'But this is not someone who's being honest about themselves though, Sara. That's what makes the difference.'

★

Later that day when they'd all finished, the squad retired to the pub and Superintendent Hargreaves joined them. Kieran had been on early shift that day and she didn't ring him to ask him to join them in the pub. She felt a bit naughty about that but lately he'd been hinting that he wanted to, as he put it, 'normalise' their relationship. That meant that he wanted to go out for dinner, meet up with mutual friends, go to the cinema on a Sunday afternoon, meet up with her and her colleagues in the pub after work and Sara hadn't wanted any of that for a long time. She was happy to conduct their relationship entirely in bed with the odd bit of conversation thrown in. Why did men have to spoil all the fun by getting serious?

Tim Norris had now returned to work after his paternity leave and was delighted with the baby daughter that he and his wife Helen had adopted. He was showing pictures of her all over the place and Sara would agree that she looked as cute as anything. It still sent a shiver down her spine though. Especially when Tim looked at her and their thoughts collided. They both hoped that their son, a baby Tim didn't know Sara had given birth to until she came to work on the squad last year, was being loved and taken care of. He'd be six now and the revelation of his existence had threatened to wreck their working relationship with obvious effects on the rest of the team. But after a tricky start it had got better, a fact for which they were both glad, even though it was still not perfect and probably never could be.

Much merriment was being made at the bar around the behaviour of the new barman, Finlay. Although he wasn't camp or obvious in any other way, he was making no secret of the fact that he was gay and that he'd taken a shine to Adrian. Sara and the Superintendent exchanged knowing looks. This could turn either way.

'You're in there, Adrian,' said Joe, 'nice to know you've got options, mate.'

Oh my god, thought Sara. They don't know what they're saying.

'Yeah well if I need to push shit up a hill I'll use a wheelbarrow.'

'Oh that's gross!' Sara cried, her face squirming.

'So is men sleeping with other men' said Adrian. 'Why it was made legal I just don't know.'

'You're not homophobic are you Adrian?' Tim asked, slightly surprised.

'It's just that there's gay this and gay that everywhere' said Adrian. 'Nobody can get away from it. It's being put across as normal and yet it's not.'

'Come on, mate,' said Joe. 'It's normal to you if you're gay and Finlay knows what the score is. He's only having some fun.'

'Yeah, well I don't get the joke.'

'Oh come on, Adrian' said Joe. 'Lighten up for God's sake.'

'Look, just because nobody, man or woman, gay or

straight, would ever fancy you in a million years, then that doesn't mean that I have to accept every pervert's attention.'

'DS Bradshaw, that's enough!' Sara charged. 'Apologise to your fellow officer!'

'Alright, Joe, I'm sorry.' said Adrian. 'I'm really sorry, I shouldn't have said that.'

'Apology accepted' said Joe. ' My shoulders are broad.'

'It's just that straight is normal, Joe,' Adrian emphasised. 'Gay just isn't. That's just how I feel.'

'It doesn't bother me.' said superintendent Hargreaves. 'I'm not gay myself but why should it bother me if other people are? I always watch Graham Norton's show and Paul O'Grady's. I think they're both hilarious. The fact that they're both gay wouldn't mean that I wouldn't want to sit down and have a drink with them. I've also got a nephew who's gay. He and his partner seem to live a normal life like any other couple. I don't even think about it. They're just good people to be around and certainly liven up any otherwise tedious family gathering.'

'Gay people do always seem to have good senses of humour' Tim agreed.

'Yeah' said Joe. 'That's why Finlay fancies Adrian.'

They all laughed but Adrian's face wouldn't budge from the stone cast he'd put it in.

'Joke, mate' said Joe. 'Just a joke.'

'Why don't you all just shut the fuck up,' Adrian fumed.

'Adrian, I'm surprised at you' said Sara. 'I thought you'd think a bit bigger than this.'

'Why is everybody jumping on the flaming bandwagon!' said Adrian through clenched teeth. He wiped his mouth with the back of his hand. 'Excuse me, I'm going to the toilet.'

There were raised eyebrows exchanged by everyone else in the squad as they watched Adrian stride very purposefully to where the corridor leading to the gents was.

'So what was all that about?' asked Joe.

'Who can say' said Sara.

'Makes me wonder if he doesn't protest too much' said Joe.

'I was thinking exactly the same thing, Joe' said Tim.

'Or maybe he's just missing his wife' said Sara. 'Let's give him the benefit of the doubt before we rush to judgement.'

Adrian came out of the toilet and bumped straight into Finlay who was on his way to the kitchen at the back of the pub.

'Have you got a tight arse, Finlay?' asked Adrian.

'Tight enough for you, big boy' said Finlay. 'I finish at eleven and usually I'm home about half past.'

'Where's home?'

'Old Trafford.'

'Give me your address and I'll be around later.'

'Okay' said the waiter who took a piece of paper out of his pocket and wrote down his name and address on it before handing it to Adrian.

'Thanks' said Adrian. ' But look, just don't flirt with me in front of my colleagues. They don't know.'

Finlay smiled. 'Oh sorry, I didn't realise.'

'It's okay' said Adrian, 'I'll see you later.'

'I'll look forward to it' said Finlay. 'You didn't tell me your name?'

'It's Matt.'

'I thought I heard them calling you Adrian?'

'It's Matt,' repeated Adrian, firmly.

'I see.' said Finlay who then looked down at big boy's

wedding ring. He smiled. 'I see.'

★

Joe Alexander got home and just hated going into his house when it was all in darkness. His coffee cup from that morning was still sitting in the sink waiting to be washed. This wasn't what life should all be about.

It was only nine o'clock and he ran upstairs to get changed. He fancied a couple of pints in the pub and he'd be down there by a quarter past.

He was just about to leave when there was a knock on the door. He opened it and Carol was stood there with her two kids and a couple of suitcases.

'I'm sorry,' she said, sobbing. 'He's found out about you and he's thrown us out.'

★

Adrian got to the flat in Old Trafford where Finlay lived and pressed the security buzzer at street level. Finlay answered through the intercom and let him in. He went up to the second floor and the door to number seventeen was slightly open.

Finlay was a good looking young guy. He had flawless skin and his blond hair was perfectly cropped. Anybody, man or woman, with a mind to be with a young guy like that would be happy that he was there waiting to please. But Adrian hadn't come for that. He hadn't come to feel the pleasure that had got him into such trouble before. Boys like Finlay needed to be taught a lesson. They couldn't just go around trying to seduce straight men like Adrian. Because Adrian was one hundred percent straight and the likes of Finlay had to learn to respect that.

'Hi' said Finlay, smiling broadly, 'I'm really glad you came.'

'You might not say that after I've gone.'

'What do you mean?'

Adrian smacked Finlay across the face from the right, then from the left, then from the right again, then from the left again. Finlay cowered and tried to protect his face with his arms but Adrian wrenched them open and made sure that his fists made contact with Finlay's face.

'Don't hurt me!' Finlay pleaded. ' Please, don't hurt me!'

'Hurt you? You think I'm going to hurt you? You have tragically underestimated me, my friend!'

Finlay wound himself up into a ball on the floor and Adrian kicked him repeatedly in the back, in the groin, in the legs.

'Scum like you are poison! Do you know that? You're poison! You get hold of decent, honest straight family men like me and twist our needs and our desires until we don't know ourselves anymore. You're scum! Twisted, immoral scum!'

What Finlay then went through would stay with him for the rest of his life. He was powerless against this much stronger man who in a matter of seconds had his trousers and pants down and was raping him repeatedly. He cried. He tried to scream but Adrian placed his hand tightly across his mouth. The ripples of pain seared through his body like bolts of electricity and his ordeal seemed endless.

'Not in control now, are you, scum!' Adrian sneered as he thrust himself violently into Finlay whose muffled groans of pain he ignored. 'Dirty, perverted scum! Enjoying yourself? Is this what you like your men to do? You freak of fucking nature!'

Several minutes later Finlay couldn't move from the position he'd been forced into on the floor. Everything seemed to hurt.

Adrian got to his feet and zipped his trousers up.

'You can relax' said Adrian. ' It's over. Oh and don't bother calling the police. I am the police and we look after our own.'

★

Sara was more pleased than she'd admit at seeing Kieran sitting in her living room when she got home.

'Hi' she said as she switched the lamp on next to where he was sitting. 'This is a nice surprise. What are you doing here?'

'I came to find you earlier' said Kieran, standing up. 'They said you were in the pub with the rest of them. You didn't call to see if I wanted to join you?'

'Oh look, Kieran, I…'

'…so anyway, I'm here to give you this back' said Kieran as he held up the key to her flat that she'd given him. 'I won't be needing it anymore.'

Sara didn't want to but she could feel her heart breaking. 'Why?'

'Sara, these past few months have been the most tremendous of my life.' said Kieran, 'We've had a lot of fun together and I wouldn't have missed it for the world.'

'But?'

'But you know how I've been feeling lately.'

'I know you've been a moody bastard.'

'Well if that's how you want to put it,' said Kieran, 'but the fact is, I need more than just great sex.'

Sara swallowed and struggled to retain her composure. This wasn't what she wanted. She didn't want to break up with Kieran. But he was right. It was only about having fun.

'I thought I did too' said Sara.

'And?'

'And I don't think I could handle it.'

'If you'd have given me a different answer then this night would be ending differently too.'

Sara put on a smile. 'Then I guess it's my loss.'

'Don't put it like that.'

'Is there someone else?'

'There's someone who I know is interested, yes,' said Kieran, 'she's a teacher at one of the schools on my beat. I've noticed her too and we've exchanged smiles, looks, you know the kind of thing.'

'Actually, I'd forgotten, but don't worry about that.' said Sara.

'Sara, I want someone who needs me for more than just sex.'

'Oh don't start giving me some moral lecture' said Sara. 'If you've found someone who'll be the boring little hausfrau you say you need then my condolences to you.'

'You don't know her so don't label her a hausfrau.'

'You don't know her yet either.'

'No, but I want to get to know her,' said Kieran.

'She'll get her narrow minded suburban claws into you and before you know it your life will be hers and you'll get no choice in anything.'

Kieran put the key down on the table. 'That's a chance I'll have to take. I want a wife, a home, kids, dogs and cats. If I thought for one second that you'd be up for all that then I'd stay.'

'Yeah, well, you know where the door is.'

Kieran placed his hand on Sara's shoulder as he passed her. 'Don't end up lonely, Sara.'

'Like you'll care.'

'I'll care because for as long as I live I'll never forget you.'

After he'd gone, Sara opened a bottle of red wine and drowned her sorrows. Then she opened a second bottle and began to cry for a little baby she'd given away and for his father who she still loved and always would.

CHAPTER TWENTY-FIVE

THREE MONTHS` LATER

COUNTY CLARE, IRELAND

Ann woke up early and decided to walk down to the end of the garden at the back of the cottage and look out over the Atlantic. It wasn't long before Brendan followed her.

'Couldn't sleep?' Brendan asked.

'I was just having a bit of a think, you know?'

Brendan put his arms around her. 'Yes, I know.'

Over a breakfast of tea and toast an hour or so later, Ann brought up the subject of yesterday's post.

'They returned my letter again,' said Ann.

'Susie and Matt?'

'Yes.' said Ann. 'They're determined not to have anything to do with me. I should've known at Bill's funeral. They could barely even look at me.'

'We didn't do anything wrong, Ann' said Brendan. 'We fell in love and we had a child. But I was married to the church.'

'Then I met Bill.'

'It didn't stop us though, did it? We carried on and we had our little girl.'

'They called her Penny,' said Ann. 'I've always liked the name. The trouble is though, Brendan, that both our kids suffered because of us. I had to dump Sean Patrick and you arranged the sale of our little girl who became Penny.'

'But neither of us were to know what would happen to them,' said Brendan, 'we acted in good faith.'

'And does that help you sleep at night, Brendan? '

'No' said Brendan. 'What helps me sleep at night is having you beside me after all these years of being so close and yet so far. I'd love to change the past, Ann. I never meant to hurt Bill or anybody else. But you and I are together now and that's all that matters to me.'

Ann threw the returned letter from Susie and Matt in the bin and then took hold of Brendan's hand. 'We've wasted enough time, Brendan. Let's get on with the rest of our lives.'

FALL FROM GRACE
A DCI SARA HOYLAND MYSTERY

Paul Foster is a social worker trying to make a difference. But what links him to an aristocratic Nazi sympathiser accused of harbouring a war criminal? And what has happened to his soldier boyfriend Jake over in Afghanistan?

In this, the first DCI Sara Hoyland mystery, the intrepid detective with a murky past enters a long-forgotten world of political intrigue. Long-held grudges and several families' secrets re-surface to further muddy the waters.